Virginia ANDREWS

CHRISTOPHER'S DIARY: ECHOES OF DOLLANGANGER

Virginia Andrews® Books

The Dollanganger Family Series
Flowers in the Attic
Petals on the Wind
If There Be Thorns
Seeds of Yesterday
Garden of Shadows

The Casteel Family Series
Heaven
Dark Angel
Fallen Hearts
Gates of Paradise
Web of Dreams

The Cutler Family Series
Dawn
Secrets of the Morning
Twilight's Child
Midnight Whispers
Darkest Hour

The Landry Family Series
Ruby
Pearl in the Mist
All That Glitters
Hidden Jewel
Tarnished Gold

The Logan Family Series
Melody
Heart Song
Unfinished Symphony
Music in the Night
Olivia

The Orphans Miniseries
Butterfly
Crystal
Brooke
Raven
Runaways

The Wildflowers Miniseries
Misty
Star
Jade
Cat
Into the Garden

The Hudson Family Series
Rain
Lightning Strikes
Eye of the Storm
The End of the Rainbow

The Shooting Stars Series
Cinnamon
Ice
Rose
Honey
Falling Stars

The De Beers Family Series
Willow
Wicked Forest
Twisted Roots
Into the Woods
Hidden Leaves

Virginia ANDREWS

CHRISTOPHER'S DIARY: ECHOES OF DOLLANGANGER

SIMON & SCHUSTER

London · New York · Sydney · Toronto · New Delhi

A CBS COMPANY

First published in Great Britain by Simon & Schuster UK Ltd, 2015
This paperback published, 2016
A CBS COMPANY

1 3 5 7 9 10 8 6 4 2

Simon & Schuster UK Ltd
1st Floor
Gray's Inn Road
London WC1X 8HB

www.simonandschuster.co.uk

Simon & Schuster Australia, Sydney
Simon & Schuster India, New Delhi

A CIP catalogue record for this book
is available from the British Library

Paperback ISBN: 978-1-47114-268-0
eBook ISBN: 978-1-47114-267-3

Printed and bound by CPI Group (UK) Ltd, Croydon, CR0 4YY

MIX
Paper from
responsible sources
FSC® C020471

Simon & Schuster UK Ltd are committed to sourcing paper
that is made from wood grown in sustainable forests and supports the Forest
Stewardship Council, the leading international forest certification organisation.
Our books displaying the FSC logo are printed on FSC certified paper.

Virginia ANDREWS

CHRISTOPHER'S DIARY: ECHOES OF DOLLANGANGER

Becoming Christopher and Cathy

The shorter days of approaching winter darkened the corners of my attic earlier and earlier every afternoon. Usually, when you think of yourself ascending, whether it's hiking up a mountain, flying in an airplane, or walking to the top floor of your house, you imagine moving into brighter light. But as my boyfriend, Kane Hill, and I walked up the attic stairway for the first time together, I could almost feel the shadows growing and opening like Venus flytraps to welcome us.

The stairs creaked the way they always had, but it sounded more like a warning this time, each squeak a groan of frantic admonition. Our attic didn't have an unpleasant odor, but it did have the scent of old things that hadn't seen the light of day for years: furniture, lamps, and trunks stuffed with old clothing too out of fashion to care about or throw away when the previous owners left. They were still good enough for someone else to use. All of it had been accumulated by what my father called "pack rats," but he also admitted to being one himself. Our garage was neat but jammed with his old tools and boxes of sample building materials, my first tricycle, various hoses, and plumbing fittings he might find use for someday.

The attic floor was a dark brown hardwood that had worn well and, according to my father, was as solid as the day it was laid. He looked in once in a while, but I would go up regularly to dust a bit, get rid of spiderwebs, and clean the two small windows, spotted with small flies and other tiny bugs who thought they had died outside. I felt I had to maintain the attic mostly because my father kept my mother's things in an old wardrobe there, walnut with embossed cherubs on the doors, another antique. Even after nearly nine years, my father couldn't get himself to throw out or give away any of her things: shoes and slippers, purses, dresses, blouses, nightgowns, coats, and sweaters.

Just like in the Foxworth attic that Christopher had described in his diary, there were other larger items that previous occupants had left, including brass and pewter tables and standing lamps, a dark oak magazine rack with some old copies of *Life* and *Time*, some black and silver metal trunks that had once worn their travel labels proudly, bragging about Paris, London, and Madrid, and other pieces of furniture that had lost their places in the living room and the bedrooms when the decor was changed.

Despite being thought useless and relegated to

this vault, to my father, they were almost a part of the house now. He said that their having been there so long gave them squatters' rights. It really didn't matter whether they had been there long or whether they would find another home, fulfill another purpose. Memories, no matter whose they were, were sacred to him. Things weren't ever simply things. Old toys were once cherished by the children who owned them, and family heirlooms possessed history, whether or not you knew exactly what that history was. It didn't surprise me that a man who built and restored homes had such respect for what was in them. I just hadn't paid much attention to any of it until now.

I was still not convinced that what Kane Hill had suggested the day he discovered Christopher's diary under my pillow was a good idea. At first, I suspected that he might be playing with me, humoring me, when he said he would read it aloud to me, pretending to be Christopher Dollanganger, the oldest of the four children who had been incarcerated in Foxworth Hall more than fifty years ago. I didn't want to diminish the diary's historical importance for Charlottesville or in any way make fun of it. He had assured me that he wouldn't do that.

And then he had added, "To get into it, really get into it, we'll read it up in your attic."

The Foxworth attic was where the four Dollanganger children had spent most of their time for years, there and in a small bedroom below. According to what I knew and how Christopher had described it, the attic was a long, rambling loft that they had turned into their imaginary world because they had been shut out of the real one for so long. The idea of reading Christopher's thoughts and descriptions aloud in a similar environment both fascinated and frightened me. We would no longer be simply observers. In a sense, by playing the roles of Christopher and Cathy, we would empathize, and not just sympathize, with them.

As soon as he had said it, Kane saw the indecision in my face and went on to explain that it would be like acting on a movie set. Movie sets in studios were suggestions of what really was or had been, weren't they?

"This is no different, Kristin," Kane said.

I pointed out that my attic was much smaller than the one in Foxworth, but he insisted that it was an attic, a place where we could pretend to be imprisoned and better understand what Christopher and Cathy had experienced.

He thought we'd get a more realistic sense of it. "It will be like reading *Moby-Dick* while you're on a ship on the ocean. This way, you'll appreciate what happens to the older sister more, and I'll appreciate Christopher's words more, I'm sure."

Of course, I had found myself empathizing with Cathy often when I read Christopher's diary anyway, but not to the extent he was suggesting. It was more like putting on her clothes and stepping into her shoes. In moments, I would lose myself completely and for a while become her. Maybe I did have to be in an attic for that. However, what frightened me about pretending to be her in front of someone else was the possibility that I would be exposing my own vulnerabilities, my own fears and fantasies. Everyone knew the Dollanganger children were distant cousins of mine.

What if I was more like her than I imagined?

The leather-bound book suddenly loomed larger than some historical discovery. It was almost as though the diary had the power to unmask me and cause me to reveal my own secrets, deeply personal ones I had yet to share with anyone, even my father. There would inevitably be questions about Cathy's feelings and how they were the same as or different from mine, especially when it came to her physical and emotional maturing. Like most girls my age, I was both excited and confused at times by changes in my body and my feelings. I wasn't comfortable chatting about them with other girls, even best friends. And here I was confronting it all with Kane more intimately than I had with anyone. We hadn't been dating that long. There was still so much about each other we had to learn, with or without Christopher's diary. Was I rushing headlong into something I would regret, all because of the diary, because of how it made me feel about myself and my own new feelings? So much of what we do and who we draw closer to ourselves makes us see deeper into ourselves. Sometimes I felt surrounded by mirrors.

Yet I had to admit that Kane sounded as enthusiastic

about and as genuinely interested in what Christopher was revealing in his diary as I was. He was as excited as I had been that day when I realized what it was. Since we could safely assume that no one else had read it, Kane made the point that only he and I would know what really had occurred at Foxworth Hall. The legend, the exaggerations, and the misinformation would all be shed, and we would know the truth about the mysteries that were thought to have gone up in flames and assumed to have been lost in the darkness of fading memories.

Kane's eyes were dazzled with excitement when he spoke about it. He looked like a little boy on Christmas morning who knew what was in the package he was about to unwrap. In his mind, perhaps, and certainly in mine, it was like opening a forbidden door, an entrance that led us back into the dark past, through the shadows, up the narrow stairway, and into a world now more like the subject for Halloween stories. Would the door slam shut behind us? Would we trap ourselves in someone else's nightmare? Would what we read and did in my attic haunt us forever because of how intimate the revelations were, both Christopher Dollanganger's and our own?

I never anticipated that I'd be in such a quandary, but after Kane had discovered the diary while he was waiting for me in my room, he was naturally very curious about it. He had only read a page. However, it was enough to force me to reveal what it was. When I explained it to him and told him that my father wasn't happy that I was reading it, his curiosity grew.

Nothing makes anything more desirable than declaring it forbidden. Kane said he couldn't wait to catch up to where I was in the diary so that we could go forward together. He sounded like a child about to begin an adventure he had imagined for a long time. I felt his excitement enliven my own and thought maybe it was a good thing he had found the diary under my pillow. Maybe it was meant to be. I even fantasized that it had the power to capture anyone who came close to it. I shouldn't have been so surprised at his finding it and being drawn to it.

And yet I had gone to sleep that night afraid that I had given my trust too easily. I thought that yes, right now, he honestly might be interested in and genuinely excited about what the diary was going to reveal, and for a while, he might find reading it aloud to me in my attic somehow as satisfying as being in a play or a movie, but what if he became bored or thought it had been stupid to start with and then mentioned it to someone at school, who mentioned it to someone else, until I was surrounded with demands and questions? As my father was fond of saying, "Loose lips sink ships." In this case, it would be my ship that had sunk, even before it had much of a chance to sail.

Would I feel like a fool? Would I feel as betrayed as Christopher would be by revealing to strangers how Cathy obviously felt at this point in his diary? I could appreciate how horrible it was for her and maybe even for him. When people whom you cared about and who cared about you seriously disappointed you, it was truly like digging farther down into a wound, sending the pain through your very being. Your heart would close around itself. You would feel naked, lost, deceived by anything and everything afterward, and you would know that from then on, you would not have faith in anyone again. You would be unable to give your trust, even to those you loved. How much more alone could you be than that? Surely, that was what had happened to the Dollanganger children. And maybe that would happen to me.

And all because I was reading the diary secretly.

Was it possible for a diary to be too dangerous to open, a Pandora's box? Was that why my father had told me not to read it? Wasn't it silly to ascribe such powers to an old leather-bound book full of some teenage boy's personal thoughts and descriptions? However, I reminded myself that there were forbidden books. Books had influence on their readers. Schools kept certain books out of their libraries, and parents forbade their children to read them. Governments forbade books. Religions forbade books they thought had been written by witches, even the devil.

Whatever had happened at the original Foxworth Hall, it still had an atmosphere of mystery and horror around it. It had been kept alive through fantastic theories printed in the local newspaper and discussed around the date of the famous first fire and always on Halloween. The diary could carry that same aura. Touch it, open the cover, read the pages, and you could be carried away in the same ugly shadows and cold wind that had carried away those children.

I had tossed and turned all night debating these thoughts and worries in my mind. Sometimes I believe we all really do have two people living inside us arguing often. One has conscience, and the other doesn't. Everyone talks to himself or herself. They would all have to admit that. Well, who *were* they all talking to? Who is the himself or herself?

The following morning, one side of me seemed to have won the argument. I was determined to tell Kane to forget it. I was even working up a good story, a fabrication, something that would end his idea completely. I thought I might tell him that my father had found me reading the diary into the early hours and was so angry that he had seized it right out of my hands. He had said he was going to burn it, and I had watched him throw it into an old oilcan in our backyard. It had gone up in a puff of black smoke.

But I changed my mind the moment I set eyes on my father at breakfast and saw how happy he was with how well his work was going rebuilding a new, more modern mansion on the Foxworth property. He was getting along with Arthur Johnson, who didn't seem as difficult apparently as other customers he had worked for. That made my father even more sweet and loving to me. I regretted even thinking of using him to deceive someone by making him sound unreasonable and angry. I couldn't do it. However, I felt trapped because I was disobeying his wishes by permitting someone else to know about the diary. I comforted myself by telling myself in this case, he would understand and forgive me.

But the questions and the doubts about what I had agreed to do wouldn't be still. Really, I had thought, what if Kane should betray me and, in a real sense, betray Christopher? *Go through with this or not, Kristin?* I had asked myself while I had dressed to go down to breakfast. I was tottering between yes and no. I could easily go in either direction. I looked at the clock. It wasn't much longer before I would have to make a definite decision. Kane was going to pick me up to take me to school again, and I knew he would be talking about nothing else. When I had told my father that Kane was coming, he paused in making our breakfast.

"Picking you up again? We're considerably out of his way, especially with morning traffic. He has to be getting himself up and out much earlier."

"Oh, please. He doesn't care about that, Daddy," I said, making it sound like he was just another parent who didn't understand what was and wasn't a priority for teenagers like us.

He shrugged. "To me—you excluded, of course— it seems young people don't want to make compromises or sacrifices too easily. They don't naturally go out of their way. It's the 'please me now' generation."

"You can exclude Kane, too, from that conclusion. Besides, you'd have driven as far as another state to pick up Mommy, wouldn't you?"

He turned and squinted at me, deepening the folds in his forehead. "I see. Getting a little serious in this first romance of yours?" he asked.

I was a bit surprised myself at how quickly I had

come to Kane's defense, but I had also compared us to my father and mother, who I knew had loved each other intensely. That comparison was a bit over the top, at least for now. And my father was right to characterize my dating Kane as my first real romance. I had gone out on dates, met other boys at parties and dances, but none of that ever became much more than one follow-up call or a few days of some additional hanging out together. Until now, those budding romances always seemed to drift away with the softening of a grip on my hand, until my date's fingers cooled into icicles and finally slipped out to find a different hand to hold. More often than not, however, it was my hand that began to avoid theirs.

You can't help but think at first that it's your fault, that maybe there's something wrong with you, especially if it happened more than once or twice. Most of my girlfriends had a similar reaction to their failed little affairs of the heart. I always felt I should have been sorrier about it. My indifference surprised me. Was I capable of having deep feelings for anyone besides my own father? *Maybe you're too picky, too sensitive, or too afraid of having a relationship*, I told myself. *Your standards are too high—impossible, in fact. No relationship will ever be satisfying, and it's mostly your own fault.*

The insecurity rocks you for a while and makes you so timid that you don't even want to look at another boy and encourage what might be another flop. Why try? Failure was inevitable no matter how promising it was when it started. It was as if the moment

I returned a smile, joined a conversation with a new boy, and then went on a date, magnifying glasses dropped over my eyes, and I could see all of my prospective boyfriend's weaknesses and faults. The only comfort I had was watching other couples fail. It was always good to have friends close enough to support me and sympathize, especially because they had been through the same challenges, similar experiences.

I was an amateur psychiatrist, especially when it came to myself, and I came up with a theory, which I told no one, especially not my father. Maybe because of how involved I was with my father's loss of his one great love, I was afraid of ever finding one of my own. People end up alone for many reasons. Many are just too selfish to share or compromise or are just too cynical. They believe love brings too many expectations that can never be fulfilled. And because you've invested so much of yourself in it, your emotions are bankrupt when it fails, and unlike with any other bankruptcy, you can't reorganize those feelings and begin again.

However, right from the beginning, I could sense that something different from any of those brief little romances was happening between Kane and me. We were looking at each other with more intensity, holding our gazes longer, smiling at each other more often, and rushing toward every opportunity to be together. It was happening whether or not either of us wanted it to happen. Every time we saw each other in the school hallways, there was almost a surge of electricity in the air. Everyone around us began to fade away, their voices drifting off, their questions lingering unanswered.

I had to believe there was something special between us, and whatever that was, it helped me relax my resistance and permit myself to believe something magical could be happening. After all, that was how it was supposed to work, wasn't it? It was finally happening to me. I felt relief about myself, as if going seventeen years without having a serious romance was close to tragic, abnormal, an indication of troubled relationships to come. I worked on convincing myself that whatever happened between Kane and me would support and justify my faith in his promises, but especially when it came to the diary, because he could see how important it was to me. Of course, he wouldn't betray me. He couldn't, I thought. Why was I even debating with myself about it? He cared for me too much. He knew I wouldn't forgive him and that everything we had would burn out as fast as a meteor falling to earth.

That buoyed my confidence and sent me back to yes, but then, almost immediately, I wondered if I was becoming another one of those ostriches my father often pointed out to me, people who wouldn't face unpleasant realities or admit to weaknesses in themselves or others they trusted.

"You can't simply will things to happen the way you want them to, Kristin," my dad had warned me. "The night owl knows sunrise is coming, and there is nothing he can do to stop it, no matter how much he enjoys the darkness."

Wisdom often dripped from his lips like honey, always kindly, always sweet. Right now, I had to answer him truthfully about Kane.

"Yes, Daddy. It's a little serious between Kane and me," I replied.

He nodded and then, turning away, added, "Let me know if a little turns into a lot."

"Why?" I demanded with a little more fervor than I had intended. Was he already suspicious about what I was going to share with Kane? Would he be upset if I had strong feelings for someone besides him?

"I'm just kidding, Kristin. I don't expect you to run off and elope or anything. Uh-oh," he added, putting up his hands to surrender when I didn't respond. Then he hummed the theme from *Jaws* as if a big shark was approaching a swimmer, and he stepped back.

"What?"

"I think I just entered that world I've been warned about."

"What world?"

"The world of sensitive teenage girls, otherwise known as bedlam."

"Very funny, Daddy. The world of teenage boys is more dysfunctional, if you ask me."

"Probably so." He returned his attention to the pancakes on the stove. "But at least that's waters I've swum in myself. I know what to expect and when to expect it. Teenage girls are more like an earthquake."

He flipped a pancake. Right after being in the navy, where he got into cooking, he had been a short-order cook in a diner-type restaurant off I-95. This was before he met my mother and got into the construction business. When I was little, he actually would juggle a couple of pancakes with two spatulas. It made my mother and me laugh. He would flip one so it fell perfectly on my plate. Somehow all that juggling made them even more delicious.

"And so for me, with a teenage daughter," he said, bringing over my pancakes, "it does feel like swimming in shark-infested waters."

"I promise, I'll warn you ahead of time before I bite," I said as he poured out just the right amount of maple syrup and added banana, which he had sliced for me. He would do all that even when I was married and had children of my own, I thought.

"I'll appreciate the warning. Oh, by the way, I might be running late every afternoon this week," he said, sitting across from me. "Scheduling all these building inspectors, dealing with different contractors, meeting with the architect. This owner is taking a very detailed interest in all the construction, too. He's a nice guy, but lately, now that this is really happening, it feels like he's breathing down my neck sometimes. He slips in behind me like a ghost stepping back into the world."

"Don't most new homeowners take that sort of interest in what you're doing?"

"Not like this," he said. "Sometimes I get the feeling someone's looking over Arthur Johnson's shoulder, too."

"What do you know about him?"

"I told you he ran a hedge fund and made a lot of money. I know as much about him as I have to, I guess. But between you and me, I think it's ridiculous for a man that young to retire, even if he can. He's married to a woman about twelve years younger. I picked that up. Her mother apparently worked for his father. I sort of got the impression that—" He suddenly clamped his lips together and scrunched his nose the way he would when he was about to utter a secret or a nasty comment about something or someone in front of me and stopped himself.

"What?"

He looked at me oddly, obviously hesitant to tell me what he was thinking.

"I'm not a child anymore, Dad. You don't have to worry about offending my innocent little ears."

"Yeah, I have to keep reminding myself. Anyway, you've heard worse and read worse, I'm sure," he added, raising his eyebrows.

"Worse than what?"

"I picked up that Arthur Johnson's father got romantically involved with Arthur's mother-in-law after her husband died. Right after," he added. I guess I didn't react enough, so he said, "Minutes after. Understand?"

"Oh. She might have picked up with him a little before her husband had died?" I asked.

He nodded. "And maybe not just a little before. His wife had died just a year or so earlier, not that her still being alive might have stopped him anyway."

The disapproval on his face was blatant. I knew he was thinking of his own tragedy and wondering how much in love with his wife Arthur Johnson's father had been if he could move on to another woman so quickly. And wondering about it even more so when he learned about Arthur Johnson's mother-in-law. For many reasons, a line from Shakespeare's *Hamlet* never drifted too far from my memory after we had read it in English class: "A second time I kill my husband dead, when second husband kisses me in bed."

It was only natural for me to wonder if my father would fall in love with someone again. When would he be ready, if ever, to kiss another woman in his bed? It was painful for me to think about it, but I didn't want to wish him endless loneliness, and I was especially worried about what his life would be like when I was out of the house. I had been filling out applications for college. An acceptance would come soon and ring a bell in this house. I wondered how often he thought about that. I knew he did. Maybe he had his own timetable for when he would fall in love again, and it would start when that bell rang; or maybe he was determined never to love again. Maybe he knew that line in Tennyson's poem: "'Tis better to have loved and lost than never to have loved at all."

"Anyway," he continued, now that he had committed to revealing the story, "afterward, Arthur Johnson met and spent time with his future wife because of their parents' relationship, and both parents were pleased when they became engaged. Then they decided to do the same thing, get engaged and get married. It was a double wedding. His father married his wife's mother at the same ceremony."

"To save money?"

"Maybe," he said, smiling. "When you question why someone rich looks for bargains, he always tells you that's how he became rich. The women shopped for gowns together, and the men bought tuxedos together. They probably did get deals. They even bought similar wedding rings from the same jeweler. He gave away his son at the altar, and she gave away her daughter, and then vice versa. It was a ceremony conducted in mirrors."

"Must have looked weird with them switching places and all."

"I would think so, but he seemed proud of it when he talked about it. 'I got a new mother, and she got a new father the same time we got each other,' he told me. Families replacing families instantly," he said, shaking his head. "Goes on a lot more these days. People accept almost everything when it comes to relationships, exes marrying exes of friends, widows marrying widowed husbands of best friends, stepbrothers marrying stepsisters. Anything goes, it seems."

"Have you seen her?"

"Who?"

"Arthur Johnson's young wife."

"Yeah, once. Pretty girl. I shouldn't say 'girl.' They have a fourteen-year-old son and a twelve-year-old daughter. Both attend a private school in another state and live in dormitories. Maybe they're just not built to raise children. More bird in them."

"Bird?"

"You know. Hatching the eggs is one thing, getting them out of the nest as soon as possible is another."

"Bird," I repeated, and shook my head. "You are a character, Dad."

He shrugged. "I call it like I see it. And if you ask me, you can learn a lot about people by watching and observing so-called lower animals."

"I guess you learn a lot about the people you build or redo houses for."

"Nothing reveals as much about people as the home they live in," he said. "And their children are products of all that, too, often through no fault of their own."

I wanted to ask, *What if you were brought up in a mansion with parents from hell like Corrine Foxworth? Would that excuse her behavior after her husband died?* But I didn't. I started to clear off the table.

"Only odd thing," Dad added, sounding more like he was talking to himself than to me.

"What?"

"Huh? Oh. The only odd thing was the feeling I got that both Johnson and his wife—her name's Shannon—that both knew a lot more about both the original and the restored Foxworth Hall than Johnson first revealed."

"How do you mean? Knew what?"

"What it looked like in detail, inside and out. He makes references to it from time to time. Where windows were and what they looked out on, stuff like that. Although it's a different architecture, with all sorts of technological updates, he wants to be sure some things are the same."

"Well, there have been pictures of it. What's the surprise?"

"No. It was as if they had been there when it was in its heyday." He thought a moment and then shook his head. "Probably just my imagination. Anyway, don't let my blabbering make you late for school."

I had been late once before because of reading the diary late into the night and then oversleeping. One time was a warning, two was a detention and a demerit, and with my pursuit of class valedictorian, any misbehavior could affect a close decision if my final grades and someone else's were practically the same, which, right now, was the case. But it wasn't just that. Ever since my mother had died of a cerebral aneurism and my father and I were the only immediate family we had, disappointing him in any way, even with something as relatively minor as a tardiness demerit, was abhorrent to me. It was as if since my mother's death, both he and I felt things more, especially sad and disappointing things.

I once heard my father say that the death of someone as close as a wife or a husband strips away the bark. "The rain, even a sharp breeze, stings more."

"I won't be late. I have someone making sure of it, remember?"

"Oh, right. Okay. I left a meat loaf in the fridge. You just have to warm it up. Don't wait dinner on me," he said, and gave me a kiss. He held on to me just a few seconds longer than usual.

"Don't worry about this bird. I'm not leaving the nest so quickly, Dad," I said, and he laughed.

"Have a good day, Kristin."

"You, too, Dad."

I turned back to the sink but paused to think. What had my father meant by people accepting more when it came to relationships these days? Would they easily accept Christopher's father and mother marrying even though he was her half-uncle? According to Christopher Jr., that's what Corrine had finally revealed, making it sound so romantic and inevitable that she expected her children would accept it. There was a time when parents actually wanted their children to marry within the family, marry cousins, believing it kept their blood purer or something, and no one thought of it as incest back then.

I glanced at the clock and finished cleaning up quickly. By the time I had my hands wiped, Kane was sounding his horn. One long beep and two short beeps, like he was sending Morse code or a spy message. *Why are we all so dramatic at our age?* I thought. When we were older, would we look back and laugh at the little things that made us cry or laugh, sad or happy? When had I become so damn analytical? Maybe because of the way Christopher described Cathy, I was thinking more about everything I did. I was finding myself blaming more of what I thought and felt on my reading of the diary. Was that a bad omen?

I scooped up my books, flicked my dark blue hooded jacket off the hanger in the entryway, and shot out the door as if I was being chased. I slammed it behind me, the echo reverberating like a gunshot. It jerked me out of my deep thoughts as effectively as a slap on my face.

Kane was laughing at me as I hurried to the driveway, putting my jacket on as I went.

"What?" I asked, getting in.

"You should see me when I get up in the morning and stumble into the kitchen for some breakfast. I have to feel my way to the table. You look so alert, so ready to go," he said, and he gazed at the front of the house for a few seconds to see if my father might be looking out the window, then leaned over to kiss me quickly. "Hi."

"I'm not raring to go. Don't remind me how tired I am," I said. "I didn't sleep that well."

"Why not?"

"I just didn't."

He carefully backed out of the driveway. It was a mostly cloudy day. Before this, I had barely noticed the chill in the air. If it had ever smelled like snow was on the way, it did this morning. Already I missed the songbirds and the sweet scent of freshly cut grass. Our short Indian summer was gone. The leafless trees looked stunned. The surrounding woods had become the sleeping forest, hibernating, and the fields of dry grass looked like faded yellowish-green carpets, corpses of hay. With the weather so unpredictable, it was difficult to know confidently what it would be like tomorrow, much less next week or next month. Normally, we didn't have heavy snowfalls this early, but there were also many Christmases without snow at all.

Kane was only in a long-sleeved khaki shirt and jeans despite the cool air. Sometimes I thought he must have ice in his veins. He could be indifferent about the weather. I thought he was that way about almost everything. Whenever I'd complain about something, he'd simply nod, shrug, and give me that "what's the difference?" smile. *What's the difference what I wear, what I say, even what I think? Just move along, and if anything, just laugh. Laugh at the changes in the weather, laugh at the nervousness before exams, laugh at the school rules, and especially laugh at the drama of growing older and closer to being totally responsible for yourself. Just laugh.*

"Did you read any more of the diary without me?" he asked as we drove off to school. He narrowed his eyes with suspicion when he turned to me. "Is that why you didn't sleep well?"

I didn't answer him. I was still thinking about reading the diary in the attic, with him playing Christopher and me being Cathy. He was so casual about everything. Why should I believe he'd take the diary as seriously as I did? *This is too big a risk,* I told myself. *You'll regret it.*

"What's wrong?" His hazel eyes darkened with concern. "Did you read something that bothered you, something terrible? I really want to do it with you. You haven't changed your mind, have you?" He looked about as sincere as he ever was about anything.

This was it, I thought. I would either deliver my fabrication and end the diary reading or go on with it. I had to take that big risk. I had to believe in someone else besides my father, didn't I? Otherwise, I'd lock myself in a different kind of attic, but it would still be avoiding the world. I had to go on with it. I really wasn't a good liar, anyway. I was often compared to a fish in a bowl, with all my thoughts visibly swimming about. My father bragged about that, telling people, "Deceit's not comfortable sitting on her face." That was certainly not true for Corrine Dollanganger, I thought. If anything, she was certainly a good liar. Were selfish people naturally better liars?

"Nothing's wrong. I didn't read any more of the diary."

"Good. That gives me a chance to catch up. What about this afternoon? What time does your father usually come home? How much time will we have?"

"He's going to be late today, maybe the rest of the week."

"Perfect. Isn't it?" he asked when I didn't say anything.

"Are you sure you want to do this, Kane, really sure?"

"What? How can you ask? Absolutely. I couldn't stop thinking about it last night. I'm excited. Besides, I remembered that I always thought my father might know more about what happened at that original Foxworth Hall fire than he admits. He's learned lots of things about Malcolm Foxworth and his family from his older customers. I just never cared much about it until now."

"Did you tell him about the diary?" I asked, my voice on the verge of panic.

"No, no. I promised I would tell no one, and that's that. I won't."

"What do you mean, your father might know more than he admits?" I asked, sitting up more. "What does he know? How do you know it's more?"

"Easy," he said, smiling. "My father and mother know we went up to Foxworth to have that picnic."

"So?"

"He asked me about the site, what your father was doing, and I asked him what he really knew about the original fire. This was before you told me about the diary. He said what he heard was that the first fire definitely wasn't accidentally caused by a servant or some electrical malfunction or gas leak. He said that the story of how it happened that some firemen describe was right."

"Which story?"

"The one about the daughter deliberately setting the fire. She had gone mad and deliberately set the fire. He said she was whisked away before anyone could ask any more questions and apparently put in an insane asylum or something."

"He definitely said 'the daughter'? He believes that to be true?"

"Yes."

"Did you ask him her name?"

"I didn't want to ask him too many questions and get him suspicious."

"That was probably a good idea. Why would she have done that?"

"Who knows? Considering how long ago that was, I'm not surprised there are so many theories and so few facts. He said no one really cared that much about them or what had happened to them. He said from what old-timers told him, Malcolm and Olivia Foxworth weren't particularly liked and were considered rich, raving, religious maniacs. It was easy to believe they were capable of doing weird things to their children and grandchildren. That's why what you found is so exciting, Kristin. We'll know the truth. We'll learn all the secrets, secrets more than fifty years old."

"I'm not really sure we should jump to conclusions about anything in the diary. We can't treat it as gospel."

"What do you mean? You said it was found on the property. It's the diary of the boy who was imprisoned there, Christopher, right?"

"Right, but we are getting the story from Christopher. Maybe . . . maybe he's not telling the truth. My father once suggested that after I had begun to read it."

Kane thought a moment and then nodded. "I'll know pretty quickly once I get into it," he said confidently. "But people don't usually lie in a diary, anyway. That's why I never kept one. I don't want to be caught telling the truth." He gave me that James Dean smile and shrug that he had become famous for in our school.

"That I believe. So how will you know so quickly if he's lying or not?"

"I have a built-in lie detector. A buzzer goes off in my head, so don't try to fool me."

"Maybe I've fooled you already."

He laughed. "You're good, angel, you're real good," he said. "My father uses that line on my mother. It comes from some old Humphrey Bogart movie."

"Too bad Christopher Dollanganger didn't have that built-in buzzer of yours to know when he was being told the truth and when he wasn't. I'm sure he and his brother and sisters wouldn't have suffered so much."

"I'll have to catch up to see what you mean by suffering so much, but don't tell me any more. I want to be objective and come to my own conclusions. I know that's what you want, too, right?"

I nodded, and Kane made the turn into the school parking lot. Others were racing not to be late, the cooler air putting more energy into their strides, because, like Kane, most were underdressed. Even though they looked like they were on treadmills going five or six miles an hour and looked as comical as silent movie stars, some boys thought it was macho to freeze.

After Kane parked and shut off the engine, he sat there for a moment.

"What?" I asked, seeing that he was still in deep thought.

"Their mother brought them there, right?"

"Yes, you'll read about how and why. So?"

"So maybe he rationalized a lot. Maybe he did know, Kristin."

"Did know what?"

"Maybe he knew when he was being lied to but put up with it and lied to himself, and that's what we'll read. So your father could be at least half right."

"Why would he lie to himself?"

"All of us are willing to forgive the ones we love, Kristin," he replied, "even for their lies."

That was a perceptive thing to say, I thought, but what was going on in Kane's life that brought him to that conclusion, a conclusion he was willing to share? I was more impressed with him every time we were together. The sensitivity he revealed was a nice surprise. My father always said that getting to know someone, someone you cared very much to know, was like peeling an onion. It took time and patience. Sometimes you peeled away too much and regretted it. I didn't think I would regret it when it came to Kane. At least, I hoped I wouldn't.

I got out of the car, but I was still thinking about what he had said. *All of us are willing to forgive the ones we love? Even for lies?*

I hope so, I thought. *I hope that in the end, my father will forgive me.*

A big secret changes you in ways you don't realize immediately, especially if you share that secret with someone and hope he or she is keeping it safe. The bigger the secret, the more vulnerable and in danger you feel. Sometimes it shows right on your face, like splattered egg yolk, especially a face like mine. Practically every moment outside of class, I expected someone to rush over to me and declare, "You have the diary? You know what really happened at the original Foxworth Hall?" Every time I heard one of my friends call my name, an electric chill would rush up my spine.

Everyone has little secrets. In our world, that was what made you more interesting. But this was very different. Anyone who found out what we had would surely pounce, and not just my classmates. Newspapers, radio, television people would haunt us. The phone wouldn't stop ringing, nor would the doorbell. People would accuse us of always having had it and deliberately hoarding the truth because it was embarrassing for our family. My mother was a distant cousin of Malcolm Foxworth, so the children were distant cousins of mine. My father would feel terrible for calling me over that day to watch him open the locked metal box at the bottom of some debris in the remains of the restored Foxworth Hall. The restoration had used the same basement walls. My father thought the builders were just not very meticulous when it came to cleaning away the original debris. His colleagues would tease him about it. Some might even be nasty and make him angry. He would hate to go anywhere, except to work and right back home. Just going to the supermarket would become a big deal. I couldn't even imagine what coming to my high school graduation would be like for him.

He might lose business. He might want to sell our house and move away.

I didn't want to imagine any of it. It was like having a nightmare while awake. That's what it was starting to feel like at school.

Physically, I was walking about with my books embraced tightly against my breasts, as if I were protecting something precious inside the covers, or perhaps really more inside me. Emotionally, I felt clogged, as if my feelings were twisted into figure-eight knots. The weight of our secret slowed my pace, no matter what I was doing. I could feel my eyes widen in expectation every time I was asked a question, no matter how innocent the question might seem. Had I revealed anything accidentally? Had I whetted anyone's interest? Had Kane inadvertently given something away already, and others were testing me? I was taking on real paranoia. This was triggered especially when one of my close friends, Kyra Skewer, asked me about Kane picking me up every morning and taking me home after school.

"Does he hang out at your house, or do you go to his or what afterward?" she wanted to know. She asked in front of Suzette, Missy Meyer, and Theresa Flowman, and all four of them gave me their full attention, their ears perked up like extraterrestrial antennae.

"It varies with my mood," I said cryptically.

"Huh?"

"Whatever," I said. "It's spontaneous."

"You and your vocabulary," Kyra complained. She had a grimace that made her look like she was being burned at the stake whenever she complained about anything.

"Spontaneous? Please. That's not a hard word to define, Kyra."

"I know what it means. I just never heard it used like that," she said.

"When you're in love, everything is spontaneous," Suzette said, and then giggled and turned her shoulders inward, which made her breasts bulge in the deep V-neck of her light blue sweater. I knew she often did that deliberately just to see where the gaze of the boy she was talking to went. "Whether it's a kiss or something more," she added.

"Then every day is spontaneous for you," Kyra said. "Every month, you fall into a desperate love that lasts as long as your period."

Everyone laughed. I smiled. It wasn't all that much of an exaggeration when it came to Suzette. Recently, she had gotten blond highlights in her dark brown hair because Tommy Clark liked blond highlights, and soon after that, she let us all know she had pierced her navel. In fact, she let everyone know, especially Greg Storm, who had his nose pierced. It did seem like she remade herself weekly to attract some new boy she fancied.

"I'd rather go to Kane's house. You'd have more

privacy," Missy Meyer said, getting serious again. "I mean, you have a nice house. It's just that . . ."

"The way the house is laid out, her father might hear what goes on in her bedroom?" Suzette suggested, her silver-blue eyes brightening like two diamonds of promiscuous excitement. "Didn't your younger brother hear what went on in yours when you brought Dylan Marks home one afternoon?" she asked Kyra. She embraced herself and mimicked groans and moans.

"Shut up."

"Well, no matter where you go after school, Kristin, he can't help you with your homework. If anything, he'll distract you," Theresa Flowman said in her nasal voice. She was hoping for that result, hoping Kane would distract me enough to lower my grades. After the last marking period, Theresa and I were neck and neck for valedictorian.

"Please, Theresa, distract her?" Kyra said. "What you need is a lot more distraction. Any distraction, come to think of it," she added, flashing a sly smile at me. Suzette and Missy laughed. Theresa turned crimson, glared at her, and walked off.

"All that girl knows about sex is that it's a three-letter word," Suzette said.

"And what do you know?" Kyra teased.

"I know Steve Cooper would like to practice the missionary position with you in his basement," she retorted, and the three of them laughed again. Steve's parents had let him move into their basement, which felt like a private apartment because it had a separate entrance. Lately, it had acquired a nickname: Steve's Sex Pit.

They looked at me, noticing I wasn't laughing this time. The chitchat had reminded me of Christopher and Cathy talking about sex, and for a moment, I was back in the attic, thinking about an older brother being a young girl's only source for information about her maturing body. Even though Christopher was coldly scientific, he was still her brother and not her mother or older sister. Any young girl would still be sensitive about asking him questions about sex, but especially a sister. I recalled how hard it had been for my father to talk to me about any of it. He finally had to ask his sister, my aunt Barbara, to speak with me about my own emerging hormones clamoring to be recognized. She had made a special trip from New York to do it.

Who would make a special trip for Cathy? It didn't look like her mother would take the time to do it. She certainly wouldn't take her out of the room to have a private conversation, one of those mother-daughter talks that my girlfriends satirized. They didn't realize how envious of them I was. There were so many little things that had become big things for all of us, but especially for children locked away like that, I thought, children locked in a room and an attic and left to their own imagination to amuse and educate themselves. Christopher would do fine, but Cathy . . . how would it end up for her? Did I really want to know? Would both Kane and I regret turning those pages in the diary?

"Anything wrong?" Kyra said. "Hello, earth to Kristin?"

"What?"

She looked at Suzette.

"We were both talking to you, and you didn't hear us. You've been acting weird all day. You didn't miss a period, did you?" Suzette asked. She would.

The three of them looked at me with one face, mouths slightly open, eyes anticipating.

"She hasn't been going with him long enough, has she?" Kyra asked.

"We really don't know how long she's been *seeing* him," Suzette said, enjoying the implication as she kept her eyes on me. "And guess what? It doesn't take that long to get pregnant. Some sperm are faster than a speeding bullet, right, Kristin?"

"Get outta here," I said, playfully nudging her. "You have a one-track mind," I added, and then spotted Kane coming around the hallway corner. "Later," I muttered, and hurried to join him.

"Hey," he said, putting his arm around my shoulders. "You all right?"

He looked back at my girlfriends, who were staring at us and giggling.

"Someone say something about us?"

"No. They don't bother me. I think I screwed up on a math quiz."

"Does the CIA know yet?"

"I'm serious. I should have aced it, Kane."

"All right. Sorry. What happened?" he asked as we walked to our next classes.

"I don't know. My mind just . . . went blank or something."

"Everyone has a day like that."

"I never did," I said.

"So now you're normal. Relax. You'll do better the next time," he insisted. He shrugged. "Isn't that why there are erasers on pencils?"

I stopped and smiled. "That's exactly what my father says when I complain about something I've done wrong."

"My father doesn't say it; my mother does. My father doesn't believe in mistakes. He claims it's not in his religion."

"What religion is that?"

"Perfection," he replied, then laughed and gave me a quick kiss on the lips, which at least twenty other students saw, their eyes blinking like the lenses of paparazzi cameras. And then he hurried off to beat the late bell for his class. Most of my classes were advanced placement classes now. He turned and waved and then pretended he had been grabbed and pulled into a room. I laughed. He could have entertained everyone on the *Titanic*.

What a mixture of emotions I was feeling. I was excited about being with him. I really did love every minute, and I loved how we were like everyone's perfect couple, but I was feeling a little numb, confused, very tentative about myself because of the plan we had made for reading the diary together. I kept coming back to it all day, and sometimes I'd be trembling. Why was I so nervous about it? Did I really think the diary had some evil magical power because it had been buried so long in the rubble of the original Foxworth Hall? Was opening it like opening Pandora's box? Did my father get me thinking like this by his wishing so strongly that I wouldn't read it?

My father always had this weird attitude about the original Foxworth Hall, never really wanting to talk about it or what had happened there, even though I was related to them on my mother's side. Maybe he didn't want to talk about it precisely because of that. When I was younger and even now, some of my classmates wondered if I had inherited any of the Foxworth madness.

It got so even I began to wonder.

Finally, I decided I was just being stupid thinking all these weird things and pushed it all out of my mind by concentrating hard on my schoolwork.

However, as soon as the bell rang to end our final class of the day, I felt my heart begin to beat faster in anticipation of what Kane and I were going to begin doing. My girlfriends, especially Suzette, continued to tease me about being with Kane before and after school, filling up every free moment with him. I thought they were just jealous.

"Will we ever see you again?" Suzette joked.

"Will you ever answer the phone when we call?" Kyra followed.

I shut them out, their laughter falling behind me like pebbles falling from a speeding, bouncing dump truck, and hurried to meet him. He was already at the exit waiting for me. He put his arm around me quickly and turned us to the door.

"I lucked out. Not much homework tonight," he said. "I can spend more time reading."

"I have my usual ton."

He opened the door, and we walked out quickly to the parking lot and his car. Practically every classmate of mine smiled licentiously at us as they passed us, some walking faster just to do that. Kane seemed oblivious to it. We had known each other a long time, even though we had just started going out together. I was still trying to understand him. Was he indifferent to most of the things that captured everyone else's interest because he was just plain arrogant, or did he simply not care? Perhaps our experience with Christopher's diary would peel that onion faster when it came to him.

"Don and Ryan were driving me crazy to go skeet shooting with them this afternoon," he said after we got into the car. "I forgot I had made plans to do that."

"You want to?" I asked, welcoming the reprieve. "We can postpone this."

"Hell no. As you know, I've got reading to do, and with your father coming home late, we have a good opportunity to get into a lot of it," he said. He started the engine and drove us to my house.

I could never imagine Kane Hill nervous about anything, but until we turned into my driveway, he talked continually, describing the most inconsequential things that had happened during the day. It was almost like someone dictating Facebook or Twitter posts. His desk in math class wobbled too much. His math teacher, Mr. Brizel, broke his green chalk, the one he used to underline answers on the blackboard when he was frustrated with class responses. It was too cool in shop class because Mr. Primack left a window open too much and no one had the nerve to complain.

I was half-listening, anyway. I was thinking that I should call my father just to be sure he was going to be late for dinner and wouldn't arrive earlier than I expected and discover us in my room reading the diary. When we entered the house, I went right to the phone in the kitchen. Kane glanced at the stairway and looked at me expectantly.

"Go on up ahead of me and start," I said. "I have to call my father."

He shot up the stairs, taking two at a time, and turned to my room before I even entered the kitchen.

He really was into this, I thought, but that still wasn't making me feel confident about it now. I called my father.

"Hey, what's up?" he asked. "Anything wrong?"

"No. Just checking to be sure you will be late for dinner."

"Yeah, sorry. I know you don't like to eat alone."

"I might invite Kane," I said. "You made enough for at least five people," I added quickly.

"Oh, so he's there?"

"Yes. We're . . . doing homework together."

"Sounds romantic. Should I be worried?" He hummed the shark theme again, just what I had been anticipating when I thought about calling him from Kane's car.

"Dad! Stop!"

"Okay."

"Is it all right to have him stay for dinner?"

"Absolutely. Later are you going to brag that your father won over your new boyfriend with his cooking?"

"No," I said.

He laughed. "Enjoy," he said, and shouted to someone just before he hung up.

I stood there for a moment thinking about it all and then walked slowly up the stairs. Kane was on my bed, his shoes off, the diary in his hands.

"You want to stay for dinner? My father's definitely going to be late," I said.

"What's for dinner?"

"It's his meat loaf, my mashed potatoes, and string beans."

"Sure. I love meat loaf," he replied, and then returned to the diary as if his eyes were pulled to it beyond his control.

I put my books on my desk and, after looking at him again, began to attack my homework. Even though I glanced at him from time to time, neither of us spoke for a good hour or so. Finally, I heard him sigh deeply, and I turned and saw that he had sat up and was holding his hands over his face.

"What?" I asked.

"This was one bright kid, this Christopher

Dollanganger. He writes well, but he sounds like he's afraid of his own emotions, afraid that he's going to explode or something. I get the feeling he was walking around holding his breath most of the time, especially after they were brought to the mansion. And how about that grandmother? She'd give Norman Bates from *Psycho* nightmares. He's putting up with a lot more than I would, even at that age."

"Yes. He's doing a great deal for his little brother and sister and for Cathy, and he has to keep the lid on."

"I can't wait to see if he does. Cathy sounds more difficult than the twins."

"She has a lot to be unhappy about, Kane. She's cut off from all her friends, everything that once made her life exciting, and look at the new responsibilities dropped on her. It wasn't fair."

He nodded. "Makes sense. So you like her?"

"Why not? It's not her fault that they are where they are."

"You sound very defensive. Maybe there's more Cathy in you than either of us knows."

"What?"

He smiled and picked up the diary again.

"Are you going to catch up to me in one day?" I asked, sounding a bit annoyed now.

"You bet."

"What about your homework?"

"I told you, I don't have that much, and besides, I'll do it when I get home."

I looked at my watch. "I'm going down to start on dinner. We'll eat in about a half hour. I hope you can tear yourself away. You're not bringing it to the dinner table," I warned.

He didn't respond. He was already back into the diary so much that he didn't hear me. I paused in the doorway and looked at him, with the book up and his face blocked. I thought of Cathy, bored in that attic, looking at Christopher and seeing him deep in one of his science books, in his own world. That was probably his only escape, but it had to be frustrating for her. She had no one else to talk to but the twins.

I didn't know why exactly, but Kane's attraction to the diary was making me irritable. Anyone might think I was jealous of how passionate he had become about it. It was as though he appreciated it more than I did or something. I banged things around a bit more than necessary and mumbled under my breath as I set the table.

Kane came down exactly thirty minutes later. I turned, surprised.

"Wow! You could break away, after all."

"Smelled the aroma and got hungry," he said. "How can I help?"

"Take this jug of water to the table. Everything else is done," I told him.

I began to bring in the food.

"It looks terrific," he said.

I began to serve him. Then I served myself and sat.

"How did you like how their grandmother fed them?" he said. "It was like leaving crumbs out for birds. I think the servants knew what was going on, or at least one or two did."

"Why?"

"Think about it. She's making food, putting together food, and taking it to them. She doesn't strike me as the sort of person who would slink about. If any of them saw her, she would tell them to buzz off."

I hadn't thought about that. Maybe it was good to have someone else reading it at the same time after all.

I started eating and so did he. "This meat loaf is the best I've ever had," he said.

"My father will be happy to hear it. I tried making it a few times, but it's never as good. He has little secrets he keeps even from me. He promises he'll reveal all when I get married."

Kane paused and looked thoughtful again.

"What?"

"There were so many secrets going on in that mansion that it's a wonder it didn't explode before it burned down. What's really going on between Corrine and her parents? Christopher is limited in what he can write, so we might not discover that. He doesn't really know what's happening in the rest of the mansion. He's never even seen the grandfather. Who knows if the old goat is really that sick?"

"You think their mother deliberately lied about that? Why?"

"I don't know." He was thoughtful for a few moments and then said, "The jury's not in on it, and maybe it will never be. As you said, we're getting it from Christopher only. Even with only what I've read until now, I can't imagine him ever calling his mother a liar. And not only because he's a respectful, obedient kid. I'd like to read *her* diary. That would be a page-turner, I bet. We'd learn a lot more if we could compare."

"I do have one other source of information," I said.

He looked up sharply. "What? Your father?"

"No, especially not him. I told you, he doesn't like me reading it, and he doesn't like talking about it."

"So?"

"It's my uncle Tommy, my father's younger brother. He met someone who claimed he had known a servant who worked at the original Foxworth Hall."

"No kidding. And?"

"He said this man told him the servant claimed their grandfather knew they were up there."

"See? Like I said, the servants probably saw the old hag carrying food and told the old man, or maybe he and the *Friday the Thirteenth* grandmother plotted together." He thought a moment and then brightened and asked, "Did your uncle say Corrine knew that her father knew?"

"He didn't say, and back then, I didn't know enough to ask many questions. I wasn't old enough to appreciate the answers anyway, and because of how my father was about it, I didn't want to think about it."

Kane sat back and nodded. "There's a lot to discover. I like mysteries. I'm not going home tonight until I catch up to you," he declared.

"I want to emphasize that I don't want my father to know about this."

"I wonder what's making him so uptight about it. Did you ever come right out and ask him?"

"No. And we're not going to ask," I said firmly.

He smiled. "Don't worry about it. I don't want to get him even slightly mad at me." I was about to smile, thinking he meant that would risk his being with me, but then he went for another forkful of meat loaf and added, "I might not get any more of his home cooking."

I laughed. Maybe my father was right. Maybe I would win Kane through his cooking.

Kane skipped dessert so he could get back up to my room. He offered to clear the table and help in the kitchen, but I told him just to go back to the diary. He'd only rush and break something. He didn't need to be told twice.

While I was finishing up, my father came home. "Where's Kane?" he asked immediately when he entered the kitchen. "I see his car's still here."

"Oh, he's up in my room doing homework."

"Enjoy the dinner?"

"You have a devoted fan."

"Didn't offer to help with the dishes?"

"He offered," I said. "Let's just say he's not used to working in a kitchen, and like you always say, when someone who doesn't know what he's doing assists you, it makes for twice the work."

"Not surprised he's unaccustomed to KP duty, but I'm surprised he left you alone. He could have at least watched. He's that into his homework?"

"He had more than I did tonight. We don't have

the same classes. How's everything at the building site?" *Get him talking about the project quickly*, I told myself. I hated coming up with all these white lies. I was with Huckleberry Finn. Why tell the truth and hurt someone?

"Usual bureaucratic delays with inspectors, but we're muddling through."

I wiped my hands. "Everything's hot and ready for you. Go sit, and I'll bring it in."

"I'm not ready yet. I want to shower and change first, baby. You better get back to that homework," he added with a bit of an impish smile.

I threw the dish towel at him and hurried up the stairs.

"Break out your textbooks," I warned Kane. "My father's here."

He nodded and slipped the diary under my pillow. By the time my father knocked on the door, Kane was doing his math.

"Smells like a library in here," my father joked when he saw us both into our textbooks.

"Hi, Mr. Masterwood. Fantastic meat loaf."

"Thanks. Glad you enjoyed it. I'll get changed so I can eat it myself and see if you're giving me a false compliment," my father said, and then he winked and left us.

Kane closed his textbook. "Gotta confession," he said.

"What?"

"I caught up to you."

"What? How could you?"

"You're not even half through it, you know, and I read fast when I'm really interested in what I'm reading."

I nodded, thinking about how I did labor over some sentences and events, always trying to imagine how Cathy was feeling. "I guess so."

"And I read another page before I realized it. I'll reread it tomorrow . . . aloud. Up in the attic," he added, and closed his textbook. "I'd better get going. I forgot to call my mother to tell her I wasn't coming home for dinner," he said. "Don't worry. I've done it before, and it's never a big shock, anyway. Tell your father good night for me."

He gave me a very quick kiss on the cheek and a playful pat on the top of my head.

I was expecting him to kiss me before he left, but not like a brother.

I had been nervous while Kane was reading the diary to catch up with me, so I hadn't done my homework as quickly as I could. I had some left to complete. Nevertheless, I went down to sit with my father while he ate. He was surprised Kane had left so early.

"Maybe he really was here just to do homework," he playfully suggested.

"Did the new owner come around again?" I asked, again looking to change the topic quickly.

"He did."

I could see that he was into one of his deep thoughts again because of my question, a thought he wasn't eager to reveal to me.

"What?" I asked.

"You still reading that diary?"

I was surprised he asked. He had told me recently that he wouldn't inquire about it anymore and that when I was finished, he wanted me to give it back to him. I had the feeling he really would burn it, so I was debating whether I ever would give it to him.

"On and off," I said, as nonchalantly as I could. The words almost got stuck in my throat.

"Has there been any mention of anyone else in the house? I mean other than their mother, grandmother, and grandfather?"

"Well, servants are mentioned but not by name," I said.

"No one specifically, then?"

"Not yet as far as I have read. Why? Who do you think was there? Someone from town knew about them?"

"It's not important," he said, and continued eating.

"If it wasn't important, you wouldn't mention it," I said.

He shook his head. "I swear, Kristin, if I closed my eyes when you were talking sometimes, I'd think your mother was sitting there."

Whenever he said anything like that, making comparisons between my mother and me to point out how much I was like her, I felt the struggle between two conflicting emotions, happiness and sadness. I loved the idea that I was anything like her, but just the reference to her stirred the well of tears that would forever be there, ready to rise and overflow before

I could do anything to stop them. If I cried in front of my father, he would cry all night, I thought, and turned away.

He didn't say anything else about it, and I didn't pursue it. *Don't bring up the diary*, I told myself. *In fact, don't bring up Foxworth Hall if you can help it until you and Kane are finished reading the diary.*

I cleared away his dishes and did everything that had to be done in the kitchen before I returned to my room to finish my homework. I knew I wasn't giving it my best. I was rushing now, because I didn't want him to know how distracted I had been. He knew how responsible I was and how dedicated I was to getting my schoolwork done and done well. He would never suspect the diary, especially because Kane was there. He would think it was because of something else, obviously something that had to do with my private time with Kane. I was confident that he wouldn't come right out and ask, "Did you guys spend all your time doing assignments from your teachers, or did you come up with your own homework?" He could tease a little, skirt around it by asking me to tell him how serious we were becoming, but making reference to something explicitly sexual just wasn't something my father would do. He wasn't a prude. He was just a shy man who was left to do and worry about things my mother was supposed to handle.

The irony was that we had done nothing my girl-friends were suspecting we did. All the girls believed that Kane was not timid about making love, and we'd been alone in my bedroom. Not only them but any parent would suspect more intimacy. All my girl-friends talked about the suspicions their parents had. Suzette went so far as to tell us her mother had given up on her, telling her not to expect her to come rushing in to rescue her. "You're old enough to know better," she'd said.

My father would never say such a thing, no matter what I did, I thought.

Before I went to sleep, I went down to wake him up and tell him it was time to go to sleep. It was a constant joke between us. He'd watch television and drift off. I would turn it off, and he'd wake up surprised. Then he would kiss me and go to his room to sleep with his memories.

I got into bed and lowered my head to the pillow, Christopher's words rambling on under it, below me in the forbidden diary.

And Kane's questions and thoughts rambling right along with them.

Kane amazed me the following day. He was so excited about what he had read and what we were going to do that I thought for sure he would be talking about nothing else, but from the first moment he set eyes on me in the morning, he seemed to know that to keep me from having any anxiety, especially while we were at school, the diary should remain under my pillow, physically and mentally. Neither of us would mention it. To show me I could rely on him for that, he talked about everything and anything else on our way to school and during the day. He went on and on about a party Tina Kennedy was planning. I knew she was always chasing him, and he enjoyed teasing me about it. He was so good at ignoring the diary, in fact, that it felt like I had dreamed the entire thing—his discovering the diary under my pillow and our plans for where and how to read it together. However, it couldn't be completely ignored until the moment we took it out from under my pillow again. For one thing, just like Christopher at this point in his diary, we were a week away from Thanksgiving. Finally, on the way to my house after school, Kane mentioned that.

"Quite a coincidence that the time period coincides," he said.

Neither of us had to say it, but we both thought that was a little eerie. Why had the diary been discovered now? And how coincidental was it that my father would be the one to locate the locked metal box after all these years? Other people, young people, searched in the debris because there were so many rumors and stories about hidden wealth at Foxworth Hall. Malcolm was supposed to be a miser, spending his money mainly on church or some religious charity. The story was that he distrusted everyone, especially bankers, and was one of those people who literally kept money buried somewhere, yet no one had managed to uncover the metal box that contained Christopher's diary—no one until my father was sent to evaluate the foundation for a new prospective buyer.

"I can't imagine what he'll write about their

Thanksgiving shut up like that. If the legendary story about them is true, they spent more than one Thanksgiving and Christmas in that attic and more than one birthday. We've got thirty-five people coming for dinner at our house," he continued when I didn't comment. "My parents don't do much. There's a full kitchen staff, waiters, and a bartender. It's more like a party than a family gathering, even though two of my uncles and aunts are there with their children, who I don't see very much. That's a good thing. Their pictures are right beside the word 'brat' in the dictionary. I'm glad Darlena comes home from college, though. What about you? What goes on in your house?"

"As you can imagine, my father fixes quite a dinner. He has a sweet potato pudding to die for."

"Just the two of you?"

"No. My aunt Barbara, my father's sister, has come occasionally and might come this time, but my father always invites his chief assistant, Todd Winston, and his wife and their two children, and Mrs. Osterhouse, who does his bookkeeping and would like to do more for him, and I don't mean at work. She's a widow who has been with him for a long time."

"Ah. Do you like her?"

"Yes, she's nice."

"Nice enough to be a new mother?"

"I'll never have another mother, Kane. Even a saint couldn't step into her shoes."

"Yeah. I'm sorry I put it that way. What about your father? Any interest? Has he dated her?"

"No. He's polite to her, but I think she tries too hard."

"Like Tina Kennedy when it comes to yours truly?"

"No, not quite as obvious as that," I said, and he laughed. "But my father likes subtlety when it comes to women."

"He's not so subtle when it comes to you."

"No," I said, smiling, "and I'm not when it comes to him, either."

"I like your father. He seems comfortable in his own skin."

"He never puts on airs, if that's what you mean. I'm proud of him."

"You should be." He paused and added, "I think I'm more like him than I am like my own father."

"Why do you say that?"

"My father's always striving to do more, get bigger, and is quite obvious about it. That's why he's on edge so much. Everything's got to come out just the way he planned. It's always the bottom line, no matter what it is. He wants to make a profit on everything, even relationships. More than once, I've overheard my mother accuse him of marrying her for her family money."

"Do you think that's true?"

He gave me a look that said, "You have to ask?"

"So you're not coming out just the way he planned, his bottom line for a son?" I asked.

He smiled. "Not exactly."

"Why not? You do well in school. They say you're the best baseball pitcher the school's ever had. You don't get in trouble, and you're passably good-looking."

"Passably?"

"Maybe a little more," I kidded.

"I'm not as ambitious as he'd like, and he thinks I waste time on too many 'unprofitable' ventures. He never stops complaining about my enthusiasm when it comes to my future. He thinks I should be just as aggressive and ambitious as he was at my age. He never misses an opportunity to say it. His favorite expression is 'Youth is wasted on the young.'"

"That's what most parents say."

"Not like he does. But from what my relatives say, he wasn't always this intense. He's like someone who wins the lottery and turns from Jekyll to Hyde. Don't quote me, especially in front of my father or my mother, but money changes you and not always for the best."

"I fear Christopher might come to that same conclusion, even though that's all they're dreaming about in that attic, lots of money."

"We'll know soon enough," Kane said, smiling, as he pulled into my driveway.

Now that we were about to start, I really wasn't sure how we were going to do this. Was he going to read it like a bedtime story? Were we going to stop to discuss things the way we might when we were studying a book in school? Was I just going to sit there and listen the whole time, or was I supposed to take over and read to him?

I headed for the kitchen first.

"What are you doing? Let's get started," he said, practically leaping at the stairway.

"I thought I'd get us something to drink and eat first. Don't you want a snack? I have—"

"Just water," he said. "Nothing else. That's all *they* had most of the time. We've got to try to replicate their situation to really appreciate what he writes when I read it."

I felt a flush come over me. It wasn't excitement, exactly. It was as if he really believed we could do it, that we really could become Christopher and Cathy while we were up in my attic. He saw the look on my face.

"Didn't you ever hear the expression 'stay in character'? That's all I'm saying."

"Okay."

I poured two glasses of cold water, handed him one, and led him up the stairs to my room. After I plucked the diary out from under my pillow, I looked at him. Now that we were about to do it, I half expected him to start laughing and say it was all just a joke, a reason to get me alone with him after school, but he stepped back instead to let me pass.

I led the way to the attic stairs. When we reached the door, I hesitated. Those creaking steps, those dark shadows, everything made it seem as if I was opening this door for the first time. It wasn't simply a door to an attic; it was a door to the past. When I did step in,

I paused as if I was expecting to see the four Dollanganger children waiting for us.

"Perfect," Kane whispered, coming up beside me. "There's furniture and old things. It really is a miniature Foxworth."

"Not quite," I said, looking at my mother's wardrobe. "It's not all other people's leftovers and such. My mother's clothing is in here," I told him, putting my hand on the wardrobe.

"Oh." He looked guilty suddenly. "I didn't know. You didn't say anything. Maybe I shouldn't have suggested we come up here."

"It's all right. I've been up here often. I even wore one of her dresses, remember? That was the night you took me to the River House."

"Oh. Right. But everything else here . . ."

"Nothing with any real memories for me, and the rest of it is stuff left by the original occupants."

He went over to the small windows and looked out. "Should I open one of these?"

"A little, but let's not forget to close it before we leave," I said.

He opened one and then turned and sat on the sofa.

"Come on," he said, obviously even more excited now. "Let's begin." He held his hand out for the diary. I gave it to him and sat beside him. He thought a moment and then got up and moved to the chair across from the sofa.

"Why did you do that?"

"Better this way," he said.

I smiled at him. "Why?"

"It's more like when Christopher read to them or something. Don't worry. You'll understand after we get started," he said, as if he already knew more about the Dollanganger children than I did. He opened the diary.

I sat back. I had no idea what to expect or what would happen next, but I couldn't help being eager to find out.

He didn't change his voice, exactly, but as he read, I could see him trying to pronounce every word perfectly and speak like a young boy who thought he was much more intelligent than anyone else around him, including, of course, his mother and grandmother. Kane even changed his posture, assuming that Christopher would never slouch.

To play along, I sat back and tried to remember what I was like when I was Cathy Dollanganger's age, when every new little discovery about myself was earth-shattering and when, like her, I needed my mother so much, a mother neither of us had.

And as he read, I could feel myself slipping out of this world and into theirs.

I think the realization that it was almost Thanksgiving shocked me as much as if not more than it shocked Cathy. I did my best to act surprised when Cathy mentioned it, acting almost carefree about it. I knew how dramatic she could be, and I was afraid of what that would do to the twins. I put on a face that said, "So it's almost Thanksgiving, so what?"

She didn't have to tell me. The "what" in "so what?" was that Thanksgivings were always wonderful in our house when my father was alive. To him, it was pre-Christmas, so he always had little novelty presents for us: a challenging mental puzzle for me, a small toy car for Cory, and fake jewelry or combs for Carrie and Cathy. It wasn't much, just little surprises at the dinner table. He didn't do anything resembling a novelty for Momma. He never gave her anything that wasn't very special. Any occasion was good for a new piece of jewelry.

"When you find your soul mate," he told me, "always treat her like a princess. Women love jewelry."

Just before Daddy was killed, it got so that Cory used to think a pair of diamond earrings could multiply somehow into a diamond necklace, too, or a bracelet by Christmas. They weren't large diamonds. Maybe they weren't even real diamonds, but Momma was always excited and happy to get gifts, no matter what the occasion and especially if there was no occasion. If he came home with something for her after work, it meant he was thinking about her.

"Oh, look, children!" she would cry. "Your father was thinking of me even when he was at work."

"I'm always thinking of you, Corrine," he would say. It made her more buoyant and beautiful, especially at Thanksgiving, because he would always begin by telling us how thankful he was for our mother. Maybe because of that more than anything, she was eager to make our Thanksgiving and Christmas dinners special. She was never the greatest cook, but she did a good job on the Thanksgiving turkey with all the trimmings, some of which were smuggled in by Mrs. Wheeler, who also made our pies.

I was carefree and indifferent about it now, because I was afraid Momma would forget to do something about Thanksgiving for us, but she surprised me when she came into the attic with some decorations for our table and announced that they were for our Thanksgiving dinner, which she promised would be hot and wonderful, as wonderful as any.

"How could it be as wonderful?" Cathy whispered. "We don't have Daddy."

"But we still have each other," I replied. "We'll always have each other."

She looked at me with grateful eyes. I always seemed to come up with the right answers for her. Sometimes, though, I thought she was sorry I had. She wanted me to be more of an ally, more impatient and disgusted with everything.

One thing that did bother both Cathy and me was that Carrie had completely forgotten what Thanksgiving was. She had been old enough to appreciate what we once had, but so much about our lives was beginning to fade and get lost in the fog of what had happened so quickly and where we were now. When the door was shut and locked, it seemed to cut off our ties with our own past, slamming down on our happier memories.

My second pleasant surprise, however, was how wholeheartedly Cathy decided to get into it, fixing the table with the dishes and place settings that she had the twins help her create. She was almost frantic about making our table joyful. I tried to go along with the same enthusiasm, but I was worried about her. She acted as if she was convinced that this dinner would be more than a typical Thanksgiving celebration; it would be the dinner celebrating our escape into a new life. I have to admit that the way Momma described it and how happy she seemed certainly gave us that impression. She promised all sorts of wonderful food from the party our grandparents were having and described the festivities just the way she would before Daddy died. All of this was going to come to a quick end and a new beginning. Momma's promises were alive and well.

However, that day, the hour for our participating in the wonderful foods and desserts came and went. Every minute, every hour, was like another whiplash. Every creak in the floor or the walls turned our eyes to the door expectantly, but there was only silence and more disappointment.

We were all getting ravenously hungry in anticipation. Momma had done such a good job of describing it all. The twins were especially irritable as time passed. Cathy tried to calm

them with whatever we had to nibble on, but
it wasn't working. I felt I was slipping myself,
losing my control. I wanted to start screaming
and pounding on the door, shouting, "Where are
you? Where's our wonderful dinner? Where's our
Thanksgiving?"

Finally, hours after she was supposed to be
here, Momma arrived. There was the Thanksgiving
food she had promised, but by now, it was cold,
and the twins wouldn't eat any, and worst of all,
Momma couldn't stay with us. What kind of a family
dinner was this? Nevertheless, I was ravenous and
couldn't get those pieces of turkey into my mouth
fast enough. The twins moaned and complained
more than ever. They wouldn't touch a thing.
Desperate to have them eat something, Cathy
prepared peanut butter sandwiches. Afterward,
Cathy didn't have to say a word to convince me. I
sat staring at the plates and thinking how miserable
we really were.

Kane paused and looked at me. "I guess I know what
we'll both be thinking about at our own Thanksgiving feasts," he said. "How would you like eating
alone with only your younger brother and sisters in
an attic? No music, no conversations, nobody telling
jokes, nothing but cold turkey and potatoes? I'll never
complain about our Thanksgivings again. That's for
sure."

I nodded. He was right. How cruel. As if he knew
what would follow in the diary, he put up his hand

before I could speak and began again, his voice firmer, the words now colored with anger so visible his face turned a shade of crimson. It riled up my sense of outrage, too. Kane had been right. It was different, more effective, to read Christopher's diary with someone else and see his reaction. I sat back, and he began again.

But the misery was yet to start. The following morning, Cory came down with a very bad cold. Two days later, Carrie was just as sick. These were very bad colds, more like flu. Momma came to treat them with aspirin and soup and juice, our grandmother following right behind her like some dark shadow cast by Death looking to get his hands on our little brother and sister. She hovered over Cory and Carrie and shook her head at the way we were making a big deal over their illness. She ridiculed whatever I suggested.

"Some doctor you'll be," she said, and insisted they just had to tough it out like any other children. I was surprised Momma had told her what my ambitions were, but now I was upset she had. I glanced at Cathy, who would always come to my defense. I shook my head so she'd understand not to do or say anything nasty now. The twins were too sick.

At one point, Cory had a very high fever, but nothing impressed our grandmother, and Momma, to my great disappointment, didn't challenge her. To impress us with how serious she thought it was, however, she claimed she had taken off from secretarial school just to care for them. I never told Cathy this, but I always suspected that Momma never went to any secretarial school. I couldn't even begin to imagine her doing that sort of work, and logically, why would she bring us here and put us through all this if we weren't going to live here but instead live in some apartment supported by her secretarial job? Of course, Cathy never thought of these things, and I wasn't going to say anything that would diminish her hope.

The twins' illness went on and on for nearly three weeks. Finally, they began to recuperate, but the illness had drained them. They were lethargic, wisps of themselves, sleeping more than usual, and difficult to get excited about any game or food.

I told Momma, and she decided that all we needed were vitamins. The words were barely out of her mouth before Cathy exploded, shouting at her to get us out or at least take the twins into the fresh air. She stomped her feet and raged. The twins were wide-eyed at her tantrum. They wanted to cry, but they were too frightened to utter a sound. She was making so much noise that I thought if no one else really knew we were here, they surely knew now. Momma pleaded with Cathy to calm down, telling her she couldn't risk taking the twins out and having us all discovered and revealed to her father. She insisted we were so close.

Cathy continued to rage. "Close, close, that's all we hear is that he's close!" she cried.

At one point, Momma cried back, "What do you want me to do, kill him?" Tears were streaming down her face. At that moment, I felt terrible for her. "There are eight servants working here," she muttered. "They're like spies, watching me all the time, especially that John Amos. I never liked him. He's like a puppet. He'll do anything my parents tell him to do."

The air seemed to go out of Cathy finally. She just glared at Momma, full of frustration and emotionally exhausted.

"You must be patient," Momma added before she left, more like fled.

Before Cathy could start, I thought I had better attack her, because I felt just like she felt, but I couldn't show it. Of course, I wanted the twins out in the fresh air. We all needed it, but I told Cathy to stop picking on Momma, especially with her incessant questions, not one, by the way, that I hadn't thought of myself. But what could I do? I had to be stronger. If I fell apart, it would all be lost, all this suffering for nothing.

Kane paused and dropped his arms to his sides, staring ahead for a moment. He looked different. Those impish eyes were suddenly dark and troubled. He sat with a posture I thought was stiff, even uncomfortable for him. Then he turned and looked at me with such a cold, impersonal expression I had to hold my breath.

"What?" I asked in a whisper. "Why did you stop reading?"

"What do you think of me?"

"You?"

"Christopher, I mean. Do you hate him? You have to hate him for defending her, regardless of the reason. From what I read up to here, he's always defending her, no matter what."

"I don't know. I don't hate him for that, but I would imagine Cathy has to be angry at him for taking Corrine's side all the time, especially now. However, she doesn't understand the danger, the risks involved with what she's asking her mother to do. It's complicated, Kane."

"Yes," he said, nodding. My answer seemed to please him, although he didn't smile. The pleasure was all in his eyes, the tiny movement at the corners of his mouth. "Of course, you're right. She can't understand the way Christopher can. She's too young. He's unselfish, that's all. He can see the bigger picture. He has the vision." He paused and looked like he was struggling with troubling thoughts again. "Although . . ."

"Although what?"

"He seems like he would forgive his mother for anything. She risked the health of the twins for three weeks, and yet he was kind of calm about that. His little brother and sister suffered unnecessarily. Kids that age need their mothers around the clock when they're sick, and they needed to be in the sunshine.

What good will all the money in the world do them if they're physically and emotionally damaged? He knows that. Don't you think he knows that?"

"Yes . . . but . . ."

He shook his head. "I don't know, Kristin. At times, I feel like he almost worships her. Maybe it's even more than that."

"What do you mean by more? You suspect an Oedipus complex?"

"Maybe. Yes. But that's not the full explanation. He wants to believe Corrine is doing the right thing for them so much he will avoid reality. And then sometimes I think he really believes her lies. I mean, come on. The old man's about to die, but he can attend a Thanksgiving dinner? What's with that?"

"I know. I wondered about that, too."

"Actually, now that I give it more thought, Christopher's pretty gullible for someone who is supposed to be so bright that he can become a doctor. I want to be on his side, but he bugs me with his understanding and forgiveness. Sorry if I show it when I read aloud."

"It's getting to you," I said, nodding.

"It has gotten to me. I didn't want to say anything this morning when you told me you hadn't slept well. I had all sorts of nightmares after reading to catch up, especially after I read that part about Cory accidentally getting locked in that trunk. I'm not claustrophobic, but I don't think I ever get into an elevator without wondering what I'd do if it broke down." He looked at the diary in his hands. "Maybe you should be the one reading it aloud."

"Oh, no, Kane, you read the diary well," I said, and I smiled. "You even read Cathy well. Maybe you should go out for the spring play. Mr. Madeo would love you in the drama club, I'm sure."

"No thanks. This is the only stage I want to be on right now, and with only you as an audience." He laughed. "If any of my buddies knew what I was doing—"

"Which they'll never know," I said sharply.

"Not from me. That's for sure."

He stood up and looked around the attic with his shoulders up, embracing himself, and for the moment looking like someone who really was imprisoned, diminished by the small space and crawling into himself. He continued to look around, turning his head slowly and pausing at the windows.

"Even convicts in real prisons get time outside," he muttered.

His gaze stopped when he reached me. It was as if he had forgotten that I was up here with him. He stared for a moment, and then his body seemed to fall back into the Kane I knew, his shoulders just a little slumped, his face framing that impish, offbeat smile that was so sexy.

"Speaking of spending time in an attic, however, I wouldn't mind being locked in here with you for a while," he said. He sounded more like himself again. He started toward me, his eyes full of passion.

I held up my hand like a traffic cop. "But I'm your

sister," I said, and he stopped. "Up here, as long as we're up here, I'm your sister. We behave toward each other like they do; otherwise, your whole theory of why we're here is lost."

I wasn't saying it to be impish or defensive. I really believed it now.

I could see his mind spinning with conflicting desires. Was this it? Would he give up reading the diary in my attic? Or reading it at all? Is that what I wanted, what I hoped to hear? Was it unfair of me to tease him with the promise that it would be different once we left the attic?

"Right," he said. He stepped back, looking insulted, taking on Christopher's posture again. "What kind of a brother do you think I am? You sound like you believe what the grandmother from hell believes about us."

I started to laugh. He was so convincing, but then I decided to get right into it and be just as convincing. "Sorry. Oh," I moaned as dramatically as I could, "I'm so sorry for doubting you, Christopher."

"Right. You should be sorry. We Dollangangers, Foxworths, whatever we are, need to stick together."

"Desperately," I said. I was expecting him to laugh, but he didn't.

He nodded instead and returned to his chair, looking even more determined.

"I guess we'll have to wait to see what kind of a brother you really are. Won't we?" I teased, but that didn't bring a smile, either. He picked up the diary, glared at me defiantly, snapped his arms out firmly, and began to read again.

Christmas Eve now loomed on our horizon, but not like Christmas Eves before. This threatened to be dark and horrible, a pending electric storm of broken promises and memories dangling like broken tree ornaments. When Cathy muttered one night that it would soon be Christmas and reminded me that we had been here just about five months, I felt panic rise through me. Five months! One look at the twins, who were still so fragile and so subdued since their stubborn colds, and I knew I had to come up with something that would stave off any more sadness and disappointment.

"We'll make them gifts," I declared. It seemed to distract her, which was my purpose, and then one night, I came up with the idea that we should even make our grandmother a Christmas present.

"Why would we do that?" Cathy asked.

"To win her over. She's still our grandmother," I told her, even though the words nearly choked me.

She stared at me. Was she going to scream or laugh? I saw her giving it serious thought. Then she smiled, realizing I was suggesting we do something to manipulate her for a change. "You really think that might work?"

I shrugged. "Why not try? Daddy used to say, 'You can get more with honey than vinegar.' "

Maybe that was underhanded, quoting Daddy for this, but I knew it would move Cathy to cooperate, and cooperate she did. She decided that whatever we made, it had to be perfect.

"We'll show her," she said, and I smiled to myself. My plan, at least for now, was working.

She came up with the idea to bond tan linen to a stretcher frame and glue on a variety of colored stones with gold and brown cording. She worked on it more intensely than she had ever worked on anything, telling me our grandmother was obviously a perfectionist and would only appreciate this if it was perfect. Whatever, I thought. At least it was keeping her occupied and not thinking about the rest of it.

And then Momma justified the faith I had in her. One afternoon, she came with a live Christmas tree in a small wooden tub. She helped us trim the tree and hang miniature ornaments. For a while, it was as though we were back home again, being the family we were. She gave us four hanging stockings and promised that next year at this time, we would be living in our own home. Cathy was still skeptical, especially since Thanksgiving, but amazingly, we woke up on Christmas morning and found the stockings stuffed and gifts under the tree. After we unwrapped our gifts, Cathy looked at me with eyes drowning in tears. I knew why. She was sorry she had ever doubted Momma.

"It's all right," I told her, and kissed her forehead. "The main thing is, she cares as much about us as ever."

Later, our grandmother arrived with a picnic basket. She said nothing, not "Merry Christmas" or anything, but I nodded at Cathy, and she approached her and handed her our gift. I held my breath. Would this be a wonderful Christmas after all? Would everything finally change?

Grandmother Olivia looked at us and at the gift, then handed it back to Cathy without a word and left. I was stunned by her insensitivity, but Cathy went wild. She stomped on the gift, smashing it and screaming about how horrid our grandmother was and how angry she was at Momma for leaving us in this place at the mercy of that monster. Her rage brought tears. I had to calm her down, embrace her, and rock her like a child, assuring her that we had done the right thing. Our grandmother was the one in the wrong.

"And you can't blame Momma, Cathy. It's not Momma's fault that she has a mother like that. Now we can understand why she was so eager to leave with Daddy and give up inheriting a fortune," I told her.

That seemed to make sense to her. Cathy saw how the twins were taking her outburst and my trying to calm her. She nodded. "You're right," she whispered, then flicked away her tears and went to them. I watched her calm them and cheer them up again, just the way a mother would do.

It wasn't a perfect Christmas; it was a Christmas, however, and Christmas always made you hopeful.

Miraculously, just at the right time, Momma

returned with more gifts, one being a large dollhouse that she said had been hers. It was done in amazing detail, with furniture and little servants. The twins were fascinated, as was I. I was sure Momma was right. It was a very expensive toy. Cathy was still very down, though, and when Momma asked why, I told her about the way our grandmother had reacted to our gift.

"Oh, you have to ignore her," she told me. "She's always been hard to please. She's not a happy woman. She'll never be a happy woman, even with all the wealth. She doesn't know how to use it to bring happiness, but believe me, I do, and I will. In fact—"

Suddenly, she burst into a new smile, hurried out, and then returned with a small television set. She told us that for now, it would be our window on the world. But even this didn't please Cathy. Finally, Momma embraced both of us, gave us each a hug, and announced that the end was near.

"This is my real Christmas gift," she said. "My plan is working. My father has called for a lawyer to put me back in his will. Step one," she declared with happy tears, "has been accomplished, and you're all just as responsible for my success as I am."

I couldn't help it. I almost burst into tears of happiness myself.

I looked at Cathy. When she was little, she didn't want me to always be right, but this time,

she looked grateful, maybe more than grateful.
I think she was looking at me and thinking I was
really quite brilliant.

And she was happier than ever that I was her
brother. I couldn't hope to replace the father we
had lost, but I was so grateful that I was able to
get as close to that as possible.

For both our sakes.

Kane set the diary on the small table beside his chair
and took a deep breath. He had read it with such intensity, the intensity of someone who had been there.
He was wiping a few tears off his cheeks. I was emotionally frozen for a moment, from both what he had
read and how he was reacting.

"Phew," he said, shaking his head. "That was intense. Do you realize how often Christopher is on
the verge of exploding, pounding on that door, and
demanding an end to it all? I can't imagine how he
sleeps at night and how he holds himself together,
seeing what's happening to his brother and sisters.
I don't care how much faith he has in his mother or
whatever."

"Christopher? How about Cathy?"

"She's always exploding," he said. He laid his head
back and closed his eyes.

I never expected him to react this way. Many times
when I was reading the diary alone in my room, I
would find myself as deeply emotionally involved
as he looked like he was now, but I just assumed it
was a girl thing, especially because of how closely I

identified with Cathy. I realized that no one knew this side of Kane Hill, his sensitivity, maybe not even his parents.

Whenever I had an emotional reaction to something in the diary, I realized that whatever it was, it resonated because of something similar, some similar fear or sadness in my own life. What was Kane finding similar to his own life, which everyone at school, including me, saw as about as perfect and privileged as life for someone our age could be?

"That's enough for today, Kane," I said, standing. "I really want to get to my homework before my father comes home."

He looked up at me with what I thought was both anger and disappointment in his face.

"I mean, we don't have to rush through it, do we? It's better if we take our time so we won't miss something important."

He thought a moment and then nodded and stood up. "Of course. You're right. Let's get at some homework, and then how about my taking you to have some pizza or something? We'll go to the Italian Stallion."

"I'll have to call my father and see what he's doing for dinner later," I said.

We left the attic, and Kane paused in the doorway to look back as though he had forgotten something. I had taken the diary from him. There was nothing else. I looked at him quizzically, and he hurried past me and down the stairs.

"Wait!" I called.

He stopped. "You want to keep going?"

"No. You opened the window, remember? I told you we always have to remember to leave things as they were."

"Oh." He started up.

"I'll do it," I said.

He waited for me on the stairway. "Sorry. I won't forget next time."

I nodded, and we headed for my room. I slipped the diary under my pillow and went to my phone while he took his books out of his book bag.

"What's up?" my father said, but not until after the third ring. I'd been preparing to leave a message.

"Are you busy?"

"Debating with the building inspector, which is par for the course. So?"

"You're not coming home in time for dinner, right?"

"Right. I might have a bite with Mr. Johnson. His architect suggested some changes that will create new issues. I don't know where some of these ideas are coming from."

"What ideas?"

"Never mind. Why are you asking about dinner? There's that roast chicken I prepared and—"

"Kane wants to take me for pizza at the Italian Stallion."

He was silent for a few moments.

"Dad?"

"Sure. Have a good time. I'll spend some time with you afterward. That is, if you have your homework done," he added almost sarcastically, which was a real change for him. Something was bothering him, I thought.

"I'll have it done," I said, then added, "Don't be a worrywart," which was another one of his favorite expressions.

"Okay. Gotta go," he said. "My torturer is getting impatient."

"Everything all right?" Kane asked as soon as I hung up.

"Yes. Just some of the usual complications involved in building a house," I said, as if I really knew.

He nodded and returned to his homework. I dug in to mine, and nearly an hour later, I heard him slap his history book closed.

"I'm starving," he said.

"Okay. I can handle what I have left later. Let me freshen up a bit first," I said, and went into the bathroom. While I was brushing my hair, I heard him on the phone talking to his mother.

I had yet to spend any real time with his parents. He really hadn't spent any quality time with my father, either. It wasn't as if we were on the verge of getting engaged or anything, but some of the parents of my friends made a big thing about meeting people they dated and getting to know them better. It was important to my father but so far not a big thing for Kane's parents. Parents wanting to get to know people you went out with seemed to be truer for girls than for boys. If some of them only knew how their daughters could be a lot worse.

It wasn't my intention to eavesdrop on Kane, but something his mother had said seemed to have irritated him, and he raised his voice.

"Yes, I'm at her house. I plan on being here a lot. Don't worry about it," he said sharply. It got quiet, so I imagined he had ended the call, but when I stepped out, he was still on my phone, listening. "You're lucky she's even coming home," he finally said, and ended the call.

"Everything all right at home?"

"Just the usual turmoil. I have to hear my mother rant about my sister, Darlena, because my father refuses to listen to any of it."

"What's the problem?"

"Darlena wants to bring her boyfriend home for Thanksgiving."

"And your mother doesn't like him?"

"Let's just say she's reluctant about it. He has a bit of Hispanic heritage."

"What? What's a bit?"

"His mother is from Chile," he said with a smile.

"And that matters?"

"She'll never come out and say it. My mother was brought up to be a princess. My parents met on some billionaire's yacht, you know. Anyway," he said, smiling, "you should hear how fluently Darlena speaks Spanish now. I think she does it just to drive my mother nuts."

"What's your father say about it?"

"If he can make a lot of money, it won't matter if

he's half Eskimo. My father is an equal opportunity capitalist."

"Sometimes you sound like you don't like your parents, Kane," I said. I was back to peeling that onion again. We were both uncovering more and more about ourselves, and I couldn't help being more interested in him after seeing how he reacted to what Christopher had written in his diary.

He looked at me. "Probably so."

"What?" I was shocked at his candor.

"We can love them, but we don't have to like them," he said. "Don't look so surprised. Lots of kids, maybe even most, don't want to be replicas of their parents."

"Doesn't mean they don't like them."

"They don't like enough of them, and they want to be different, right?"

"I guess so. But not for me," I added quickly.

"Yeah, but maybe that's what eventually happened to Christopher and Cathy when it came to their mother. Maybe they still loved her but they didn't like her. I don't like her," he added. "Even if Christopher does."

"But you really don't like your own mother?"

He shrugged. "Let's put it this way, Kristin. I don't have trouble imagining her locking me away in an attic if it meant she'd inherit a fortune."

"You don't mean that."

He smiled. "Wait until you get to know her better," he said. "When she lets her hair down. Sometimes my mother reminds me of Lady Macbeth."

He made me think. I had been at the homes of many of my friends, eaten dinner with their families, watched television with them, and slept over, but did I really know what their family life was like? How much of it was a show for me, the nearly orphaned girl? *Don't let her see any family problems. Be grateful you're not in her situation.*

The neighbors the Dollangangers had before Christopher Sr. was killed probably thought of them as a precious little family full of love and beauty. Could any of those neighbors and friends, any who had been waiting for Christopher Sr. at his birthday party that fateful night, ever have imagined those children locked away by their own mother and grandmother for years?

We left for the restaurant.

"Promise me you won't read the diary without me," Kane said after we had sat in a booth at the Italian Stallion and ordered our pizza. "To make this real for us, we have to make the discoveries together."

"I won't."

"I can tell from the expression on your face if you do," he warned.

"You want me to make your famous blood oath?" I asked.

"Maybe," he said, and then he laughed.

We talked a lot about events in the earlier part of the diary. Kane found it hard to believe that Christopher Sr. had left his family so destitute.

"The man has no life insurance? He had four

children. There's something odd about it, about the way they behaved together, anyway. It was like a family of children. They lived in a bubble, and the bubble burst. They thought all they had to do was change their name to Dollanganger, and they could make the past disappear. You know what I think? I think by the time we get to the end, Christopher Jr.'s going to think his parents were just plain irresponsible. You saw the way he began to doubt his father, thinking he might have been some kind of dreamer who talked a good game but never had his grasp of anything substantial. Even his job might have been all fluff."

"You were supposed to be the objective pair of eyes here, Kane," I said. "No preconceptions. Wait until we get to the end before making judgments."

"I know, I know. I get . . . frustrated too easily. But you'll keep my feet on the ground," he added, reaching for my hand. "Just the way in the end Cathy will keep Christopher's. That's a bet."

We stared at each other, but I felt as if we were looking through each other, looking at our visions of Christopher and Cathy rather than ourselves.

"I still have some work to do," I said, "and I'd like to spend some time with my father before I go to sleep."

"Sure." He signaled for our check.

When we pulled into my driveway, I could see my father was home. His cherished pickup, Black Beauty, was parked there. He treated it like some revered old friend, full of mechanical arthritis but still ambulatory.

Sometimes I would catch him just looking at it and stroking it affectionately, lost in some memory that involved it or perhaps thinking about my mother sitting beside him.

"Maybe I could get your dad a good deal on a new truck," Kane said. "I'll talk to my father."

"Don't bother. Even if you brought one over for free, he'd drive his. He says they grew on each other. He even named it: Black Beauty."

Kane laughed. "Tell him people like him will put my father out of business."

"I will," I said.

He kissed me softly. "I would have preferred being the older child in my family," he said. "I kind of like the idea of looking after someone the way Christopher is doing, without the situation, of course."

"You will someday, with your own children," I said.

He nodded, but I could see he meant something else. "See you in the morning."

"You sure? I mean, I could drive myself and—"

"Absolutely not. I'm looking after you as if there was no one else," he said. "As if we had no one but each other."

It sounded like something I should appreciate, but it followed me all the way to the front door, the way something eerie and haunting might. He backed out, waved, and drove off. I gazed up at my bedroom window. In my wild imagination, I saw Christopher Dollanganger peering out between the curtains. The image disappeared as quickly as it had come, but a night that had begun with a warm, cozy feeling suddenly had a chill.

I didn't hear the television when I entered. It was too early for my father to go to bed, and he wasn't at the desk he used in the den for his paperwork at home.

"Dad?" I called. Either he hadn't heard me or he was in the bathroom. Nevertheless, I went into the living room and saw him sitting in his chair, staring at the television. It wasn't on. "Dad?"

He turned slowly. "Oh, Kristin. I didn't hear you come in. Have a good time?"

"Yes. What's happening? Why are you just sitting here practically in the dark?" I asked. He had turned on only a small lamp next to the sofa.

"Oh, I must have nodded off a little."

"Aren't you feeling well?" I asked, not hiding my nervousness.

Ever since my mother's sudden illness and death, I would practically panic when my father complained about an ache, developed a cough and cold, or just looked exhausted. His health actually was very good. I couldn't recall a time when he had missed work or even gone in late, but for that matter, I couldn't recall my mother ever showing signs of any serious illness before she had her cerebral aneurism. Like most young children, I took it for granted that my parents would always be there, would live forever. Many nights I woke up crying for her. It took months for me to get past expecting her to be sitting where she always sat, standing where she stood in the kitchen, hearing her footsteps in the hallway or her voice somewhere in the house. I kept pushing the reality of her death away, thinking of it as only a bad dream.

For Christopher, Cathy, and even Corrine, the appearance of those policemen who had come to report their father's fatal accident surely became the basis of nightmares that would follow them into every sleep, perhaps for the rest of their lives. Cory and Carrie were still young enough to fail to grasp the impact of the tragedy. Every day, just like I expected to see my mother miraculously appear, they expected to see their father come through that front door, calling for them, eager to embrace them, and maybe, even though they didn't say it according to Christopher, they were hoping he would come and take them away from Foxworth Hall, too.

The younger you were, the longer it took for death to find its way completely inside you. But they all felt lost, vulnerable, and frightened, even Christopher, who portrayed himself as older and mature. No wonder they were so willing in the end to do what Corrine demanded. They could rage, throw tantrums, cry, and moan, but in the end, they would tolerate far more than ever, because they had only her now. Maybe Kane ascribed other motives to Christopher because he didn't understand this, never having lost a parent.

"Yeah, I'm fine," my father said, but he rose as if he had aged years in hours.

"You didn't hurt yourself today?"

"Oh, no."

"Something's up," I said. I reached back into

myself, perhaps into that part of me that was my mother, to sound firm and demanding. "What is it, Dad?"

He looked at me and instantly knew he couldn't get by with some lame excuse. He took a deep breath and tried anyway. "Things just got a little more complicated at the site, that's all," he said.

I stood my ground. "Why?"

"It's probably nothing. I'm just a stickler for perfection, for everything I do being clean and straight."

"Dad," I said, and I put my hands on my hips, something he would do when he wanted to get to the bottom of things.

"It's really nothing you'll be interested in, Kristin."

"Which means it is," I said.

He sighed deeply and sat again. I came around and stood in front of him, my arms crossed over my breasts. He looked up at me and smiled.

"What?"

"You look just like her doing that. Whenever I tried to keep something from her, she would plant herself in front of me and fold her arms, practically singing, 'I will not be moved.' You even hold your head the same way."

"And you told her what it was?"

"Always," he said.

"So?"

"Okay. I had occasion to look at the paperwork on the property late this afternoon. Not the architecture or materials, none of that."

"What, then?"

"The title, who owns it."

"I don't understand." I sat on the sofa. "I thought Arthur Johnson owned it."

"So did I. Turns out it was bought by a trust, and the trustees are not revealed."

"What does that mean?"

"I'm not sure. I'm not even sure Arthur Johnson and his wife will live there."

"But you said he was so involved—haunting you, I believe, was the way you put it."

"Yes, that's true."

"So?"

"I don't know. That's what irks me. Maybe I'm just spooking myself. Like I said, it's not anything to talk about. As long as I'm paid, I guess."

"It still matters to you, and there's some reason for that."

"I just don't like mysteries involving something I'm doing. Especially on that property," he muttered.

"What could it be? Who would want to keep the fact that they had bought and were building on Fox-worth a secret?"

"I don't know."

"Someone from Charlottesville?"

"Maybe. Look, I'm tired, Kristin," he said, getting up again. "It was a longer day than usual. We'll talk about it some other time, maybe when I find out more. Okay?"

He did look tired. I didn't want to keep nagging him and making it all worse. "You're right to think it's weird," I said sharply, then turned and went upstairs.

How much of this should I tell Kane, or should I tell him anything about it at all? What could it possibly have to do with Christopher's diary? I stood staring at my bed and thinking about the diary. Should I do what I had promised and not read it until Kane and I could read it together? Or should I read ahead and be more prepared for what happened? Would Kane realize it, as he claimed he would? Probably, I thought, and then he might be the one who felt betrayed, and who knew what would happen then?

No, despite the temptation, I would have to wait. Nevertheless, I went to sleep thinking that maybe including him in reading the diary would turn out to be a big mistake in the end for many reasons, some unforeseen.

My father looked surprised the following morning when I told him that Kane was picking me up again. He was thoughtful a moment, and then he smiled.

"Well, I guess we'll save a lot on gas and tires," he joked. He didn't seem as bothered by what he had discovered yesterday, so I didn't bring it up again. "Let me know when I should sell your car."

"Like I would," I said. "Ever."

He laughed. "I'm going to get down to business about Thanksgiving," he said, changing his tone. "It's only days away. I reserved a fourteen-pound turkey."

"Sounds bigger than last year."

"Just in case we have another guest or two," he replied, his eyebrows up in expectation.

"Not Kane," I said quickly. "His family has a big Thanksgiving with lots of relatives. He has to be there."

He nodded. I was sorry that the way I had said it made it sound like I was unhappy with our small group. "Your aunt Barbara might still come. She was invited to her boss's home, but . . . she might still come."

"Whatever. We'll have the best dinner for miles around," I told him.

It brought a weak smile to his face. "Did I ever tell you about your mother's and my first Thanksgiving together?"

He had, but I shook my head.

"I was still at the diner, and I made a six-pound turkey just for the two of us. We ate late, after the crowd had gone. We ate in the kitchen. It was the best Thanksgiving we had until you were born and could sit at the table with us. She was the one who said, 'No matter how good the food is, it's better when you share it with people you love. Otherwise, it's just good food.' Sounds like it should be on a greeting card, huh?"

"Yes."

He was thoughtful for a moment and then snapped back quickly. "She'd sure bawl me out for doing or saying anything to diminish ours."

"You didn't, and you won't," I said. "Besides, you're with someone you love and who loves you." I got up and kissed him. I heard Kane's horn.

"He's early."

"Eager to get to school and learn," I said, and left him laughing as I rushed out the door.

Kane put up his hand as soon as I got into his car.

"What?"

"We don't talk about the diary ever until we're up in the attic from now on."

"Well, I agree, for reasons I've said. I don't want us to talk about it in school in case someone overhears, but when we're alone, too? What's brought you to that conclusion?"

"I thought about it a lot last night. We've got to give it authenticity, and that will come only when we're in it, when we can feel it on us. I don't want to make this into some school project. You know, like we're studying a book in English class or for an exam. Do you?"

"No, but—"

"So good. Good," he said, and backed out. He looked up at the attic before driving off. "It doesn't exist except up there," he added firmly.

At first, I thought his attitude was a bit extreme. Of course, I liked the idea that it would be kept an even better and tighter secret, but there was still something about it that bothered me. It didn't frighten me or anything, and I certainly agreed about not turning it into some extra-credit book report. Like him, I wanted to step away from that sort of thinking. There was nothing personal about that. Maybe what bothered me was what had begun to bother me from the start. Kane seemed even more into this than I was, and I had far more reason to be. As distant as

the relationship was, the Dollanganger children were
still related to me through my mother. And it was my
father who was working on the property and who had
found the diary. What got me thinking harder about
it was wondering why Kane was so into it. What was
he bringing to it that I had never expected or could
have known? At times, he seemed to be very critical
of Christopher, but then he would suddenly embrace
him. Our English teacher, Mr. Madeo, who also directed the school plays, once told us that an actor
has to find something with which he can identify in a
character he plays, even if he plays a villain.

What was it that Kane found in Christopher and
the whole Dollanganger situation that enabled him to
get so into it? Maybe there were some resemblances
to his own family. The Dollangangers were a loving family at the start of the diary, but it was clear
that with the loss of their father, the children were
drifting away from their mother. They were almost
like orphans. Kane did admit that he didn't like his
mother; he'd said he loved her like a child should love
a mother, but he didn't particularly like the person
she was.

Even though I never spent any time with Kane and
his sister together, I could tell that he had a very good
relationship with her. Was she as critical of their parents as he was? Did they complain about them to each
other? She surely must be complaining to him about
her mother's attitude toward her boyfriend. In how
many families that I knew only on the surface were
the children allied against their own parents? Even if

I had a brother or a sister, I couldn't imagine the two of us being adversaries of our parents, especially my father.

How ironic this was all becoming. In the beginning, I was afraid that I would be the one who revealed too much about herself, but it was starting to look like it might be Kane who did that. Was I ready for the revelations? Did I want to know them? What sort of a Pandora's box had I opened by agreeing to read the diary with him? Of course, I didn't bring up any of this, even after the school day had ended and we were on our way to my home. All day, I had tried to distract myself from these heavy thoughts.

The girls were all talking about Tina Kennedy's party the coming weekend. Unlike Kane's recent party at his home when his parents had gone on a trip, Tina's party was promising to be wild. Her father owned lots of real estate, and one of the properties was an adult bar outside of Charlottesville, so everyone imagined there would be a good supply of booze, and Tina had an older brother in his third year of college who seemed to have an endless supply of mood-enhancing drugs. Lately, she had practically dared me not to attend. In her effort to win Kane's attention, she was portraying me as the class "goody-goody," who was capable of turning "state's evidence" when it came to whatever my girlfriends and the boys did. She didn't want me to be trusted. I complained to Kane about it, but he didn't want to take any of it seriously. That was beginning to annoy me.

To counter her insinuations, my closer friends, like

Suzette and Kyra, were telling everyone that Kane and I were really getting it on at my home after school almost daily. I wasn't happy about any of that and was even a little irritated at Kane's indifference to the chatter. Until now, that was his charm, his "coolness," as most girls put it, but I had seen him be quite the opposite in the attic.

I suggested that he and I boycott the party.

"Why give her the satisfaction?" he said. "We can handle it. Don't worry."

We both had a light load of homework that day, which Kane took to mean we could spend more time on the diary.

"We'll order in Chinese or something, okay?" he asked.

"Sure," I said. He drove a little faster than usual. Neither of us said anything more until we entered my house and went up to my room to get the diary.

"I just want to freshen up a bit," I said when he turned to the door.

"Go to the bathroom?"

"Just freshen up. Go on ahead if you want," I said, and to my surprise, he did just that.

I was even more surprised at what he had done by the time I got up there. He had moved furniture around so it resembled the Foxworth Hall attic as much as possible.

"Gives a better idea," he said when I just stood there looking at it all. "Okay?"

"We have to move it back before we leave."

"Oh, absolutely. No problem." He got into the chair and looked at me. I moved to the sofa. He began.

Momma had told us about the grand Christmas party her parents were having, and Cathy pleaded and pleaded for us to be able to see it.

"How can I let you do that?"

"We'll hide and watch. We'll be careful. Please," she pleaded.

Momma looked at me. I knew she was hoping I would disagree with Cathy or help her explain why it wasn't possible, but I was just as tired of being confined and seeing nothing beautiful and fun. She read it in my face, thought for a moment, and then pulled us aside so the twins wouldn't hear us.

"Okay. I know a place where you can hide and watch. Just the two of you. The twins wouldn't be able to contain themselves, and they would give us all away. Promise not to tell them, and promise to wait until they are fast asleep."

We did, and she promised to come get us and take us to where we could watch the party unseen. I thought Cathy would be ecstatic about it, but the moment Momma left, she took on a long face.

"What?"

"She won't come back. It will be like our wonderful Thanksgiving dinner. Something will prevent her."

"Give her a chance," I said, but in my heart,

I bore the same skepticism. Momma was good at making promises and then finding explanations for why they were broken. But that was something I thought I would never tell Cathy.

Fortunately, this time, I didn't have to consider it. Momma showed up looking more beautiful than ever. She looked like a princess, a movie star, in her formal gown, which showed more cleavage than I expected, especially in this house with our grandmother. I couldn't take my eyes off her. Even when I was younger, but not too young to appreciate a naked woman, I wasn't as moved, even when she had paraded nude in front of us. Maybe it was because it was so long since I had seen her so bright, the crests of her breasts so crimson with excitement, her eyes as dazzling as her diamond and emerald earrings, that I found myself so taken. It was easy for me to imagine how my father had been so smitten with her beauty and impervious to any suspicions of incest. I could feel my own sexuality stirring, and I was admittedly ashamed. How could I have these thoughts and feelings about my own mother?

Kane paused and looked at me with a strange expression of guilt on his face. In fact, he seemed to cringe in the chair.

"What?" I asked. "Why did you stop reading?"

I expected him to go into his theory of the Oedipus complex again, but he surprised me. "I remember when I first had a similar feeling."

"What similar feeling?"

"Feelings about my mother. I've never told anyone. I've read about it, of course. I don't have an Oedipus complex," he added firmly. "The jury's still out on whether that even exists."

I didn't know what to say. I just stared at him.

"I was just a little more than twelve. For the previous year or so, my mother had become very careful about undressing in front of me or appearing undressed where I could see. She always closed her door, but one time, she didn't, and . . ."

"You saw her naked?"

"Worse. She and my father were on the verge."

"Oh."

"I couldn't help becoming aroused. Sometimes you just can't help it," he quickly added. "It just happens, especially for boys. Understand?"

"Yes."

"It never happened again," he said. He looked angry now.

"I'm sure it's quite normal, especially at that age, when you were just . . ."

"Breaking out," he said. Then he smiled, which gave me an instant sense of relief. "And not just with pimples." His expression changed again, returned to a cross between anger and guilt. He looked around the attic and nodded to himself.

"What?" I asked. What was he thinking now?

"This is our special place now, Kristin, our attic of secrets, right?"

"Of course. We both took blood oaths."

"I'm serious."

"I am, too. I was the first to demand that, Kane. And I would never repeat anything we say to each other up here, especially because of the diary."

He nodded, looking satisfied. "I'm sorry. I just . . . I've never been so honest with anyone else, even my parents or my sister."

"Then I'm flattered," I said, and his smile returned.

"You're very special, Kristin. I mean it. I'm happy you trusted me with this. I know what that means to you." He looked down at the diary in his hands.

"Go on," I said. "It's all right. You haven't done or said anything that would change my mind."

I told him that, but I wasn't as confident about it as I made it sound.

Nevertheless, he nodded, smiled, and began again.

Momma smiled at me as if she knew how intoxicatingly beautiful I thought she was. Why should I be surprised? She was always good at reading my thoughts.

She warned us not to stay out for more than an hour, as the twins might waken, and then she took us to a place she said used to be her own hiding place from which to spy on adults, a massive oblong table with cabinet doors underneath. There was barely enough room for Cathy and me to crawl under, but through the fine mesh screen, we could see the grand ballroom below, all lit with candles. The elegantly dressed men and women, the women with glittering jewels, the huge Christmas tree with what looked like hundreds of lights and ornaments, the dozens of servants serving champagne, the display of foods being served by chefs, and the music made it the greatest display of wealth we had ever seen. Momma hadn't lied about this. They were rich, very rich! She hadn't exaggerated about that.

I looked at Cathy. Her face was so full of wonder it brought tears to my eyes. All these months of boredom and depression, sickness and cold, and reams and reams of cruel words spewed at us, all of it paled at this moment. A curtain had been lifted and showed us what could one day be ours, too! Oh, how worth it our struggle has been, I thought.

I looked at my sister and smiled at the way she was dazzled before my eyes. She could easily grow into one of those beautiful women below, as beautiful as Momma, I thought. We watched Momma, who was talking to a man about my father's height. Suddenly, he took her hand and kissed it. I felt like an arrow of ice had just been shot into my chest. Cathy nudged me.

"Did you see that, what she let that man do?"

Of course I had, but instead of talking about it, I talked about what our parties would be like when we were finally accepted and living in this grand mansion.

I thought we had seen all we would that would shock and amaze us, but suddenly, our grandmother from hell appeared, only now she looked as elegantly dressed as any of the other women. Cathy was astonished, too, but could only remark about her size. Somehow, among other women, she looked even taller than when she loomed as she stood above us.

And then the most astonishing thing of all happened. Our grandfather was brought in, in his wheelchair.

"It's him!" Cathy muttered.

He paused and slowly raised his head and looked up in our direction. I was positive he was smiling. Instinctively, I pulled back, but Cathy remained staring down at him.

"He looks like Daddy, only older," she said.

"Why wouldn't he? He's Daddy's half brother."

"But—"

"Shh," I said. There were two people nearby talking, a man and a woman. They talked about our mother. The woman was uncomplimentary, but the man, whom she called Albert Donne, raved about Momma and wished she was his instead of belonging to someone named Bartholomew Winslow. They confirmed that Momma was once adored by her father and would inherit the fortune, but neither was happy for her. They drifted off.

"Who's Bartholomew Winslow?"

"Let's go," I said, instead of trying to come up with an answer. I knew it had to be the man who had kissed her hand and was paying so much attention to her at the party. "The twins might have woken up."

Cathy wanted to stay longer, but I made her leave and return to our little bedroom. The twins were still fast asleep. Both of us stood there looking at them, stunned and dazzled by all we had seen and heard.

"Is Momma going to marry this Bartholomew Winslow? Is that what those people meant?"

"How do I know?" I snapped back at her. I shouldn't have, but I couldn't help it. The woman I had seen below at that grand party was different from the woman who had brought us to Foxworth Hall, and I was afraid of what that difference might mean.

Suddenly, I felt defiant and excited about a new idea. Why not take advantage of this opportunity to explore the house and really understand where we were? Momma was occupied, I told Cathy, and the door was unlocked. We wouldn't get a better opportunity. She was worried that our grandmother would find out and whip us, but I thought I would go up to the attic, find some clothes to use for a disguise, and then go out. I found an old dark suit that fit well. Cathy stared in amazement as I paraded boldly before her, pretending to be some old gent.

"I'll never be recognized," I declared. She still looked quite terrified but told me to go explore. She made me promise I wouldn't be too long. I pretended to be a hero about to embark on a

dangerous venture to save us both by learning the
secrets of the mansion. She smiled when I swept
her up in my arms, and for a moment, inhaling the
sweet scent of her freshly washed hair and feeling
the smoothness of her skin and the closeness of
her body naked beneath her new nightgown, I felt a
rush of passion, heat rising from my thighs, through
my body, and into my face. I kissed her cheek,
and the kiss was such a surprise to both of us that
we stood motionless for a moment. Then I forced
a laugh and, pretending to be a knight in armor,
rushed out of the room and into the mansion of
secrets.

Kane paused, looked at me, and then jumped up and
came over to kiss me.

"Why did you do that?" I asked, smiling.

"Christopher kissed his sister. You said we had to
do what they do when they do it."

"I didn't mean literally," I said.

"Maybe you did and you didn't realize it." He returned to his chair. "You hear anything that surprised
you?"

"Don't try to be a teacher, Kane. Remember, this
is supposed to be different from a school assignment."

He laughed. "Sorry. Okay. You heard how the old
man looked up at them and smiled?"

"Christopher said he thought it looked like that.
He wasn't sure."

"The old man knew they were there," Kane said,
nodding. "Your uncle's contact was right, I bet."

"Okay, I'll play along. What do you think it all means?"

He sat back, looking like a junior Sherlock Holmes, full of self-confidence. "I'm thinking the old lady told him right from the start, and he approved of keeping them under lock and key. They both believed the children were the devil's children or something, didn't they? Maybe they thought they'd grow horns and tails and confirm their nutty ideas."

"But what about Corrine? I admit that what she's doing, what she's permitting, most mothers wouldn't, but I really believe she thinks she can pull it off, don't you?"

He shrugged. "Maybe they played her, too."

"Played her?"

"You know, conned her into believing the plan had a chance. Granny told her she was keeping the kids a secret from the old coot until he kicked the bucket. She forced Corrine to do the things she did, convincing her that was the case. All the while, she kept the old man in the loop."

"But why would he do it?"

"He gets his slow revenge for her running off with Christopher Sr. He puts her through all this hell first."

"It doesn't sound like she's going through hell now."

"Yeah, not now. Now she's back to being Daddy's little girl. She's been whipped and made to do what they want her to do with the children. He's letting out the leash little by little, her own car, money, clothes, and jewelry. He keeps her obedient, and that keeps the children locked up. She's all he's got left, with the brothers dead. He sounds to me like someone who wants his legacy. He's probably got too much of an ego to see the end of the Foxworths. Her return, molding her into the woman he wants her to be, is satisfying, maybe even keeping him alive at this point," he continued, obviously thinking it through as he spoke.

"Maybe," I said. What he was saying did make some sense, at least with what we knew now. "But I still think we shouldn't jump to any conclusions."

He smiled. "That's okay. Keep your options open. One of us should always be challenging what the other thinks, anyway. Cathy's really challenging Christopher's theories most of the time, isn't she? You challenge mine."

"Yes, but—"

"So let's keep going. I want to see what he discovers. It's still early."

I checked the time. "Okay."

Pleased, he returned to the diary. As he began, I thought again about what I had considered might happen, how by reading the diary and putting ourselves as best we could in Christopher's and Cathy's place, we might expose things about ourselves that we'd told no one. He had already done it. Soon it would be my turn, I was sure. Would this all make us closer, or, in the end, would it drive us apart?

As quietly as I could, I opened the door and slipped into the room, but when I turned to look for Cathy, there was Momma. I had never seen such rage in her face. Her whole body looked swollen with it. Before I could speak, she slapped me hard on the left cheek, and when I recuperated, she slapped me even harder on my right. Stunned, I stood there, my face stinging.

"Where were you? Where did you go? If you ever do anything like this again"—she practically spit at me—"I'll whip you. I'll whip you both the way I was whipped. Do you hear? Do you?"

I couldn't speak.

Was this the mother who had so often embraced me, petted me, and covered my face with kisses, telling me how much she needed and depended on me and how like my father I was to her in almost every way?

Was this the mother who looked to me to help her get through this crisis, because she believed I was more an adult than a child and I could understand her and what she needed more perhaps than someone her age?

Who was this woman now standing before me with such fury in her eyes?

For a long moment, it was so quiet we could hear the walls and floors creak. Then my mother's expression changed so quickly it took my breath away. It was as if she had been possessed by some demon and, realizing what had happened, driven him out.

"I'm sorry. I'm sorry!" she cried. "Forgive me, please. Forgive me!"

She reached forward with soft hands now

and cupped my face as she stepped toward me, muttering how I shouldn't be so frightened or afraid of her, how her threat to whip us as she had been whipped was, of course, ridiculous. She flooded my stinging face with quick kisses, apologizing, embracing me, and bringing my face, my lips, down to the warmth of her breasts, my lips pressing to them, drawing out the warmth and love I always thought she kept safely there for me.

She released me, and I stepped back, but then she kissed me again, but this time, she kissed me on the lips the way I had seen her kiss my father so many times. It wasn't simply a smack on the lips; it was a kiss that cried for forgiveness. When she pulled away, she stroked my hair and smiled that soft, loving smile I had known so well all my life.

"Will you forgive me? Will you?"

"Yes, Momma," I said. "I forgive you."

She burst into a wide, ecstatic smile and reached for Cathy's hand. I could see that Cathy was trembling with fear. She had never seen our mother like she was moments ago, either. She looked at me, her face slowly hardening now more into anger than surprise or fear. I gave her a look of reassurance, but she wasn't ready to accept any. Momma could see that, too.

Momma told us she had overreacted because everything was finally going our way. That perked up Cathy.

· "How?" Cathy asked. "Tell us how it's going our way."

"I can't right now," Momma said. "I've got to get back. Perhaps I'll have time to tell you everything tomorrow. Forgive me, Christopher," she said, and kissed me again before going to the door. And then, before she walked out, she said something that sounded out of place, even stupid. "Merry Christmas."

She closed and locked the door.

Cathy turned to me. "For a while there, I thought our grandmother from hell had gotten into her body," she said, and then, slowly, she gazed at all the presents. Suddenly, everything looked out of place for both of us—these gifts, being locked away, us being our little sister and brother's parents, and a grandmother threatening us with a rainstorm of hell if we broke any of her ridiculous rules. "Merry Christmas," Cathy said bitterly.

"She didn't mean it, Cathy. She got frightened when I wasn't here. She thought I had been discovered and it was all over," I told her.

She moved quietly, silently, looking like her tongue had hardened into stone in her mouth, and then she got back into bed with Carrie.

I got undressed quickly and decided to lie beside her for a while. Without a word, she rested her head on my chest, and I slipped my arm around her.

To my surprise, Kane lowered the diary and looked at me. He had been reading so well and was so into it that I truly felt as if I was there alongside Christopher. I hated for him to stop. We still had plenty of time.

"What?"

"That sofa you're on."

"What about it?"

"It's a pull-out."

"So?"

He rose. "Let's do it," he said. I sat looking up at him. "Re-create the scene," he added, and held out his hand. I took it, and he helped me up and then removed the cushions and lifted out the sofa bed. There was a cloud of dust. We waved our hands in front of our faces. "We should clean up this place a bit. They cleaned up their attic," he said.

"Just what I need, more housework."

"I'll help." He looked around and went to one of the trunks, opened it, and took out an old comforter. "This will work for now," he said, and spread it on the sofa bed. Then he put the pillows back on the bed. "Ta-daaaa."

"What are we doing?"

"We're Christopher and Cathy lying on that mattress." He picked up the diary. "Come on," he said, and lay down on the sofa bed.

I remember thinking that maybe we were going too far with this, but it also intrigued me. I did what he asked. He sat up, pulled off his shirt, and lay back again, patting his chest. I knew what he wanted and laid my head against him. He held up the diary to begin reading again, his right arm slipping comfortably around my shoulders.

"Wait," he said.

"What?"

"You've got to get more into it, get closer to the way Cathy was at this point."

"I don't exactly have a nightgown up here, Kane."

He looked at my mother's wardrobe. "Maybe there's something in there."

I hesitated.

"I'm overdressed, too," he said, and sat up to take off his pants.

My heart began to race. I could feel a warm sensation of excitement building in the pit of my stomach and spreading like tepid water just beneath my skin, into my thighs. I rose quickly and went to the wardrobe. Two nightgowns were hung on the right. I plucked one out and began to undress. He was in his underwear, lying back, watching me and waiting. With my back to him, I went down to my panties and slipped the nightgown over my head. Smoothing it down, I returned to the sofa bed and lay beside him, placing my head on his chest. He ran his fingers through my hair and then began to read.

There was no longer a doubt in my mind.

We were in the Foxworth Hall attic.

In the short silence that passed between us, I felt my sister's warmth in a way I never had felt it. It's difficult to explain, but perhaps because of our circumstances, all that had happened, the emotional roller coaster we were on, I wasn't thinking of her as my sister. I was sensing her more as a girl, young,

of course, somewhat frightened, but also desperate
for my touch, my warmth. It aroused me in ways I
hadn't expected.

I started babbling about everything, defending
Momma again, and talking about how we had all
changed. She perked up, now interested in how I
thought she had changed. It was on the tip of my
tongue to tell her she was more mature, she was
even prettier, but something kept me from saying
it. I was afraid to say it.

Instead, I started to talk about what I had
discovered when I had snuck out. I told her I
heard the party winding down and went to spy on
them and that many of them looked drunk. I saw
the nurse wheel out our grandfather. Moments
after, I saw Momma come up the stairs with
Bartholomew Winslow, who asked to see her
special bed. I thought it was just a clever way
to get into her room with her. I hesitated to tell
Cathy any more, but she insisted. I had to tell
her about how they kissed and how he touched
Momma. I knew it would make her angry but not
angrier than it made me. I told her how he still
insisted on seeing the famous swan bed, which I
had overheard had been our great-grandmother's.
To get off the topic, I described wandering into a
trophy room with dozens of animal heads on the
walls and the portrait of our grandfather, Malcolm
Neal Foxworth. She didn't want to hear any of
that.

Again, I hesitated, but I had promised I would

tell her everything I saw, so I couldn't leave it out, even though I knew it was going to disturb her. I described what I had seen of Momma's suite of rooms, with that enormous swan bed, when the door opened. There was no way not to say it; it was the bedroom of a princess.

Momma was living in luxury, while we were wallowing in a small room and an attic full of antiques, dust, and no sunshine. The air was stale. We were shut away and drawing closer to each other daily to find the comfort and the hope anyone our ages should have the moment he or she opens his or her eyes. Maybe legally we weren't orphans, but the only thing that separated us from them was a second death certificate—our mother's.

Darkness was never darker; silence was never deeper. We were in a world where it was futile even to cry. Who would hear us? Who would wipe away our tears? How different we were already from the children who had been brought here. We were frightened, and we were unhappy, but we had been dressed in hope. Momma's voice had been so full of promise. Really. Where else could we have gone but to her to find a reason to continue, to grow, to dream again of any future for ourselves?

Kane stopped reading and turned to me. "If I were really there with her in that bed, I would say, 'More and more, it's looking like we're going to have only each other, Cathy.'"

"Their mother does seem so deceptive, complaining about how difficult it is for her and telling them how patient they have to be."

"I think Christopher knows that but can't say a word. You can understand how alone they must feel, locked away. I can see a mother unconcerned about them in the interim, but those two little ones."

"Yes." I could feel the tears coming into my eyes, and he could see them. He leaned toward me and gently kissed my eyes, his lips feeling like slightly damp tissues. Then he kissed my cheeks with small pecks, as if he was exploring and finding his way to my lips. I wasn't terribly experienced at it, but I could sense that Kane was a very good kisser. He pressed just so hard and held his lips on mine just long enough to keep the tingling lingering after we parted.

"And we can understand why they would need more from each other, more comfort, more love," he whispered, his lips just under my ear and just close enough to graze the peach fuzz on my cheek. He caressed my breasts, lifting my left breast gently, and with his left hand, he reached down to get under the hem of my mother's nightgown, sliding it softly but quickly up my thigh to my waist and turning me to him more for another long and passionate kiss that seemed to draw the last drops of resistance from me.

When he started to draw back, I was the one who pursued, bringing my lips back to his. Then I stiffened when his hand reached my breasts, naked under the nightgown. His fingers nudged my nipple as he lowered his mouth to my neck. I was surprised at how I suddenly stiffened and pulled back. I could feel myself sliding down that dangerous slope my aunt Barbara had described, when she had come to visit and play the role of a mother educating her daughter about her own sexuality.

"It's all right," Kane said, kissing my forehead and trying again to bring his fingers to my erect nipples, but I moved back even farther.

"They wouldn't do this," I told him. I knew it was a strange thing to say the second after I said it.

He smiled. "Right, right. We'll continue this downstairs. I think we've done enough today, anyway," he said, and rose. He looked down at me to see if I would follow, if I wanted to continue. The candles he had lit inside me were still flickering and did not go out. So many places on my body still longed to be touched. Now it felt like I had suffered sunburn. My skin tingled.

I nodded and started to get up. As he dressed and then began to put everything back to the way it was, I dressed, too, and rehung my mother's nightgown. I closed the windows, and then we left the attic, both of us pausing first to look back at it, me to be sure it didn't reveal what had been happening in it and him looking back with the expression of someone who was remembering having been there for years and finally leaving.

He took my hand. The passion that had blossomed between us was still as heavy as honey on our lips. My body still tingled, and both of us were as flushed as the moment we had touched and caressed. Neither of us spoke. We were hurrying down to my bedroom, where I was almost certain now I would do what my girlfriends and I jokingly referred to as "crossing the Rio Grande."

We had just gotten down the stairs and started toward my room when I heard the front door open and close. We both froze for a moment. Without speaking, I hurried him to my room.

"Does anyone else have the key to your house?" he asked.

"No. It has to be my father," I said, slipping the diary under the pillow and flopping onto the bed with my history text open to where I was actually supposed to be reading.

Obviously frustrated, Kane reluctantly took his books out of his bag and slapped his math text onto my desk. "If there's anything that could keep you from feeling romantic, it's studying math," he muttered.

We could hear my father coming up the stairs. I brushed back my hair and gave my clothes a once-over just before he knocked.

"Hey," I called, and he opened the door.

He peered in at us. Kane turned as if he hadn't heard him coming because he had been so entranced with his intermediate algebra.

"If this keeps up, you'll both be competing for valedictorian," my father said.

I could tell from the look in his eyes, the way he tightened his lips and moved his ears slightly back, that he really didn't believe what he was seeing. I imagined we looked too perfect, too innocuous, or perhaps our faces were still flushed. We hadn't had time to throw cold water on them. He didn't look angry as much as he looked a little more concerned this time.

Seeing the knowing expression on his face made me wonder why any teenager, boy or girl, believed he or she could completely fool parents, anyway. My father wouldn't tell me, I'm sure, but in his youth, he was surely in some similar circumstance. Yes, teenagers today were probably more sexually active than they were in my dad's time, I thought. Eighth-graders were getting pregnant. The attitude about virginity seemed completely upside down. Once, a girl could be proud she had held out until she met the man she loved and who loved her, but now, girls even considered carrying virginity into their late teens to be some sort of failure.

My father worked hard. He didn't socialize as much as everyone else's parents did, but he wasn't oblivious to the way things were today. Just because he trusted me not to get into trouble, that didn't mean he would never worry that I would, maybe especially now that I was dating a boy as carefree and privileged as Kane Hill.

"Hey, Mr. Masterwood," Kane said. "No worries. Kristin is so far above me in grade point average, I need a telescope to see her scores."

Dad smiled. "I bet."

"What are you doing home so early? I thought you said you would be late all week," I said.

"I have to change and put on some formal duds. I've been invited to dinner at Spencer's."

"Spencer's? *Très* top-notch," Kane said. "My father goes there to close deals."

Dad nodded.

"Who invited you?" I asked him.

"Mr. Johnson. He wants me to meet someone," he added. I knew he didn't want to say any more in front of Kane.

"Your blue suit was dry-cleaned a month ago," I said. "It's on the right side in your closet."

"I was thinking about that. Good."

"And wear the light blue shirt with that tie I bought you last Christmas," I added as he started to back up.

He glanced at Kane, a little embarrassed, but nodded and backed out, closing the door softly.

The look on Kane's face made me laugh.

"Yes?"

He shook his head. "You really take care of him, don't you?"

"We take care of each other, Kane."

He looked very sad for a moment and then turned back to his math homework. "Let me know when you're hungry," he said. "I'll order and go pick it up."

"I can just throw something together here, but you had better remember to call home and tell your mother this time," I warned. "Stay on your homework. I'll be back," I told him, and went down to see what I could make us for dinner. I was pretty good at pasta with olive oil, cheese, and some eggplant. Everything was there, so I started.

I heard someone coming down the stairs about twenty minutes later and saw my father standing in the doorway.

"Well?" he asked, gesturing like a six-year-old boy waiting for his mother's approval.

"You look very handsome, Dad." I walked over to him and brushed his hair back a little before kissing him on the cheek.

"I always feel a little awkward in a jacket and tie, especially after a day in the field." He looked back at the stairway. "Staying for dinner, I see," he added, glancing at my preparations.

"Yes, I thought I'd do a nice pasta, some salad. Defrost and heat up that Italian bread we have in the freezer. Nothing fancy."

"You'll probably eat better than I will. I don't like dinner meetings. Everyone waits for the right pause in chewing and drinking to say the important things after the mandatory small talk."

"You and Uncle Tommy are really different, from the sound of how he runs his business. He says the better the deal, the better the restaurant, or vice versa."

"He was spoiled from the get-go."

"So who is going to be at this dinner?" I asked, and then held my breath to see if he would tell me.

"Someone who flew in just for it, apparently. I don't know whether to be flattered or nervous."

"You don't know his name?"

"I was simply told it was a major stockholder in

the trust involved. I'm beginning to think I'm deep in some tax-avoidance scheme. I was starting to suspect that this whole sweet deal was too good to be true. Anyway, don't worry about it. It will all work out."

"You used to say it would come out in the wash."

"Yeah, but no one's doing any washing in particular right now. Enjoy your dinner," he said, then kissed me and started out.

He did look handsome, as handsome as I could ever remember him being, but I didn't have to be a sophisticated, mature older woman to realize there was still something very important missing. There was a light, that joie de vivre that a truly happy man had. He had carried his sorrow too long. It had lost no weight and still put darkness in places where there should be none. It kept his enthusiasm for almost everything contained, chained to a sense of guilt, perhaps. How could he be happy without her? The moment he laughed, felt a smile break out on his face, let something exciting quicken his pace, he felt his loss, remembered she wasn't there beside him to share in the joy. Every laugh, every smile, gave birth to another tear. He went to sleep apologizing for being alive.

I knew all this, and it broke my heart. Right now, it made me feel even guiltier about what Kane and I were doing. I had never kept anything this serious a secret from him. How was I going to explain it to him afterward? My fear was that I would not only hate myself for having done it but also hate Kane for encouraging me with his own obvious interest and excitement. Could I explain this to him and stop? Had we gone too far to stop? And would the effect on our relationship be the same? Would he now feel betrayed? Already, he had confided in me about himself and his family more than he had confided in anyone else.

I returned to preparing dinner, these thoughts like little pinpricks on my heart. I cut some onions for our salad, but the tears that came to my eyes were not a result of that. I tried to pull myself together when I heard Kane descending.

"You didn't come back up," he said.

"I thought I had better get started on dinner. I'm hungry, aren't you?"

"Yeah, for lots of things." I smirked, and he smiled. "I left a message on my mother's cell and a message with Martha, the maid who looks after her things, which include me," he added. "Your father left?"

"Yes. He hates business dinners."

"My father has business breakfasts, lunches, and dinners. He once even had a business New Year's," he said, and leaned against the doorjamb.

"Oh, c'mon."

He raised his right hand. "I kid you not. He invited all these car company executives and their wives to our home on New Year's Eve, and they talked about business right up to the clock striking twelve. I was only eleven at the time, but I remember it well, because my sister and I were spying on the party just the way Christopher and Cathy were spying on their grandparents' gala. We got bored, however, and returned to our own rooms. I remember thinking that if that's what adults did to celebrate, I was going to remain a kid."

"And you have," I said.

He laughed. "I'll set the table this time." I looked at him, surprised. "Hey, I'm not spoiled. I'm corrupted but not spoiled," he said. "I think I was two when my mother had me instructed on how to place silverware, fold a napkin, and organize the wine and water glasses."

"Not two."

"Well, close to it. I had to live up to being a prince, didn't I?"

He went for the dishes and silverware, and I continued preparing our meal. Occasionally, we gave each other a look that reminded us of the passion that had just passed through us, but neither of us said anything. It was just dinner now and more discussion about what we had read of the diary.

"I really have to get to my homework this time," I said, when we were cleaning up. "I have a test in history and a quiz in English tomorrow."

"Don't throw me out. I promise I won't touch you," he said. "I'll just work on my own."

"Why is it I get the impression you're in no rush to go home . . . ever?"

"Maybe because I make it so obvious," he said.

We returned to my room, and we did do our homework. Close to nine o'clock, he closed his books and declared that I was turning him into a better student. He couldn't stand it any longer. We both laughed, and I let him kiss me, but he could feel that we were going no further. I was anticipating my father returning any moment, anyway.

"I'm off," he said. "I'll be in your driveway waiting for you in the morning."

"I'm going to forget how to drive."

"If you would agree to bring the diary to my house . . ."

"No," I said sharply. He put up his hands and then, with that cute smirk on his face, began to back up toward the doorway.

"Don't shoot. I'm going, I'm going. " He threw me a kiss and disappeared.

I went to the window and watched him leave. Literally seconds later, I saw my father pull into the driveway. I could tell from the way he came into the house and started up the stairs that he was tired. I stepped out to greet him in the hallway.

"Hey," I said. "How was your dinner?"

"It was okay. The steak was a little overdone for me."

"I don't mean the food, Dad," I said.

He stood there looking at me.

"So?"

"Remember how I once told you that getting to know someone is like peeling an onion?"

"Yes."

"Well, getting to know what's behind the building of a new mansion on the foundation of Foxworth Hall is like peeling an onion, too."

I thought he was going to leave it at that, but it was just a long pause as he put his own thoughts about it together. I waited.

"The man I met tonight still isn't the man behind the project. Arthur Johnson was one layer of onion, and the man I met tonight is another. You know how I feel about navigating through mazes."

"Who did you meet tonight?"

"A Dr. Martin West," he said.

I saw that he was waiting to see if I knew that name from reading the diary. I shook my head. "What kind of a doctor is he?"

"He's a psychiatrist."

Again, he waited for my reaction. Again, I shook my head. "How is he involved in all this?"

"He didn't come right out and say it, but I'm sure he worked in the clinic Corrine Foxworth was taken to after the fire here," he said.

"Corrine was his patient?"

"My guess is that's how Arthur Johnson and his wife know so much about the interior of Foxworth Hall. Dr. West knew it all from what she told him during whatever they call that treatment psychiatrists do. You know, patient on a couch or something, babbling."

"So Arthur Johnson works for this psychiatrist?"

"Not exactly. I mean, he's not on the title document. As I've told you, it's a trust, and the owners or partners, or whatever they call them, aren't mentioned."

"But the doctor is a wealthy man?"

"I don't know if he's the one who's wealthy. Although he didn't say it, I had the feeling he was working for someone else, someone who's a major investor in Johnson's hedge fund. That's all I can tell you. My head's spinning with all the intrigue. I'm going to sleep," he said.

"Are you upset about it?" I asked quickly.

"Upset?" He thought a moment. "I'm not sure if 'upset' is the right word. I'm more . . . confused about it, but maybe, if I just stick to what I have to do to build this turkey, I'll be fine. Which reminds me. Mrs. Osterhouse is going to pick up the turkey I ordered. I've given her a list of what I need to prepare it. When does your holiday start?"

"Next Wednesday. We usually pick it up and do the extra shopping."

"I know, but she wanted to do something. Sometimes being generous means letting someone do something for you. It doesn't sound like it makes sense, but it does. You and I will get the rest of it on Sunday along with our weekly food, okay?"

"Yes. I understand," I said. I didn't want to elaborate and reveal that I knew Mrs. Osterhouse was working so hard to become a member of our family, but it was one of those times when my father knew what I was thinking. He left it dangling in the air.

"Right." He started to turn away and then stopped. "Oh. So how was your dinner?"

"Pretty tip-top," I told him, which finally brought a smile to his face.

"I bet," he said. "You're a chip off the old block. Get to sleep."

I watched him walk to his room, and I hated how old he suddenly looked, his shoulders slumped now with the fatigue of work, along with the weight of the deep and enduring sorrow he carried plus the weight of worrying that he was doing what he could and should do for me.

Seeing how upset my father was, I realized that I had another reason to get through Christopher's diary: to solve the puzzles for him. Who wanted this large home on the Foxworth property, and why? I hoped that the clues were somewhere in the diary. Of course, I would say nothing of this to Kane. I had no idea what it all meant or even if it meant anything that concerned the Dollanganger children, and the one thing I didn't want to do was start a conversation about it in school.

Talk among our group of friends was centered on Tina Kennedy's upcoming party, anyway. Kane knew how I felt about going. Nevertheless, he enjoyed teasing her by saying we still weren't sure of our schedule. "We hope to be there, but there are a few things in the works."

"In the works? What does that mean?" she asked him, and he just looked at me and then gave her a smile and a slight shrug, leaving her gaping after us.

"Why do you tease her, Kane? Don't you know that especially for a girl like Tina, any attention breeds hope?"

"I'm not teasing. It's the truth, isn't it? We have things in the works. Maybe we'll go, or maybe we'll be up in your attic."

"Not when my father is home," I said. "And if he sees us spending so much time in my room, especially on a weekend, he's going to get suspicious."

He gave me the oddest look, his head a little tilted to the right, his eyes smaller. "Sure you're not exaggerating his attitude about the diary?" he asked.

"I'm sure. He's made it crystal-clear a number of times."

He still looked skeptical, which annoyed me. In fact, I was irritable for the rest of the day. I know I didn't seem myself to my girlfriends. I had nothing funny or flattering to say about Suzette's new shade of lipstick, which she was proudly demonstrating on her perky little sexy mouth. She had used that description of herself, the girl with the perky little sexy mouth, ever since her older brother's college buddy described her that way and set her eyelids fluttering for a week.

But I wasn't ignoring just Suzette. Kyra's father had given her a black and gold pyramid stud wrap watch this morning, because her birthday was falling on Thanksgiving this year, and he wanted her to feel the impact of a special day. He and her mother would give her gifts every day until Thanksgiving and probably the day after, too. All of us had expressed interest in such a watch, so I knew I should have been happier for her when she showed it to us.

I was having moments like this ever since Kane

first proposed reading the diary together. Without reason, I would find myself trembling and slinking away from contact with my girlfriends. The moments passed quickly enough. They were like tiny puffs of black smoke after a match was struck. Kane always seemed to be able to bring me back with his jokes and offbeat smile.

However, he knew he had annoyed me by doubting that my father was so against my reading the diary. He apologized at lunch and broke his rule that we shouldn't talk about the diary outside of my attic, or at least outside of my house.

"It's a very sad, even at times brutal story, but after some of the stories lately concerning people locked away for years, it's not full of black magic or anything for me. That's all I meant."

"We haven't reached the end, Kane. You might change your mind."

He nodded. "I might," he admitted. "But that's more reason for us to do it like we're doing it. We can comfort each other, right?"

"Comfort?"

"Just like Cathy and Christopher did," he said. "Everything unpleasant is more unpleasant when you're the only one feeling or experiencing it. That's why as soon as something bad happens to us, we like to share it. We need the empathy and sympathy to help us get through it."

"Apparently, they didn't have anyone to do that for them, even their own mother," I said bitterly.

"Looks like it," he said.

"What is making you two look like you lost your best friends?" Serena Mota asked us as she was passing our table.

Kane looked at me and quickly said, "We're upset because we might have to miss Tina Kennedy's party this weekend."

Serena looked at us, dumbfounded for a moment, and then shrugged. "I might miss it, too."

As she walked off, we both laughed, but the lesson was learned. We looked at each other and repeated it word for word. "Don't talk about the diary in school!"

I was afraid that Kane's obvious anticipation of my meeting him at the end of the day and our usual rather quick departure from the building, both of us avoiding contact or conversation with any of our friends who might delay us even for a few minutes, would attract even more attention and interest in how we were spending our afternoons together. Of course, as with most things, he didn't worry about it and just smiled and shrugged when I mentioned it on our way to my house.

It had been a while since my closer girlfriends had called me, too. I knew they were all getting a little upset with me, probably telling each other that I was getting snobby because I was going with Kane.

However, I noticed that he was acting a little different this time. As usual, he brought his book bag in to leave in my room so that later we could employ the cover activity we had been using, doing our homework together. But then he suggested that

I get us a snack of some sort, since by now the Dol-langangers would have something like that, too, perhaps leftovers from the holidays. While I was doing that, he said he would go up to the attic and arrange things. I knew it was silly to feel it at this point, but I couldn't help being a little reluctant to give him the diary to take up with him without me. It was a ridiculous anxiety. After all, he had been alone in my room reading it, hadn't he? It was just something about it being up in the attic without me that made me uneasy. I was like the Keeper of the Book or something in a science-fiction movie. As if he could read my thoughts, before I could say anything, he told me to bring the diary up with everything else and then charged up the stairs.

I went into the kitchen, cut up cheese for some crackers, got some cups and lemonade, put it all on a tray, and walked up, stopping in my room to get the diary and put it on the tray. I could hear him moving things around above. I stood there for a moment thinking about it. Corrine had given the children a television. When they were in the attic, they were playing games. The twins weren't big, but their constant scuffling about and all the other sounds surely must have been heard by someone, some servant below. What did their grandmother tell anyone who commented about it? That maybe it was mice or rats or raccoons that had gotten into the attic? Kane's insistence that they weren't as big a secret as both Corrine and Grandmother Olivia told them they were was beginning to sound more credible to me. It could even have something to do with the mystery my father was discovering.

I walked up the stairs carefully, balancing everything on the tray. Kane had left the attic door open for me. I entered and stopped dead in my tracks. Kane had unfolded and set up the sofa bed, but that wasn't what surprised me. It was what he was wearing, what he obviously had kept hidden in his book bag all day.

He was wearing a wig with a shade of flaxen gold hair nearly identical to my hair color. I didn't speak. I just gaped at him and had this eerie feeling shudder through my body.

"Say something," he said. "It's pretty good, isn't it? I stole some of the strands of your hair from your hair brush a few times and put them together to give the wig store guy a pretty accurate idea of the color I wanted. This was specially made for me. I'm assuming Christopher's hair would be this long by now. I have the feeling he wore it this way, anyway," he added. He kept talking, because I was making him nervous just standing and staring at him. "I mean, I don't have your color eyes, but we can skip that one, or I might get color contacts of plain glass. So? Doesn't this help you envision him—them?"

"Yes, I guess it does. It was just such a shock seeing you there."

He smiled. "You thought Christopher might have appeared?"

"Not quite that," I said, putting the tray on a small table. "It was just a shock."

He nodded and picked up a cracker and some cheese. "I'm a little hungry," he said, smiling.

I looked at the bed. "Why did you do that?"

"Before I closed the diary yesterday, I glanced at the next page. You'll see," he said. He poured himself some lemonade and ate another cracker and cheese. I took some and sat on the bed. We just stared at each other a moment. I was shaking my head. "What?"

"That wig. Changes your whole look."

"That's the idea. Actors don't want the audience to see them; they want the audience to see and hear the character they're playing. Let's get started," he said, swallowed some more lemonade, and then plucked the diary off the tray and opened it to where we had left off. I sat on the bed while he walked around reading, but it was taking me a little while to get used to him as a flaxen blond.

During January, February, and most of March, we rarely went up to the attic. It was so cold, some days we could see our breath, and the twins were very uncomfortable, their misery level going up a few notches every time we attempted to go up there. So what we had to do was stay in our claustrophobic bedroom, huddled up in bed together, watching television. I understood why people in foreign countries liked to watch American television. They could learn English and much more. Suddenly, for us, too, the television Momma

had brought wasn't just a window on the outside
world; it was a teaching device, because the twins,
and even Cathy, had questions raised by what
we saw.

Kane paused, nodded at me, and then made himself
comfortable beside me on the sofa bed. He looked so
pleased with himself that I almost laughed.

"Big shot," I said.

He blew on the tips of the fingers on his right
hand, and I poked him. Then I lay back beside him,
and he continued, his voice softening until he was almost whispering.

It was inevitable that I would see Cathy's body
maturing right before my eyes. She was at that age
when some girls advance in leaps and bounds. I
always believed she would be one of them. I could
see she wasn't reacting well to it. I caught her trying
to pluck her sprouting pubic hair and saw that she
was self-conscious about her budding breasts. My
maturing had become obvious, too. When she
discovered the stains resulting from my seminal night
losses, she thought I was peeing in bed and wanted
me to tell Momma. I tried to explain it, and then I
realized it was time Momma had a mother-daughter
talk with her, not about me so much as about what
was soon to happen to her. As Momma was leaving
us one day, I caught her arm at the door and turned
her toward me to whisper.

"You've got to explain the facts of life to

Cathy, Momma. She's going to experience menarche," I said.

For a moment, I thought Momma didn't know that word, which meant a girl's first period. Then it suddenly dawned on her, and she nodded and told me she would handle it. I should take the twins up to the attic and let her have that conversation when she was ready to do it. I wonder if she would ever have done it if I hadn't brought it to her attention. Like some parents, was she hoping her children would just suddenly, almost miraculously, know what they had to know about their own bodies? We weren't in school, where Cathy or I could get the information in some health class or science class, either.

One day soon after, Momma finally had the conversation with Cathy that I wanted her to have. Afterward, I assumed it had gone well, because Momma was so proud of me for alerting her. I was actually a little embarrassed by her over-the-top affectionate kisses and hugs. Out of the corner of my eye, I saw the twins looking at us jealously, and I tried to get Momma to pay them more attention, but all she could do for now was smile and whisper, "My little doctor. Menarche." She left laughing. When I glanced at Cathy, I saw a look of pure rage on her face. I realized she didn't like the facts of life. None of us wanted to be dragged into adulthood this soon, but life at Foxworth Hall was making it impossible not to be. You could pretend it away just so long. Cold reality was there to greet us in the morning and especially at night when we went to bed.

The warmth of spring made it possible for us to spend more time in the attic again. The twins needed the space more than Cathy and I, the chance to move their legs and arms and hopefully grow normally now. Momma continued to lavish gifts upon us, especially on Cathy's birthday and then the twins' birthday. They were now six. It was when Cory began to take to the musical toy accordion and piano that Momma finally sat and told us about her two dead brothers. She said Cory had probably inherited their penchant for music. Then she described the death of her older brother Mal, who, eerily like my father, had been killed in a car accident. What happened to her younger brother, Joel, was even stranger. She said he had run away from home the day of Mal's funeral.

"He didn't want to become his father," she said. "He didn't want this life. My father didn't appreciate Joel's love of music."

"Where did he go? What happened to him?" I asked.

"He went to Europe. He had taken a job with a traveling orchestra. I think he was always planning to do that. My father wouldn't have permitted it, of course. He wouldn't even hear of it. And then . . ."

"Then what?" We were all glued to her,

the dreadful expression on her face, the way she hesitated. Even the twins, who didn't quite understand it all, were entranced.

"We learned he had died in a skiing accident in Switzerland. We were told he went off into a ravine, and something of an avalanche had followed. It was too high up to melt away enough for his body to be discovered. At night, I would wake up after having a nightmare in which he emerged from the snow, still frozen, still dead."

None of us spoke. Cathy's eyes were big with fear. Momma realized it right away. She had gone too far.

"But I haven't had that dream for years and years, and when your father came into my life, he washed away the sadness," she said quickly, with her beautiful smile born out of the memories she obviously cherished.

Cathy's face softened and then grew sad again. "He's gone, too," she whispered. I decided to pretend I didn't hear her.

Afterward, to lift the gloom and doom, I suggested to Cathy that we take on a big job: teaching the twins to read and write. At first, I didn't think she would be interested, but she was, and she was good at finding ways to overcome their resistance and make learning fun. One night, I told her how proud of her I was. The twins were asleep, exhausted from their lessons and their playtime, which Cathy ran like a school monitor and then followed with more lessons. I slipped onto the bed beside her. She opened her eyes with surprise.

"You were wonderful today," I whispered. "I watched you. You were so into it."

"What else is there to do?" she replied bitterly.

"It's going to get better . . . soon," I said.

She put her fingers on my lips. "No more promises, Christopher. I'm tired of promises. It's like waiting for rain in a drought."

"We're going to get through it," I said. "You'll see. That's not a promise. It's a prediction."

She smiled. I was just realizing how cute a smile she had. It had something of Daddy in it but more Momma's lips. I leaned forward and kissed her on the forehead. As I drew back to return to Cory's and my bed, she grabbed my wrist and then, to my surprise, kissed me quickly on the lips the way Momma often did. The instant she had done it, she turned quickly. I lay there a few moments more. I could see the graceful turn in her neck to her shoulder. I wanted to touch it, but I retreated.

That night, I woke during a seminal night loss that lasted so long it actually frightened me for a moment. Right before it happened, I had dreamed of touching Cathy in her private places, pretending I was explaining things to her like some health education teacher. In my dream, she saw what was happening to me as a result and then decided she should be able to touch me, too.

And that's when it happened.

Kane put the diary down beside him and stared up at the ceiling. Then he turned to me slowly. I saw a deeply serious look of yearning in his eyes.

"What?" I whispered.

"Last night, I had a wet dream, what he calls 'seminal loss' . . . thinking of you. It was almost an identical dream."

I did not know how something you heard could embarrass you and yet fascinate and excite you at the same time, but that was exactly what his revelation did. My close girlfriends and I trusted one another with confessions about our sexuality. Sometimes we told things to one another simply to confirm that our experience was normal. I know that for most of the girls, it was easier to tell one another these things than it was to tell their mothers or even their older sisters. They wanted to disclose their secrets to someone who wouldn't impose any judgments. None of us would be critical or make fun of one of us for what she had told us.

But I couldn't remember any of my girlfriends ever telling something as personal as this that her boyfriend had revealed to her. Even Suzette had nothing like this to tell us. Of course, Kane would trust that I would never tell any of them what he had said. I don't know whether he expected to hear something similar from me, but I did feel that I should give him something to show him that I had as much trust in him as he had in me.

"I fantasize about you, too," I said.

He smiled, and then we kissed. "Maybe we should

live our fantasies," he whispered, his lips so close to my ear that it felt like his words caressed me. "What was your fantasy?"

I hesitated.

"If you can't tell me, who could you tell?"

"Maybe I should tell no one."

"Okay. Don't tell me. Show me," he said.

Just the idea brought a flush into my face. I started to shake my head, but he leaned forward quickly and kissed me.

Then he said, "Please."

My two voices that usually argued didn't even begin. A wave of delicious warmth rose up my legs, consuming me in a rush of desire just like I had experienced in my fantasy, desire that had awakened me to the sound of my own moans of pleasure. And just like in my fantasy, my fingers moved to the buttons of my blouse. As I began to undress, Kane lay back on the pillow and watched. I saw his lips tremble when I unfastened my bra and then began to undo the belt on my jeans. As I lowered them, he put the diary down.

"What did I do in this fantasy?" he asked, sounding fragile, almost helpless.

"You just watched," I said. "To prove to me that you could control yourself."

His eyes widened when I stepped out of my panties. "That's cruel," he said. It looked like tears had come into his eyes.

I smiled and lay beside him again. "Just kiss me," I said.

He did, and then he smiled. "You put words into my mouth unfairly in your fantasy." Then he brightened with a thought. "This is a fantasy Cathy might be having just at this point."

"Maybe," I said. "We're not reading her diary, though."

"Christopher is very intelligent. He knows she's having it," he insisted, and then he began to kiss me everywhere, moving randomly at first over my breasts, my stomach, and then my thighs.

I could feel my resistance rapidly defrosting, but I had a surge of caution and gently pushed him back.

"I'm dying here," he protested.

"You insisted that I show you my fantasy," I told him, and he groaned. I looked at him seriously and thought lovingly. "Not yet," I said.

"When, then?"

"I don't know. I just know . . . not yet," I said. "Please."

I felt his disappointment. It was that clear in his face, a face that was usually very good at hiding thoughts and feelings. He realized it, too, and gave me that smile and a shrug. "I promise I'll respect you in the morning," he said.

"But will I respect myself?" I countered, and put on my panties.

"Next time, I'll keep my mouth shut, I think." He put his hands behind his head and watched me finish dressing. "Was it the wig?" he asked when I was almost finished.

I looked at him. Was it? I wondered. "Maybe," I said.

He reached for the diary quickly, so quickly it was as if he was positive that my hesitation would diminish somewhere in the pages to come.

And that was more eerie than anything.

Summer came, and because of the warmth, the attic was once again tolerable for us. Momma knew we needed more and more to keep us occupied. She began bringing us books that looked like they might have come from the library in the house, especially the history books. Sometimes I read things aloud to Cathy, and sometimes she read them to me. The twins would listen for a few moments and then get bored and distract themselves with their toys, Momma's precious dollhouse, or just a nap.

One afternoon while they were napping, Cathy and I lay together on the stained old mattress by the attic window and had one of the most intimate conversations between us. We talked about what nudity could lead to and then about her menarche. I was honest about the changes in me, too. I was sure that the honesty we shared made us closer than most brothers and sisters. I pressed my face to her hair and assured her that what was happening to her and to me was right and good and nothing to be ashamed of. We clung to each other silently, as if the whole world swirled around us and we had no place else to go to be safe but into each other's arms.

Before we parted, she asked me if I thought it was odd that Momma had kept us locked up so long, that she had put up with our grandmother's demands no matter how it affected us. "She seems to be doing well," she added. "Much better than we're doing."

I couldn't deny that Momma seemed to have more money, beautiful clothes, and jewelry. I had to admit that I had the same thoughts, but I told her we had to have faith in her. She seemed to know what she was doing. She had a plan, and we had to let her work it out.

And then, after a time when she hadn't been by to see us, Momma came and told us that, finally, her father was very ill. He was much worse than he was when we had first arrived. She was confident that he would die soon, and as soon as he did, we would be free. How happy Cathy and I were all those days as we waited, hopeful. I didn't even feel guilty about wishing for my grandfather's death.

And then one day, Momma came to our door, poked her head in, and told us he had recuperated and the doctors said he had passed through a crisis. She left before I could ask a single medical question.

Neither Cathy nor I could speak. We put the twins to bed that night and looked at the calendar.

With rage in her fingers, Cathy made an X through
the day, then turned to me and said something
I had either deliberately forgotten or just hadn't
realized.

It was August.

We had been here a year!

When Kane stopped reading and lowered the diary,
neither of us spoke. A dark pall of silence fell between us. Without looking at me, he got up and went
to the windows and looked out. I watched him and
waited, as if no matter what I said or how I said it,
the sound of my voice would shatter us both. For a
few moments, with him standing there like that and
wearing that wig, I could easily imagine Christopher
by a window in the Foxworth Hall attic, gazing out
at the warm sunshine and the full-blown woods that
surely resembled a green sea with waves of maples and
oaks flowing toward the horizon. Perhaps he looked
longingly toward the lake where Kane and I had
picnicked. Perhaps he watched birds enjoying their
freedom, soaring onto higher branches and enjoying
their power of flight, and envied them. How torn he
had to be, struggling to balance what he knew was
their need to grow and mature in a world with others their age and his mother's desperate plan to bring
them back into financial security and promise for their
future. Surely he was wondering if the price they were
paying was far too high, especially after a year. Maybe
he was wondering how he could have lost track of that

fact. Maybe he was more afraid now about what was happening to him. If he lost it, what would become of his little brother and sister? What would become of Cathy?

"How long were they really up there, exactly, you think?" Kane asked, without turning back to me.

"I only know from the same stories you read and heard, Kane."

He turned to me. "Your father never offered an opinion, a hint at what was true?"

"I told you, he doesn't like talking about it. He said my mother hated hearing about it. It disturbed her, and he can't forget that."

"To keep your children locked up for just one year is crazy enough, especially those little ones. How confused and frightened . . ." His voice trailed off. He wiped his head with a quick motion and swiped off the wig. He held it for a moment, turning it slowly in his hand as though he was looking for something, and then he opened one of the trunks and dropped it inside. "I have to go home for dinner tonight," he said, coming back to the sofa bed. "My sister might be back from college in time for dinner."

"Oh, that's nice."

"With her boyfriend," he added. "Should be interesting. It will be the first time my parents have met him. I hope my mother doesn't put him in the maids' quarters."

"She wouldn't do that, would she?"

"My sister would turn around and leave if she did."

I stood up, and we began to put the attic back to the way it was.

"Maybe we should skip tomorrow," I said. "Sounds like you'll have lots to do."

"No, no," he quickly responded. "She'll be showing him around all day. We want to get as much read as we can while your father has this schedule, right?"

"I'm not sure what his schedule will be. I'll find out tonight."

"Well, even if he's back for dinner, we still have a few hours after school. I don't want to whiz through it, but I can't help but wonder where this is all heading."

"Okay," I said.

He smiled, but I could see that he was still quite disturbed. We walked down to my room. He started to pick up his books, paused, and flopped back on the desk chair. I stood there for a moment and then sat on my bed. He looked emotionally exhausted, like a shadow had darkened his eyes even more.

"Do you want to stop reading this?" I said, holding up the diary. "Because if you're saying what you're saying and doing it just for me . . ."

"Oh, no, no. I can handle it."

"Then what is it? I see that something's seriously upset you."

He smiled. "I'm still reeling from your fantasy and the frustration that followed."

"No, you're not. Don't try to joke your way out of this. I'm getting to know you too well."

"You mean I'm losing the famous Kane Hill mystique?"

"What is it, Kane?" I persisted.

He nodded, a sign of surrender, and then leaned forward, thinking. When he looked up, I could see he had decided on something very important to him. I held my breath. My mind raced from one end of the spectrum to the other, ranging from thinking he might tell me about some terrible illness he or someone in his family was suffering to imagining a confession about something terrible he had done. If it involved one of the girls in our classes, I was hoping he wouldn't reveal it.

"I'm still a virgin," he confessed instead.

If there was anything I did not expect to hear, it was that. For a moment, I couldn't speak. Of course, I was sure I looked skeptical.

"I know, I know," he continued, putting up his hand before I could say anything, not that I knew what to say. "I've got this reputation. Funny, the girls I have been with would never say we hadn't gone that far if they were asked. It would reflect more on them than me, I guess. It's not that they didn't want to; it's more that I didn't want to with them. Do you believe me?"

"No."

He nodded. "Understandable."

"Why tell me that, anyway?" I asked. "You think that is the reason I've held back, that you've been with so many other girls, and I'd just be another?"

"Well, it could be your reason."

"If I thought you believed that, I would certainly be even more skeptical about what you're saying now, wouldn't I? Naturally, I'd think you were manipulating me."

"I guess, but you're about as easy to manipulate as a steel rod." He leaned back.

"Remember that conversation we had once about why some girls are easy and some aren't? You've tried to get me to go further, Kane. You're not exactly Mr. Shy. You don't come off as a virgin."

"I wanted to, yes. I wanted to upstairs just now. I don't think I ever wanted to more. I want to every moment I'm with you. You think that's dirty or something?"

"No. I didn't say that."

"I think it will mean more with you. I hope you think or will think the same. I suppose all I'm trying to say is, when you're ready, I'm ready."

I smiled.

"What?"

"I think you've been ready from the first day."

He held up his hands. "Guilty," he said, and stood up. "I'd better get out of here before I confess too much more." He scooped up his books and turned toward the door.

"What brought on this confession, Kane?"

He stood looking at the floor.

"It was Christopher, wasn't it?" I asked him before he could leave. "The things he wrote about sex, his feelings? That's what got you to tell me this, isn't it?"

I didn't think he would answer. He looked like he just wanted to leave, but after a moment, with his head still down, he said, "Yes."

"Why? What exactly was it that pushed your buttons? Don't try to make a joke of it," I added quickly. "What will make anything between us significant is honesty."

He looked at me and said, "My sister is only a few years older than I am. She's very pretty."

"I know. I've seen her. So?" My mind began spinning with the possibilities. What else was he going to tell me? Did I want to hear it?

"Enough said for now, maybe," he replied. "I'll see you in the morning."

If I had ever felt I was hanging off a cliff, it was right then. He was already halfway to the stairs. I got up to follow him down and to the doorway. He paused and turned to me. Suddenly, he looked more like he did in the attic, more like Christopher than Kane. I even imagined that wig. The light in his eyes seemed to flicker. He had never looked as serious and less Kane Hill–like than he did at this moment. It made my heart flutter.

"I feel like we have something very special because of the diary, don't you? Like we're privileged by being granted entry to someone else's most private, painful, and yet at times strangely wonderful thoughts. Do you feel it, too, this . . . this possession? I mean, it's really as if Christopher Dollanganger is talking to you and me. Right?"

I could see he thought he might be going mad and wanted confirmation. But it was true. I did feel the same things. "Yes."

"Let's not do anything that might make us lose it."

"Okay."

He smiled, gave me a quick kiss on the lips, and started for his car. I stood there watching him get in and then back the car out. He waved and drove off. Little butterflies of panic were fluttering in my head. I couldn't help but think that he was more than right, that we had crossed some forbidden line. The diary had led us into a world where emotions whirled, fears crawled about like electric spiders, and private secrets locked in our hearts began popping around us like bubbles.

Suddenly, I felt lonelier than I had felt in a very long time. I remembered myself as a little girl for no apparent reason turning away from my toy world and rushing to my mother, who seemed to instinctively know she had to embrace me and kiss me and smile softly, lovingly.

It was only natural for very young children to be overtaken by inexplicable fears, perhaps the leading one being the fear of being deserted, to suddenly turn around and be afraid that you were all alone. I thought of the Dollanganger twins literally shoved into that strange, cold world and left to cling to each other, to a sister barely old enough to comfort herself and to an older brother who was struggling to be a man with a man's responsibilities long before that should happen.

My mother couldn't stop herself from comforting me. It was essential to being a mother. What inside

Corrine was stronger than that need? When she went to sleep at night, did she toss and turn, thinking of her children locked away yet so close? Did she imagine their moans? Hear them calling for her? Did she struggle with the urge to go to them and rip them out of that dark world, where nightmares danced around them?

Among other things, like me, Kane felt some of this, understood their pain. I was sure, but I was also sure there was some other feeling, some other memory that had just been exposed in today's reading. Whatever had kept it from resurfacing had been ripped away. Did I want to know, to pursue it until I found out? Maybe it was better if we remained somewhat strangers to each other.

I had started to return to my room when the phone rang.

"Hey," my father said.

He had heard something in my voice when I said hello. I wasn't surprised. Because we were so dependent on each other since my mother's death, we were both sensitive to the smallest changes, the slightest signals in our voices or in our faces. We both knew when something troubled or annoyed one of us. Loving someone meant being able to understand him or her better than anyone else.

He paused and then asked, "Everything all right?"

"Yes, fine," I said. In the small pause, I knew that he knew that wasn't so, but he chose not to pursue it.

"Free for dinner?"

"Yes."

"Good. I'm home in an hour. I feel like Charley's. Is that all right?"

"Sure," I said. I wasn't in the mood for anything more formal. My father liked Charley's Diner because it was his chance to meet some of his old friends and toss around stories and their form of gossip. Charley's was a sort of hangout for men involved with the construction industry.

It was designed like an old 1950s diner, with faux-leather red booths with pleated white centers and chrome edges and base tables. There was a long counter with swivel barstools, lots of Formica and chrome, but there were also a dozen retro dinette sets, again with lots of chrome and Formica. The floor was a black and white checker, and although some of them didn't work, there were miniature jukeboxes at the booths and on the counter. Consequently, there was always music but nothing anyone my age would appreciate. Actually, I never saw any of my school friends there.

Charley Martin was the original owner. He was well into his seventies, although he looked ten years younger, with his full head of salt-and-pepper hair swept back and on the sides as if he had just run a wet washcloth over it, maybe with a little style lotion. He was stout, with the forearms of a carpenter, both arms stained with tattoos he had gotten in the Philippines when he was in the navy. Dad called him Popeye. He pretended to be annoyed, but I could see he liked it.

"Is it just the two of us?" my father asked cautiously, obviously assuming that the note of sadness he had heard in my voice had something to do with Kane. Perhaps my little romance had crashed on the rocks like a little sailboat.

"Yes. Kane went home. His sister is arriving for her Thanksgiving break tonight," I quickly added to wash away his suspicions.

"That's nice," he said. "I'm going to cook up a storm for us." I knew what he was thinking now. Kane's family's preparations for a family get-together on Thanksgiving would remind me of the hole in my heart, too. "See you soon."

After I hung up, I went to get into some of my homework so there wouldn't be much when we returned. I had left Christopher's diary on the bed. When I picked it up to put it under my pillow, I was so tempted to open to the page where we had left off. Maybe it was a good idea to read ahead now, I thought. I would know what to expect and how to react to the way Kane would react, especially after seeing the way he was today. That was a good rationalization for it, but then I feared he would know I had read ahead and that would break our trust. Besides, I really had to get into my homework. My father could linger at Charley's.

And linger we did. Everyone there wanted to hear about the new construction on the old Foxworth property. I listened politely as they debated some of the new materials and techniques versus the old tried-and-true. I didn't want to interrupt or complain that we were staying too long. I could see how happy my father was talking shop with some of the men he'd known since he had first begun in Charlottesville. With any reference to my mother, even a passing one, he would shift his gaze to me and then find a way to change the topic. Finally, he was tired himself, and we left.

"Some of those guys are so set in their ways they're like petrified trees," he joked on our way home in Black Beauty. It rode rough, but he kept the engine purring.

He hadn't mentioned this at Charley's, but as we drew closer to home, he decided to tell me.

"The darndest thing," he said, "but I was given quite a challenge today. 'Course, there's enough time to adjust things, and I suppose it works with the architecture. No structural problems with the roof."

"What is it?" I asked, wondering if he would ever say.

"Oh. There'll be no attic. I mean, there'll be a crawl space but no actual attic. 'Course, lots of houses don't have attics today. Wasted space for most. Things go to these storage places you rent or just get given away. No one wants memories."

"So why is it so weird?"

"Oh, it's not so weird. It's just that the original plan had a sizable attic, and then this new order came down the pike," he said. "But how does that saying go? Ours is not to reason why . . ."

He didn't finish the line, and I didn't want to finish it for him: "Ours is but to do and die." Either he didn't want to mention it or he really didn't care to make the connection, but eliminating an attic in the new structure suggested to me that the new real owner didn't want even the idea of an attic on that property, and yet other things were shared with the old structure in this new one, like views from windows; it was a puzzle.

When we got home, I went right to finishing my homework and studying a bit for a history quiz. Unlike on most nights, my father didn't fall asleep in front of the television. He did some paperwork, then decided to turn in early and stopped by to say good night.

"Tomorrow's Friday. You have any plans yet?" he asked.

"Nothing for Friday yet, but expect to," I replied. "Tina Kennedy is having a party Saturday night, which we might attend, but tomorrow night there's a new movie we both want to see. I guess we'll go for something to eat first. Are you working till the same time?"

"With daylight savings time, it gets dark now, not much choice," he replied. "Don't worry about me. Have a good time."

"I can do both," I said, and he laughed.

I had a message from Kane on my voice mail. He just said to call him when I could.

"Problems for Darlena?" I asked as soon as he answered. I was thinking of their first dinner with Darlena's boyfriend.

"No, not really. My mother was cordial, as cordial as a queen might be to a servant, but we got through it. My father grilled him as if he had come to ask for a job. Darlena should get herself and him through the maze and return to college after the holiday with only minor scars."

"Is your mother really that bad?"

"Let's just say when she's seventy, she'll be a leading candidate for the Olivia Foxworth award."

"Oh, stop," I said, and he laughed.

"What I really wanted to tell you was I'm all right. I could see you were a little concerned when we said good-bye today, but don't worry about me reading the diary. I'm not usually that emotional about anything."

"Tell me something I don't know."

"You're good, angel, you're real good."

"I know. Are we going to the movies tomorrow night? I told my father we might."

"Sure. After we—"

"Do our session in the attic. I know. I can't believe I was once more enthusiastic about this than you were."

"Were you?"

"I've got to go to sleep. I have a test tomorrow."

"You can practice your answers on me in the morning," he said. "I'll go to sleep counting the minutes until I see you."

In the morning, my father told me that he had forgotten to mention that my aunt Barbara wouldn't be coming to our Thanksgiving after all. It wasn't because she felt she had to go to her boss's dinner. She had come down with a bad chest cold. I saw that he was quite disappointed, enough to suggest that we might visit her in the spring. He wasn't fond of going to New York. He claimed he was too much a small-town boy.

This was going to be the ninth Thanksgiving for us without my mother. There would always be that gaping hole in our holiday happiness. Aunt Barbara's presence would have helped us get through it a little, so I shared my father's disappointment. Feeling this way brought back the terrible Thanksgiving the Dollanganger children had soon after they were brought to Foxworth Hall. For them, there would never be another with their father, and that first time, they didn't even have their mother. Just like mine, their holidays would be forever a mixture of sadness and joy, no matter how fast their freedom was returned and how rich they would all be.

When Kane arrived in the morning and we started for school, most of his conversation was about his sister and her boyfriend, Julio Lancaster. Kane told me he was named after his maternal grandfather. He was the fourth of four children, with two older sisters and one older brother.

"How is he taking your parents?" I asked.

"My sister prepared him well. He's overly polite. I have to believe he went overboard on his conservative appearance, too. He has a haircut like my father's, wore a tie to dinner, wore shoes with a shine better than my father's, and had sharp creases in his pants. He looked like he had taken a graduate course in dinner etiquette, too. If I didn't know better, I'd have thought he was satirizing my mother especially. I loved the way she pronounced his name: Jewel-o. Darlena kept correcting her, and he kept saying, 'It's all right. My father's mother calls me Jewel-e.' Even my father had to laugh at that."

"Why is it I suspect your sister might be going with him and brought him home just to get at your mother?"

Kane smiled. "Could be, but he's not bad-looking, and he is a bright guy. Slim, swimmer's build, about six foot one, with those sexy dark Spanish eyes and a voice as melodic as Julio Iglesias's, whose singing my mother likes, by the way. It's like those racists who watch *Oprah* regularly."

"Hearing you talk about your mother helps me to understand why you're so ready to condemn Corrine Dollanganger," I said.

"Yeah, I know, but something keeps me from all-out condemning her. But I can't help believing she's going to break Christopher's heart."

I nodded, and Kane changed the topic. He described how his close buddies were teasing him about me. Already, he had been seeing me longer than he had any other girl in our school.

"I'm losing my playboy reputation. It's even caught my mother's attention."

"Oh? Is she upset?"

"No, but she quipped that I might have to bring you around to introduce you to her if my 'new fling' continues much longer. I think some of her trusted gossips mentioned it to her. Brought up like a princess, you naturally assume you'll be queen."

"If you keep talking about her like that, I'll be terrified of meeting her."

"That's the idea. She likes people being a little terrified of her."

"Stop it," I said, and he laughed. The difference between him this morning and the way he had been when he was leaving my house the day before was like night and day.

The school day always seemed to go faster on Fridays. Maybe it was because of how hard we wished for the final bell and the beginning of the weekend. Tina Kennedy tried to up the excitement for her party by revealing that her parents had agreed to pay for a disc jockey. Her family had a large ranch-style home with a beautiful five acres just outside of the city in the opposite direction from ours. Besides the adult bar, her father owned five Burger King franchises and a number of triple-net properties renting to drugstores and two supermarkets. Tina liked to brag about all this in front of Kane, as if she was giving him another reason they belonged together. She practically came out and said, "The rich belong with the rich," the implication being that Kane certainly didn't belong with the daughter of a middle-class construction worker.

Despite how hard she tried to get him to commit to attending her party, Kane held out the possibility that we might not be able to make it. He kept the reason vague and was so convincing he had most, if not all, of my girlfriends believing it and tugging at me to tell them what we would be doing instead. I hadn't done a very good job of hiding my lack of interest in her party, anyway.

"I can't say, because it might be a surprise," I told them, which only intensified their curiosity.

Suzette suggested that it might have to do with Darlena. She knew Darlena had brought her boyfriend home from college. Her mother was a member of Kane's mother's gossip club. "Maybe they're going on a double date," she told the others.

Going on a double date with a college junior and senior probably seemed very sophisticated to them. It set off a flurry of conjectures and more questions, but neither Kane nor I offered any further details. At the end of the day, we both hurried out of the building, laughing about the buzz we had created.

"My phone will be ringing all day tomorrow," I said.

"I'll just have to keep you too busy to answer," he replied, and we drove off to my house.

Right from the beginning, I believed that reading the diary together would either draw us closer or drive us apart. Seeing how he had reacted and knowing how I had been reacting did make sharing it something special between us, as he had said. Would I have felt this strongly about him if he had never found the diary and we had never started this? Maybe, I thought, but I would always be carrying the deep secret of the diary inside me, and he would wonder if my silences, my drifting back into something I had read, meant I was getting bored and losing interest in him. He might have pursued the reason, and that probably would have driven me away from him in the end.

Christopher, I thought, *you never dreamed you would do this, that you would become a bridge between a boy and a girl, taking them across to a place they would fear and despise and yet be attracted to, maybe even in their special way cherish. You had no reason to believe that all that you felt and experienced would be understood and shared as if it belonged to someone else, maybe to everyone.*

Kane and I walked up the stairs, now more than ever feeling like two explorers traveling to another country inside themselves. He went right to the trunk. I thought he had cast the wig aside, maybe feeling foolish about it, but I was wrong. He put it on and smiled. "Hi, Cathy," he said, and began to read.

So much of what we did and how we lived the following year was the same as the first year that I can simply say another year passed.

Never in my wildest imaginings did I see us living in that small room and this attic for this long. Every day, I awoke the same way, with the same thought: Today, our grandfather will die, and we will return to the world. And every day, he lived on.

Momma wasn't visiting us as frequently. A heavy wave of resignation settled over Cathy and me. We were the twins' parents now, caring for their every need, teaching them what we could, amusing them every way we could, healing them when they had colds or bruises and cuts, and comforting them when they had nightmares. Nevertheless, it was good that they had each other. I didn't tell Cathy this, because I knew she would go into some sort of rage, but I found an old book on the care and breeding of dogs. It was highly recommended that there be at least two if the owners were not going to be able to pay them enough attention. Children were certainly no less than dogs. They needed company.

For Cathy and me, expanding our territory somehow became paramount. I realized that on Thursdays especially, when the servants left for town, she and I could crawl out onto the roof and sun ourselves. It became our outing, our little trip to someplace else. We went there during the day and during the night. It gave us the desperately needed sense of some freedom.

Time wasn't simply marked off on calendars. We had three, one dedicated to the death of our grandfather, because that was supposed to be the birth of our freedom and new life. Time was also marked by our own physical maturing. Cathy was far more aware of hers than I was of mine. Girls usually mature faster in so many ways. I knew she was intrigued about it because of her constant questions, the answers for some of which I had to research.

What happened next was my fault more than Cathy's. One day, I found her gazing at her naked body, exploring the changes in her breasts, the curves in her figure, even touching herself between her legs. Suddenly, she sensed my presence and turned to look at me. I must have looked fascinated, because she didn't rush to cover herself. Then she reached for her dress, and I said, "Don't." She held the dress but made no effort to put it on.

I kept thinking I shouldn't be doing this, but I was so drawn to her sex, and I could see she was realizing her power over me. She didn't tease me. At least, I don't think she did, but all she said was, "You shouldn't."

I tried to explain myself, to compliment her on her growing beauty, and then we heard the door being unlocked. She rushed to put on her dress, but she didn't get it on fast enough to avoid our grandmother's startled eyes. We watched as she gave a cold, satisfied smile. At last, she said, she had caught us.

Caught us doing what? I protested. I knew what she was going to accuse us of doing, but Cathy had no idea what she meant when she said she was positive now that Cathy had been permitting me to use her body. She made it seem like Cathy's body, her beautiful hair, were all designed for sin. Of course, Cathy had no idea what she meant by "using her body." Suddenly, our grandmother left.

Fortunately, the twins weren't down from the

attic to see and hear this. When they came down, I heard our grandmother returning and told Cathy to get into the bathroom, but she was in and on her too fast. She had brought a pair of scissors and said she was going to cut Cathy's hair down to her scalp.

Cathy and I refused to let her, and she threatened that until Cathy cut her own hair, we all would have no food, even the twins. I thought it was an empty threat. Momma would be around soon, anyway. She left the scissors behind and shut the door. We had a little food left. The twins, of course, were so terrified they trembled. By now, Carrie had come to call Cathy "Momma," and she often crawled into bed with her so Cathy could embrace her and comfort her. Cory always looked a bit stunned to me, his little mind twirling in confusion. How unnatural it all seemed even to one as little as he.

I didn't know how long this terrible situation would last, and I had no idea that it would get even worse. The following morning, I awoke late and discovered that during the night, our grandmother from hell had snuck in, injected Cathy with some sedative she had probably taken from our grandfather's medicine so that Cathy wouldn't wake, and then poured tar into her hair. When Cathy realized it, she started to scream. I calmed her so that the twins wouldn't be even more terrorized, and then I tried to shampoo it out while she sat in the tub. It didn't work, no matter how hard I scrubbed. Hair was coming out in my fingers. I tried mixing some chemicals from a professional set Momma had brought me to keep me occupied with my scientific studies, but nothing worked. The twins kept asking about it. Cathy pretended she had done it to herself. She didn't want them to know how horrible our grandmother was. It would give them even more nightmares and cause her presence to send cold shivers of fear through their little bodies. They trembled enough as it was for some reason or another every day.

And then it began. She was true to her threat. There was no food brought to us. I was afraid she would sneak in and cut Cathy's hair anyway, so I tried blocking the door, and we planned to take turns playing sentry. We soon realized there was no reason to do it. She wasn't coming back until she got what she wanted. She didn't even check to see how we were doing without food. She brought us no supplies, either. Our toilet bowl got clogged. The twins were listless. All of us were weak without any food. Then I thought that if I cut off some of Cathy's hair and she wrapped her head in a scarf, that could fool her. We thought it might work, but she still didn't come with food. I even tried to feed the twins some of my blood for nourishment.

We were desperate. I planned to make a sheet ladder for an escape from the attic. I even

prepared dead mice for us to consume for the
strength we would need, and then, perhaps
believing she had punished us enough, she
left us a basket of food. What we discovered,
however, was that she had removed every mirror
and smashed the one in the bathroom. Cathy
wondered why, and I told her I had read that the
devil loves vain people. "She believes it and thinks
she can stop us from having any pride or what is
known as vanity."

We were in the hands of an insane woman, and
deny it as hard as I could, I couldn't answer Cathy
when she asked why—why would our mother let all
this happen? All I could think was she didn't know
what her mother was doing to us.

Kane looked at me and stopped reading.

"Are you all right?" he asked. "You look sick to
your stomach."

I nodded. However, for a moment, I couldn't
speak. I actually ran my fingers through my hair as if
I believed it had been magically bathed in tar and then
cut off.

"He had to feed them his blood?" I said. "I felt my
stomach churn when you read that."

"He felt he had no choice. How could she do that
to children so small? I have to say he was clever to cut
her hair that way and make it look like she had obeyed
the old lady's insane demand. What would she have
done if they had all died? Could she cover up something like that?"

"I don't know. It gets back to whether anyone else in that house knew about them."

He held up the diary. "I still say, how could they not? If I understand this correctly, he's saying they've been there two years. That's a long time to go without anyone else knowing they were there."

"I suppose."

He thought a moment. "You know, Kristin, maybe the Halloween stories are not that exaggerated. Some of the stories I've heard range from two to five years. We know now that there are people who have been kept locked up that long without anyone realizing it. If he was ready to create a sheet ladder for them and escape because she was starving them to death, why didn't he do it?"

"I don't know, Kane. All of it is disturbing, but this part made me sick."

I didn't want to say it again, but maybe this was why my father didn't want me reading the diary. And yet how would he know what was in the diary? Could he know what really had happened at Fox-worth Hall? Was that why he hated the property so much that he literally attacked the rubble when it became time to clear it away? Had my mother known any of this? Was this why she hated hearing about it? There were so many questions rolling around in my brain I felt dizzy. And here I had thought reading the diary would bring answers, not more questions.

Kane put the diary down. He stared at me strangely,

as if I was going in and out of focus. Maybe he was having a similar reaction.

"What?"

"Maybe he didn't want to escape."

"What? Why not?"

"Same reason he didn't come up with an escape plan earlier. He didn't want to ruin his mother's plan."

"I know, but how could he not want to give up on it by now? Especially after what their grandmother did to them. Who knew what she might do next?"

He was silent a moment, but I could almost see his mind working.

"What?"

"We were just talking about this in my English class recently, something called the Stockholm syndrome, where hostages actually sympathize with their captors. In a way, that's what Christopher is constantly doing, sympathizing with his mother's plight, blinding himself to the truth. It sounds crazy, especially after what we just read, but if you're penned up that long, you might grow comfortable with the situation, especially after years. It sounds like the twins have fully accepted things as they are. They don't scream for their mother as much." He paused and then added, "Even Christopher and Cathy seem to be accepting their relationship in a way. I don't know if it's so unexpected under the circumstances."

"What do you mean?"

"The way they treat each other, comfort each other. Sometimes I forget that they're brother and sister, don't you?"

"I don't know." I didn't want to say yes, but he was right.

"It's not unusual. I mean, it could happen to people that age even if they're not locked away together for years."

"I'm not sure I understand what you mean, Kane."

"That scene he described, coming in on Cathy looking at herself . . ."

"Yes?"

"You've done that, stood naked before a mirror. It's only natural to be interested in yourself, right?"

"Yes. Of course."

"Women would be doing that more than men. There are more changes to observe. I mean, breasts, curves. Men can see hair grow, some size, but looking at yourself . . . that's not sick or anything." He seemed to want confirmation from me.

"No, Kane, it's natural to be curious about yourself. Why do you keep talking about it? What does that have to do with what you're saying?"

"I don't know. The way Christopher's describing it . . . does it make it seem weird?"

"He's gazing lustfully at his own sister," I said. "He feels guilty."

The way Kane sat there and continued to stare at me suddenly convinced me that I knew now what he had meant by telling me his sister was beautiful. "Are you trying to tell me that you've done that, spied on your sister?"

He shrugged. "When I was younger. I would never do anything like that now," he quickly added.

It was my turn to shrug something off. "I bet every boy who has an older sister has done that one time or another," I said.

"You think? None of my buddies ever told me such a thing."

"I don't think they'd talk about it, brag about it. If they did, then they'd be weird."

"I just did."

"You didn't brag about it. All you did was admit to having done it and admitted it to me after what you read. That's not what I mean."

"Yes, that's true. I mean, I've done that, the spying, but I didn't have the kind of thoughts afterward that he had."

"I'll say this much. When it came to his being interested in girls, he didn't have much choice at that moment. That's all I think it means, Kane."

"I suppose. Yeah, I guess Christopher and I are not so different, even at this point in the diary," he said, holding it again. "I mean, he's not turning into a child monster or anything, the way some of those stupid stories depict him."

"Oh, no, definitely not. There's so much about him to admire. You've made understanding it all easier. I mean, the way you read it, our being up here and trying to understand what being shut up meant to them, even that wig." I started to smile.

"Maybe next time we're up here, you should wrap a scarf around your head." At first, I thought he might be kidding, but he didn't smile.

"I still have my hair, Kane."

"But if you want to feel what she feels . . . it's just a suggestion."

I nodded but wondered whether we were taking this too far now. The expression on Kane's face was so different, especially while he was still wearing the wig. Maybe my own imagination was going wild, too, because I thought he even sounded different, and not just when he read the diary. Every time we entered the attic now, he lost that casual, carefree posture for which he was so well known. There was an intensity about him when we were up here. He didn't shrug anything off or give me that wry smile, the way he often did at school or when we were with others our age. When he gazed at me now, he looked like he was gazing at someone who was suffering as much inside as he was or, maybe more accurately, as much as Christopher had.

Why wasn't I happy about all this? Wasn't it our intention to feel and appreciate what Christopher and Cathy had endured, to use the diary as a doorway to the past and discover what really happened and who they really were? It was working. His ideas made it all more authentic. Why be upset about that?

I had put on my mother's nightgown for the scene we read. It wasn't a big leap to wrap a scarf around my head. "Okay. I'll see."

He smiled, looked at the diary, and then stood and handed it to me. "Maybe we should think about getting something to eat. The movie starts early."

"Well, I'm not going out without a shower and changing," I said.

"Shower? Sounds good to me."

"Just a shower," I said firmly, and he laughed.

We restored the attic to the way it had been and went down to my room. I could see what he had on his mind. The thought brought back that rush of excitement I had when I demonstrated my fantasy in the attic. Every part of me tingled in anticipation. How much longer could we be this intimate with each other without "crossing the Rio Grande"? I would be a liar if I said I didn't want it to happen.

Whenever my girlfriends and I had serious conversations about this, a few questions were inevitable. Who among us would admit to being afraid of it, and not solely because we might become pregnant? There were obviously ways to avoid that. Who among us thought we should be as casual about it as any boy? Who among us thought she shouldn't do it unless she was really in love with the boy or expected to marry him?

As we grew older, we stopped asking one another these questions. We waited for one of us to admit she had done it. We all joked about it. Most of us believed Suzette had lost her virginity before she was a junior, much less a senior. I thought she enjoyed everyone believing that. Now she was the one teasing everyone else. She didn't tease me as much. I knew it was because my mother had died. Somehow she believed it would be unfair, perhaps because I had no one at home to run to and confess or ask the important questions.

If there was any reluctance to believe it about me or tease me about it before, it was dying a quick death now that I was "hot and heavy" with Kane in the eyes of my friends. The assumption was that no girl could go with Kane Hill more than two weeks and not have slept with him. If they only knew, I thought, and then I wondered why it was important for them to know anything, really. Did it bother me or make me feel older, more sophisticated, to have them think so? I knew it would bother me if my father thought so. How much, I wondered, would it really bother him? Whatever was left of his image of me as his little girl would evaporate, but did I want to be forever a little girl?

These thoughts and growing pains were hard enough when your hormones took center stage. But to have it happening with no one to compare notes with? That had to be twice as hard. Yes, Cathy missed having friends, for sure. She missed everything girls her age were enjoying out there, but I could speak from experience. Surely she missed having a mother most of all.

Kane watched me move around my room, choosing the clothes I would wear and preparing to take my shower. When I glanced at him, I saw him pretending to be interested in one of my magazines. I smiled to myself, got down to my panties, and went into the bathroom to shower. Maybe it was just natural for a female to be a tease, I thought as I got into the shower. Moments later, I got my payback.

He got into the shower beside me as he had suggested he would. How many times had I seen a movie scene like this? I thought when he kissed me. The warm water cascaded over our heads and bodies. I turned my face into it, thinking that it was a baptism of some sort. It was the first time I was totally naked with a boy who was totally naked. I don't think I was more than eleven when the image had occurred to me, and along with it, the waves of sensual excitement washed over me so quickly I was afraid I would drown in my own fantasies.

This was no fantasy. My nipples hardened; my legs felt weak. I leaned against him for support as he turned me toward him. His hands moved around my thighs and gently lifted me to him. I felt his excitement building and tensed up. My heart fluttered with panic, not because he was being aggressive as much as because I was quickly losing resistance.

"Kane," I said, my voice so weak and tiny I wasn't sure I had said it or thought it.

"Don't worry," he said. "When it happens, it will be a lot more comfortable for both of us."

That made me laugh, but I was in a terrible conflict. I was happy we were under control, but I was also disappointed. It wasn't the first time in my life when two conflicting emotions had raged inside me simultaneously, and I was sure it wouldn't be the last. There were those two parts of me again, arguing through every pore in my body, disagreeing along every nerve, only pausing when I brought my lips closer to his. We kissed again and again, his hands gently lifting my breasts toward his lips when he lowered his head.

We kept pulling away from each other and then rushing toward each other, each time closer, tighter, more passionately, and then truly like someone who had come upon a fire. I reached for the shampoo and poured some of it over his head. He cried out when it burned his eyes. He laughed, and then he poured some over my hair.

"I'll do it," he said when I reached up to begin washing my hair. I turned to let him go at it. It's not as hard as trying to shampoo out tar, I thought, when he started to wash my hair for me like a professional beautician.

"Thanks."

"I'll do it every night if I can do it in here," he said.

He stood back as I rinsed, and then he began to work on his own hair. He remained in the shower after I got out. I dried myself, slipped into my panties, paused to catch my breath and let my heart stop pounding. And then, quite contented, I stepped out of the bathroom.

I started for the clothes I had chosen and then stopped. I could feel something different, and not because of what had just happened in the shower.

It was my bedroom door, I realized. We hadn't closed it when we entered.

But it was closed now.

How do your parents adjust to the new you once you've crossed over from dolls and toy teacups, from cartoon shows and picture books, once you've lost your childhood faiths, including all the make-believe you cherished, like waiting for the tooth fairy after you lost one of your teeth? How long does it take them to realize you are your own person, more and more responsible for all you do, for what you think and what you say?

All parents must fool themselves for a while into believing their children would remain young and innocent longer. Perhaps out of fear of what really lay in wait for their children, parents surely cling to the belief that the children's world was somehow safer. There was all that protection they could layer over it, making sure that they knew exactly where their children were going all the time, filtering out what they heard and saw, locking them safely under wing when curfews came. With a kiss and a hug, they could always drive away goblins and ghosts, monsters and creatures invading their children's dreams. They could tuck them in securely and watch them fall asleep in the bubble of security they created. Every day for as long as they could do it, they could advise and counsel, demand and receive the obedience that helped tie their children to them.

"Time to go to sleep. You don't want to be tired and sick."

"Who's taking you home from the party?"

"Are any of your friends doing that? Has anyone suggested it?"

"No, you can't go."

"You're not old enough yet."

"I'll tell you when."

Layer after layer of orders ensured that sanctuary with only a moan or two in protest. In the morning, the rules and demands they made firmly still resonated. The little protests were forgotten, at least until the next time.

Gradually, all this began to fall away. It fell in small ways at first, but soon every rule they set down, every demand they made, was challenged more vigorously and bravely. Defiance crept in alongside anger and self-pity. In how many households could we hear, "Everyone else's parents let them do it! Why can't you trust me?"

Slowly, their grip weakened. They relented in more ways, and before they knew it, certainly before they wanted it to happen, their children were out there, vulnerable to all the dangers they had somehow escaped. Other parents, psychologists, and advice columns in magazines all warned them that clamping down too hard, tightening the restrictions, forbidding things, would drive their children to be defiant and perhaps even to do something they wouldn't have done if they hadn't prohibited it so inflexibly.

My father liked to joke whenever anyone commented on how grown-up I was now, "Yeah. Little kid, little problems, big kid . . ."

Whoever heard it laughed, but behind the laughter, you could see the belief that there was more truth in jest than anyone wanted to admit openly. Who wanted to be a bigger problem? Certainly not me, not now, not for my father, who was already afraid he wasn't doing all he could to ensure my safety and who felt a bigger burden and obligation to my mother's memory. To fail in any way with me would have a resounding, deep effect on him, twice as resounding as it was for parents who shared the responsibility with a spouse.

I knew all this, I felt it, but I was also a young adult now. Because of my mother's unexpected early death, I had been hurried along in so many ways my friends had not been. How many nights did I choose to stay home with my father rather than do something with them? My father thought I was just being very picky about whom I associated with and when I would join them for some event. I let him believe that was true, because I knew how much it would bother him if he thought I had declined something because I felt sorry for him or thought he'd be too lonely.

I was older and surely more mature than everyone with whom I associated. I could see it in how casually they treated the risks they took, whether it was drinking and driving, recreational drugs, curfews, or, yes, sex. But I tried desperately not to preach or make anyone else feel guilty. I knew I wouldn't hold on to any friends if I said what I thought. Ironically, there were many times when I wished I didn't have these thoughts, when I wished I was more like them, when I longed to take those risks and fly without a parachute. There was an excitement just beyond me, something I never had tasted, something I never had felt. Despite all I knew was right, I resented my own self-control.

So now, when I left this room and confronted my father, I knew he would be looking at me differently. He would do his best to disguise it; he might even make one of his silly jokes or try to ignore what he had just witnessed. Surely, with the bathroom door open, he had heard our laughter in the shower. I hoped he hadn't stepped up to the door and looked in, but I couldn't be sure.

The thing was, I didn't want to feel ashamed or guilty. I wanted the way he and I had often conducted ourselves, like two equal adults and not always a father and a young daughter, to carry over into this. I wanted him to trust me, but I knew in my heart that even if he wanted to do that, he couldn't. As he would say, it was not in a father's DNA.

Before I started down, I looked in on Kane, who was dressing in the bathroom, and said, "My father's home. He's been home a while."

He paused. All the possibilities began to flash before him like trailers for an upcoming movie. He knew, of course, how close my father and I were. Was he going to face a man in a rage? Would he have to deny and lie? Was it better for him to somehow slip away? Would my father forbid us ever to see each other socially again? Would my father call his father and mother to complain? Would the turmoil spread quickly to his house, and would it leak out to the community, our friends? Some would ridicule us, some would joke about it, and some would actually envy us, but it would all make us uncomfortable, especially if our teachers found out. How bad was this?

"Did he . . ."

"I think so," I said. "Let me go down first. Wait a few minutes and follow."

He nodded.

I practically tiptoed down the stairway. He wasn't in the living room, and he wasn't in the kitchen, but I saw a note taped to the refrigerator door: *Just stopped in to get an important invoice I needed. See you later. Dad.*

Just like him to let me know he was here, I thought. He wasn't going to pretend he wasn't just to let me off the hook. He might not bring it up, but he wasn't going to let me believe he didn't know. We knew each other too well for false faces.

Kane came down the stairs slowly and paused in the doorway.

"He went back to work. He was here only to pick up some important paper."

"Oh." He looked relieved. "Then maybe he didn't . . ."

"He saw your car, Kane. He wouldn't just walk in, get the paper, and walk out. Even though he left this note that implies just that," I added.

Kane looked at it. "What should we do?"

"Nothing. We should do nothing."

"I'm sorry. I didn't want to get you into trouble. I just assumed we would be alone. I mean . . ."

"Let's not apologize to each other for what we do

together, okay? If we think we might have to apologize for something, then let's just not do it."

He smiled.

"And if and when we see my father soon, do not apologize to him or look guilty."

"Yes, ma'am," he said, and saluted. He took a deep breath. "I'm still hungry."

"I will be once my stomach twists out of the knot it's in," I replied, and we headed out.

While we were eating, Kane got a text from his sister.

"You'll be happy," he said when he looked up.

"Why?"

"My sister and her boyfriend want to take us out to dinner tomorrow night at La Reserve, without my parents. Of course, if we feel generous afterward, we can stop by Tina's house. Sound good?"

"La Reserve? That's *très* fancy."

"So we'll dress up, okay?"

"Yes," I said, but without the enthusiasm I would have had before my father had come home unexpectedly.

Kane knew me well enough to see the hesitation. "You don't think your father will ground you, punish you or anything?"

"No. My father doesn't punish me for things I do wrong. He just looks at me with disappointment, and I punish myself," I said.

"We didn't do anything wrong," Kane said, his eyes more like I imagined Christopher's would be, with that look of intensity and confidence. I almost anticipated a long, scientific explanation for our behavior, supported by references to the situation we were in. He did add, "It's only natural for me to want to make love to you, Kristin. Both of us are really adults. We're both less than a year away from being able to vote. Right? We drive cars. We'd be in adult court if we did something illegal, I'm sure."

"What a relief to know that," I said.

"I just meant . . ."

"It's all right. Don't worry. I'm okay."

"We can't legally drink alcohol, but in some countries, we'd be married with children by now," he added. He was on one of his Kane rolls.

"I'm not leaving the country," I said, and he laughed.

I was glad we were going to a movie, and for a few hours, at least, I didn't have to think about anything else. Some of our friends were there, but we didn't sit near them. When the film ended, we rushed out before anyone could suggest we join them for something. We tried to talk only about the film. When Kane brought me home, he wanted to come in to face my father.

"No sense in running away. I've got to face him sometime."

"He wouldn't say anything to you, Kane. If he's going to say anything, which I doubt, it will be to me. It's late. He's probably asleep in front of the television."

"What time should I come over tomorrow? He's working, right? The construction guys always work on Saturdays around here."

"Yes. He'd work seven days a week if he could."

"Then we can get much further into the diary."

"Maybe we should just take a breather," I said. Even in the dim glow coming from the light on the garage, I could see he looked like he had just lost his best friend.

"Why?" he protested. "I thought you were into it as much as I was. We should take advantage of every opportunity."

"We'll see." I relented. "I'll call you in the morning, okay?"

"Whatever," he said, his disappointment drifting into a shade of anger.

"Kane, I'm just a little nervous. I was hoping you'd be understanding."

"I am. I am. I just feel as if it's almost . . ."

"Almost what?"

"Almost unfair to Christopher."

"What? How?"

"In my mind, he's trusting us with his words. I know his diary was hidden and locked away, but I bet he's thought about it often since he left the original Foxworth Hall, and he's hoped that whoever found it would hold it sacred."

I couldn't help smiling.

"What?" he asked.

"I can't help but think we've completely changed places here. Those were my feelings when you first discovered it under my pillow and wanted to read it aloud with me. I was afraid you would end up making fun of it or something."

He grimaced. "You thought that of me?"

"Kane, come on. You haven't exactly been Mr. Serious before this. You're not disrespectful or a cutup in school, but you have a way about you."

He turned completely to me, putting his right arm on the top of the seat. "Go on. You're on a roll. Don't stop with the Kane Hill description."

"Your family is one of the most respected in Charlottesville, but you're not conservative. I don't mean how you dress. You've got rebel in you. You enjoy being an individualist. It's what makes you kind of . . . dangerously attractive," I said. "You're unpredictable. That's all I meant. So I wasn't sure how you would react to the diary once we were into it. Okay?"

He smiled, his eyes capturing the illumination from the light above the garage and dazzling me with their twinkling deep affection. "Kristin Masterwood," he said, "I can't imagine falling in love with anyone else would ever be any better than the way I feel about you right now."

Slowly, he leaned toward me to kiss me. It was a gentle kiss, more loving than passionate, a sign of truly deep feelings and not just a call for sex. It was the sort of kiss shared between people who have been together for a very long time, reminding them how important each was to the other. The sincerity surprised me.

"Speechless finally?" he asked, when he pulled back. His words did make my heart flutter, as if I'd had a baby bird emerge from its shell under my breast, and stole away my breath.

"Yes," I managed.

"I'll wait for your call in the morning," he said.

I got out. He watched me walk around the car and up to my front door before he started his engine again. Then he pointed toward the attic and backed out. I didn't open the door until he drove off. I wanted to gather my wits and not look like I had just stepped off a cloud.

I wasn't surprised that my father was awake in front of the television tonight. He would have been no matter what he had seen or heard earlier. Whenever I went out, he stayed awake and only half listened or followed whatever he was watching. He turned when I entered. Maybe he heard me enter; maybe he just knew whenever I was suddenly near him.

There are so many little ways to read someone's face, especially a father's. There was no anger in it, and he didn't look hurt, exactly. I would say he looked a little stunned, the way he might look if he had just heard or seen something very unexpected. But at the same time, he was obviously trying to hide it, hide his feelings.

"Hey," he said. "How was the movie?"

"It was very good."

"What was it?"

"*Someone's Watching*. It was about these two teenagers about my age, a boy and a girl. The girl's mother married the boy's father, and they all lived together, only the father was a degenerate and started abusing his wife's daughter, so she and her stepbrother ran away and camped out in an old, deserted hotel that wasn't really deserted. The aged owner's grandson lived in the building, a sort of recluse, not mentally deficient but socially. And he was big. Slowly, they get to know him. He comes to their defense when the stepfather hunts them down . . . sort of like Boo Radley from *To Kill a Mockingbird*." I rattled on out of nervousness.

"I remember that book and movie. It was one of your mother's favorites," he said.

All my life, I would be moving through my father's minefields of cherished memories, I thought. I would mention something, do something, or just look like my mother for a moment, and it would happen. I didn't regret it, but I couldn't help feeling some of his great emotional pain when one of those memories burst out and confronted us both again with her unexpected death.

"Yes. We read it last year in English class," I reminded him. Almost every time I held the book in my hands, he would smile, with the vision of my mother doing the same thing.

"She was always after me to do more reading."

"Nothing to stop you now," I said, and he smiled.

"I have to be there a little earlier tomorrow," he said, looking eager to change the topic. "Seems crazy to be working on this before I'm halfway finished with the house, but we're setting up the pool, doing the dig, running electric and plumbing."

"I've never really looked at the plans," I said.

"Oh. Right. There's a set on my desk." He nodded at it, and I went over to the desk and unrolled the bound plans. He remained seated, watching me as I perused them.

"Looks bigger than Foxworth Hall."

"No, it's about twelve thousand square feet smaller, but of course, there's more patio. There's no ballroom as such, but there is a rather big living room. Six bedrooms, all with en suite bathrooms, and a den about the size of the one that was in Foxworth."

"All the bedrooms are upstairs?"

"Maids' are downstairs," he said. "There's a kitchen Charley would love to have in his diner."

"How long is all this going to take?"

"I've put on more crew, but it'll still be the best of a year and a half, with all the detail in the woodwork and landscaping."

I realized I had done all I could to avoid talking about Kane and myself. "Kane's sister and her boyfriend have invited us to dinner tomorrow night."

"That so?"

"He's her boyfriend from college. I haven't met him yet, and I haven't seen her for years, it seems."

"I remember her vaguely. Nice girl, I think."

"I'll give you a full report."

"Okay."

He rose. "I'd better get to bed. I want to get as much done as we can before we break for Thanksgiving."

We looked at each other. When two people knew each other as well as we did, they said a great deal in their silences.

"You ever wish you had a boy instead?" I asked. I

could see the question came out of nowhere as far as he was concerned, but my implication was clear. Parents generally worry less about their sons' romances.

"A boy?"

"So he could be there to help you with the actual work? You know how I am with a hammer or a screwdriver."

"I can't even imagine how bad my life would be without you standing there, Kristin."

I ran to him. He embraced me, kissed my hair, petted it, and held me as long as I held on to him. I didn't say anything else, and neither did he. I turned away and ran up the stairs.

I overslept the next morning, but it was a Saturday, so there was no need for an alarm. When I did get up, dressed, and went down for breakfast, however, I was disappointed that my father had already left for work. My breakfast setting was on the table, with a note telling me he had worked up an egg batter for my scrambled eggs. He said he would call later just in case I had to leave for dinner before he got home.

I prepared my scrambled eggs. He seasoned them so well and uniquely that it was difficult eating them without thinking of him sitting across from me. It wasn't until I was nearly finished that I noticed he had left the morning newspaper on the table where he'd sat. It was still open to an inside page. I looked at the stories. The biggest one was about the construction of a new home on the Foxworth property, "the site of one of the most horrendous child abuse stories in our city." Almost always, whenever any reference to

Foxworth was made, it was followed with that phrase: "most horrendous child abuse stories in our city."

The new owner was listed as Arthur Johnson, so the facts my father had uncovered were still not general knowledge. There was a short biography of Johnson, mentioning his successful hedge fund and his wife and children. He came from Norfolk, Virginia, attended William and Mary College, majoring in business, and then went to work in his father's company before starting his own hedge fund. They had managed to get one quote from him: "I don't know anything about the history of the property, which frankly doesn't interest me. Every place and every thing has a history. You judge it by what it is, not by who owned it. That's just good business."

My father's company was mentioned, but he had made no comment other than that the work was going well. There was that now-famous picture of Foxworth Hall, depicting it more like a Gothic old house in which ghosts dwelled, the picture that was usually run on Halloween. Some people swore the cloudy spots in an upstairs window were Malcolm and Olivia Foxworth's ghosts, their souls sentenced to be imprisoned for what they had done to their grandchildren.

The article whetted my fascination and my need to get back to Christopher's diary. I called Kane.

"I've been sitting around with my phone on my lap hoping you would call early."

"Did you see the article in today's paper?"

"I didn't, but my father did and mentioned it. I

acted like I had little or no interest. My sister was interested. She'll probably bring it up at dinner."

"Then let's get started," I said.

"I'm already out the door," he replied.

I cleared the table, washed the dishes, and went up
to my room to finish dressing. At one point, I paused
and looked at some of my silk scarves. It came over
me. I couldn't help it. I wrapped it around my head,
and when Kane saw me, he smiled with glee. We were
like two children rushing ahead to unwrap Christmas
gifts, only both of us knew that what was wrapped in
this leather-bound book was not anything either of us
would wish for.

We set up the attic, and he began, quickly drifting into Christopher Dollanganger, wearing his wig,
changing his voice and posture, and filling his voice
with that constant stream of pain and disappointment,
wonder, and mystery that was dragging Christopher
into adulthood far too soon.

At the beginning of the last week in August, I was
mumbling to myself about how hot it was for us in
the small bedroom and especially up in the attic,
when an exciting idea suddenly occurred to me. I
was staring at the sheet ladder I had created when
I thought we had to escape from starvation. When
I proposed my new idea to Cathy, she thought I
had finally gone nuts, but I convinced her we could
do it. We would climb down from the attic on the
sheet ladder and go for a swim in the lake at night.
Of course, it occurred to us both that we would be

standing on the ground for the first time in more than two years.

Despite her timidity, she climbed down that sheet ladder as if she had been doing it all her life.

Once we were down and moving hand in hand through the darkness, the thrilling sense of freedom overtook me. Everything looked fresh and new and exciting. I had never appreciated the stars more and realized how important were all the little things I had once taken for granted. I was so entranced I didn't notice how frightened Cathy was, but when I did, I put my arm around her, and her trembling subsided.

Finally, the lake loomed before us, with all its promise of pleasure. For a little while, at least, we could be young again; I could be like a boy of nearly seventeen and she could be a fourteen-year-old girl.

We decided to swim in our underwear instead of completely nude, although Cathy had no bra. She embraced herself and touched the water with her toe. I saw that she was hesitant about getting in, so I pushed her into the water, and suddenly we were young children again, splashing each other, dunking each other. I clung to her and she to me, laughing and spinning each other about. We swam until we were both exhausted, and then we walked out and fell on the grass to lie on our backs, catch our breath, and gaze up at the stars.

Lying there beside her, her blossoming breasts

captured in the starlight, her face gleaming wet,
I couldn't help but reach for her hand. What if
she weren't my sister? I thought. What if I was
here with some girl I liked? What would I do next?
Cathy looked at me and saw how I was staring
at her.

"What?" she asked.

"Nothing," I said, shaking my head and turning
away. Whatever she saw in my face, it made her
think of being with someone you loved. I shouldn't
have been surprised. Girls mature faster than boys.
She would have all these feelings, too, and maybe
even stronger ones than mine.

It occurred to Cathy first that we were now
the ages our parents were when they first met. I
suspected she was thinking that they were related,
but it didn't stop them from falling in love.

"Do you think it was true, Christopher?" she
asked me. "Do you think they really fell in love at
first sight? Is that possible?"

I wanted to believe it. I wanted to believe that
there was something more between a male and
a female than mere physical attraction. I told her
that whenever I was physically attracted to a girl in
school and thought that maybe, maybe, it could be
love, I was disappointed once I talked to the girl,
who nearly always was too silly or stupid for me.

"Am I too stupid for someone to love?" she
asked.

"Absolutely not," I replied, and told her how
talented I thought she was. Her problem was that

she had too many talents and would have trouble settling on one. She drew closer to me. I put my arm around her, and she rested her head against my shoulder.

The night, the stars, and our sense of freedom relaxed us both like we hadn't been for more than two years. Before we had been brought here, I wouldn't have dreamed of being as open and honest with her as I was now. It was nearly impossible for me to think of her as a little girl anymore, and I felt sure she could never think of me as just her older brother. It was too late for us to go back to that sort of innocence. I'd be the first to admit how confused I now was about my feelings. I didn't like that. I didn't like the insecurity. It made me angry.

Cathy sensed it. "Where do you think our mother is?" she asked. It had been so long since she had visited us.

I looked for as many reasons as I could to explain her neglecting us. Maybe she was sick. Maybe she had gone on a business trip. Cathy shot down every rationalization I presented. That only fired up my own frustration and anger.

When she asked me if I loved and trusted our mother as much as I used to, I snapped back at her, not because she was wrong to wonder but because I didn't want to admit that I didn't. She quickly changed the subject to what it was like to date, and her questions suggested that neither of

us would know what to do because we had been
out of socializing so long.

God, she was so right, I thought, and I
exploded, revealing how angry I was at Momma.
I raged about being shut away from life and
feeling more like a first-grader when it came
to my emotions now. I know my outburst
frightened Cathy. Maybe because we were out in
the open, I didn't contain myself. I didn't care
who heard me. She hadn't seen me this way for
a long time, maybe never. She wanted to leave
immediately.

"We have to get back to the twins," she said.

On the way back, she suggested that we climb
down with the twins, maybe make a sling to hold
them so we could bring them down and escape.
We had found a way. I knew she was saying all
this because of how I had behaved. She was
probably worried that I was losing it fast now and
that if we stayed much longer, who knew what
would happen? I couldn't blame her for thinking
that.

My mind reeled with the possibility of making
an escape, but I didn't want to give Cathy any false
hope. After all, where would we go? How would
we go anywhere? We would need money. How
far could we get, considering we would be two
teenagers traveling with small children? Everyone
would look at us and wonder. Eventually, we were
bound to attract some policeman, and then what?

If we told him who we were, we might be returned to Foxworth Hall, but this time, we would be returned only to be thrown out with Momma. We would be children with a single parent who had nothing. What then? All Momma would do would be complain how we had destroyed our chances, our opportunities. She'd hate us, at least Cathy and me.

No, I thought, better to ignore her for now, even though the pleasure of being free was so great I couldn't calm myself down enough to not think about it.

I let Cathy start up first. About three-quarters of the way, she lost her footing on the bottom knot and screamed in panic. I quietly, calmly told her how to regain her control, and she was able to continue up. By the time I joined her, we were both exhausted, but all Cathy could think of was what would have happened to the twins if she had fallen from that sheet ladder.

"I can't believe I'm happy to be back here," she said.

I didn't say anything.

Instead, I thought, look what had happened to us if we could even for a moment be happy we were here.

Kane paused and stared at me for a moment before he swept off his wig, as if he had to do that before he could talk to me now as Kane Hill.

"You ever go skinny-dipping?"

"No."

"My sister did at our house. She had a party for a half dozen of her friends in early June of her senior year. Our parents were away for the weekend. I had gone to an early movie, got bored, and came home early. I heard the laughter out at the pool and made my way there, sort of sneaking up on them. I remained in the darkness and watched."

"So your sister didn't know you were there?"

"No. I remember being more angry than amused."

"Angry? Why?"

"I resented my sister being nude in front of those boys. Finally, I turned around, disgusted, and went back into the house."

"Did you tell her how you felt about it later?"

"No."

"So she never knew you were there?"

"No. The thing is, I've been at skinny-dipping parties but didn't react like I did spying on hers."

"Probably just . . . natural. You were embarrassed for her."

"No, for myself," he said. "What just happened between Christopher and Cathy has made me think of something."

I smiled to myself. It hadn't just happened to them, as he had put it, but also to us. Reading the diary this way, it was as if we were doing what he had done at his sister's pool party, staying in the shadows and observing something happening right before us. "What?"

"Say you never met your sister your whole life. Say you didn't even know you had a sister, and you met this girl and dated her and went skinny-dipping and did it all. Would it be sinful?"

"I don't know. It might be sinful but not your fault, if that makes any sense," I said.

"But the point is that every desire the brother had as a boy and every desire the sister had as a girl would still be there. No wall would go up between them miraculously. Nothing would click in their heads and stop their sexual activity."

"I guess not."

"Whatever thoughts Christopher has and whatever he does with his sister are not his fault, even though the situation isn't the same. I mean, he knows she's his sister, but it's as if they're on a desert island or something, just when things are happening to them, to their bodies."

"I'm not blaming them for anything, Kane," I said. He was acting as if he thought condemnation was on the tip of my tongue. "It's too soon to be judgmental."

"Right," he said, nodding.

Look how important it is for him to defend Christopher, I thought. I wanted to smile, but something kept me from introducing even an iota of amusement into it.

"If there's anyone to blame for anything, it's Corrine and, despite her high-and-mighty moral attitude, Grandmother Olivia. Right?"

"You don't have to convince me, Kane," I said.

"Yeah, well . . . yeah," he replied, and put his wig on.

Momma had been gone more than two months now. Every time the door opened, all of us would stop whatever we were doing and shift our eyes quickly to see if it was finally Momma, but it was always our grandmother, silent, looking like she was tiptoeing through a field of snakes, eager to get in and get out. Neither Cathy nor I had the courage to ask her where our mother was. Besides a tirade of threats and horrible predictions for us, she might add the one thing I think both of us feared to hear: "Your mother has run off. She realized what evil she brought into the world."

Cathy would look away quickly, and when she looked to me, I would turn away and focus on something I was doing, as if our disappointment didn't matter, but oh, how it did. The little ball of anger rolling around inside me night and day was like a rock gathering moss. Sometimes I would wake in the middle of the night, the rage inside me so hot and strong my teeth were clenched and my jaw ached.

Cathy talked endlessly about escaping. Our swimming adventure had crystallized the possibilities for her. I wouldn't deny that I still savored every second of that time at the lake, that wonderful sense of freedom we had walking hand in hand through the darkness, seeing the stars, and feeling the cool night breeze. It was as if we had come back to life again.

Every afternoon, I would go to the window,

sometimes twice a day, to see the train pass by, the same train that had brought us here years ago. Sometimes it sounded mournful, like a train carrying a famous dead person, like Lincoln's train, and sometimes it was more like it was calling me directly, telling me it was there. It would be there for us to take us away from all this. It bounced back and forth from being a train that reminded me of our situation, growing more horrid every day, every week, to being the sound of hope, the call to a new future, a new life, and a place where we would all grow naturally again.

Cathy could sense this mix of feelings inside me. The longer Momma was away, the more stridently she pleaded for our escape. "You're always watching for that train," she said. "You know you want to be on it, want all of us to be on it."

Her constant prodding and nagging were wearing down what resistance I had left in me. Why would we wait for a mother who had neglected us so long? Why would we wait for an old man to die if it hadn't happened in all this time? How would we know if he had without Momma being here? Would our grandmother come rushing up, happy to unlock the door and bring us into the bosom of her home? Would she say, "Now you can be my grandchildren, and you can forget all the terrible things I had to do to you"?

Hardly, I thought. I had no good answers for her. Maybe it was cruel to do it, but I fanned her dreams, her hope.

"Where would you go if we did get out of here?" I asked.

She talked about going farther south, being on beaches, soaking up the sunshine like someone who had been dying of thirst and crossing a desert. I let myself daydream aloud, too, and talked about things I'd like to be doing out there, the fun I'd like to be having. Those were weak moments for me. Cathy pounced on them. "Why are we staying? You hate it as much as I do."

Of course I did. I hated every moment, actually, but I reminded her how important money was in this world and how the old man had to die soon. It was just logical. He was sick. We saw him in the wheelchair. He couldn't live much longer, he just couldn't, and then we'd have the money. I reminded her how important it was for me to become a doctor and how expensive that education would be. "Without money, I'll never be anything. What job could I do to keep us alive out there? Who'd even give me a job? Whatever I could manage wouldn't pay enough to keep the four of us alive."

Of course, Cathy promised to take any job to help. We were going back and forth about it. The train was coming again. And then our grandmother appeared and told me to get away from the window. I tried to defy her. When she called me "boy," I told her to call me by my name.

"Call me Christopher, or don't call me at all."

I thought she would rant and deliver another punishment, maybe starve us again for a week, but she smiled coldly at me instead and went into what I could only call her rationalization for how she was treating us, how she had treated our mother. She hated my name because of what she said our father had done to her and her husband. She claimed she was the one who got her husband to take in his half brother when he had no one, and how did he repay them? He ran off with our mother to get married. He had the nerve to come back, as if they could ignore that he had married his own niece. When our grandfather threw them out, he had his first heart attack, so his terrible health was their fault, my mother's fault. She did this to her own father. She was so passionate about the story she seemed to lose her breath.

Both Cathy and I were shocked at the outburst. I thought, okay, they did that to you, but why take it out on us? I told her we weren't to blame.

Then she went into how sinful we were in this small room.

I challenged her and blamed anything that had happened or would happen on her, on her locking us away. How could she think of herself as good and pious if she would starve little children? I didn't know where the strength for my rant came from, but it came, and I let it all out with as much venom as she directed at us.

Cathy kept pleading with me to stop, but it was too late. Our grandmother ran out. I thought, okay, she'd find a way to punish us, but maybe it was worth it.

To my surprise, she came back instantly, with a green willow switch in her hand. She had it so fast I knew she always kept one nearby. She ordered me to strip down and said that if I didn't, she would starve us again, starve the twins. I had to submit to her whipping me in the bathroom.

Afterward, because Cathy was screaming and crying, she did the same to her, only she went wild, breaking the switch on Cathy's naked body. I could hear Cathy's defiance, which I knew would only drive the old lady to be crueler. She pounded her so hard with a hairbrush that she finally knocked her unconscious.

She left her there on the floor and came out, her bosom lifting and falling, her face still red with rage. I was in great pain, but I didn't cry.

"God sees everything you do," she said. She had said that before.

It was on the tip of my tongue to reply, "Then you will surely go to hell," but I said nothing. I looked down. I was terrified now for the twins. Would she turn on their small bodies? She did look at them, clinging to each other.

"The devil's spawn," she muttered, and walked out.

I got the twins to go up to the attic to play so they wouldn't see how bad Cathy was. Then I carried her out of the bathroom and began to treat her wounds. When she woke up, I told her I was worried she might have a concussion. She sobbed, and we held each other. We were both still naked, and I couldn't help it. I had to kiss her. The feel of her body against mine seemed, for the moment, to make me forget the pain. We had never held each other naked. I could see it was affecting her as much as it was me.

She felt my erection and whispered, "Stop, Christopher. This is what she thinks we do, making love."

"Making love involves more, Cathy," I said. I smiled at her, and I described it in as much detail as I could. Her expression went from fascination to fear and then to guilt for even imagining it.

"We can't. We won't. We never will, right?" she asked.

I didn't say anything. I wanted to say no, but at the same time, I didn't trust fate or my own emotions anymore. So much had happened to us and between us over the years that we were confined, so much of what I would never, even in my wildest dreams, have imagined. All brothers and sisters have a deep love for each other, even if they're close in age and go through sibling rivalry. I had read so much about this, even before we left our home. As all my teachers knew, I read and understood on a level at least three grade levels above my age.

But that love had a different nature to it. It came from being part of something greater than yourself, your family. An attack on your sister or brother was an attack on your family. Protecting and cherishing your sister or brother was a way to protect and cherish your family, especially your parents. When another sort of feeling even suggested itself, you instantly retreated from it, were ashamed of it, and forced yourself to bury it. You didn't nourish it.

Could I say I wasn't doing that now?

I continued to attend to her wounds and then had her attend to mine. Neither of us mentioned again how close we were to doing exactly what our grandmother believed we had been doing.

Later, I kissed her good night after we had put the twins to sleep—kissed her, I hoped, the way my father would have kissed her good night. She held my hand for a moment, as if she wanted another kiss or to kiss me back, and then she let go and turned away.

But it was too late, I thought. We had touched each other in ways I was sure we had both begun to imagine we might.

And now we had to live with whatever dreams might come of it.

When Kane stopped reading and lowered the diary, he saw that I had covered my face with my hands. It was as if the tears in my eyes were so heavy that I couldn't keep my head up. He rushed over to me, kneeling beside me. I lifted my face away from my hands slowly, the tears still trickling down my cheeks. He rose slowly and started to kiss them away, petting my hair as he did so.

"Cathy, Cathy," he said. "Don't cry. I can't stand it when you cry."

At first, I thought he wasn't serious, calling me Cathy, but when I looked into his eyes, I saw he was, and it gave me a chilling feeling for a moment. He was really into it now, and it both frightened and excited me. I realized he was just as into it as I was, and it was natural for him to call me by her name at that moment. I took a deep breath and nodded. Crying for them now wouldn't do anyone any good.

"Their grandmother was so cruel. I could feel Cathy's pain with what Christopher described as a seemingly endless whipping," I said, my teeth clenched with the rage I felt toward that evil old woman who justified her cruelty with biblical quotes. Religion cloaked her sadism, I thought. Someday I'd like to know what turned her into this dreadful person, not that any of that would justify what she was doing to her own grandchildren. Maybe nothing did. Maybe she was simply born that way, and that was what my mother's distant cousin liked about her.

"And I felt his pain. I really did, but I also felt how it brought them closer," Kane added, and he kissed me softly, the way a father or mother might kiss away a bruise or a sad moment. "Their pain and suffering drove them to be more to each other," he said, his voice a whisper now. "We can understand that, can't we?"

"Yes," I said.

"They desperately needed to feel each other beside them, to comfort and love each other, especially at that moment, no matter how it might look to us," he said, his face full of intensity to drive home his conclusion.

"Yes, you're right."

I held on to his shoulders. I felt like he was trying to bring me the same comfort Christopher brought to Cathy. Surely, she would have drowned in her sorrow and agony otherwise. I could easily imagine her curling up in a ball in the corner of that attic, refusing to eat or drink, fading away and dying as would any flower without the sun, which in this case was the love of a mother who had apparently deserted them.

Kane brought his hands down to my waist, and we turned together on the sofa bed. His fingers moved up to the buttons on my blouse. After he slipped it off me and undid my bra, he raised himself and took off his shirt. I knew what he was doing, I knew what we were going to reenact, and I didn't try to stop it. We had been naked together in the shower, but somehow, up here in the attic, turning ourselves into Christopher and Cathy at this precise moment in the diary, it seemed like the first time.

As he moved himself so I could feel his erection where I should, I could tell he was waiting for me to say it, almost as if it was a line I had rehearsed many times in a scene we could finally perform.

"Stop, Christopher. This is what she thinks we do, making love."

He laughed the way I saw Christopher laughing when Kane was reading. "Should I describe what making love involves, too?" he asked.

"If you can, but the way Christopher did," I challenged.

He turned to lie on his back. I rested the palm of my left hand on his chest, feeling the quickened beat of his heart, and looked at him. He tried so hard not to be comical about it, to explain it the way Christopher might have. He was doing a very good job of it, too, when I finally had to stop him.

"You read up on this, memorized some textbook or something, didn't you?"

"Sort of," he admitted. "I'm pretty good in science, you know. That's my best subject, just as it was Christopher's. It's funny now, but when I read things in the science text, I actually imagine Christopher explaining them and think I should be able to do that, too, sound as confident of my explanations. When I answer questions in class, Mr. Malamud looks more impressed these days. How did I just sound to you?"

"Too good. Too clinical and definitely not romantic," I replied, at first to tease him.

"But wasn't that what Christopher really wanted to do at that moment? He was avoiding being anything like romantic with his sister, right? I think doctors hide behind their facts in order not to get too emotional over a patient. It's a technique Christopher's already mastered because of the circumstances. That was what he wanted, right?"

Suddenly, we were like two drama students discussing a scene we had just seen performed. It was like someone throwing a pail of cold water over me. "I'm sure," I said, then turned away and began to dress.

He watched me for a moment and then began to dress, too. I thought he would protest. Now that we were moving away from what had been a very passionate few moments, I was surprised he had given up so easily, surprised and maybe a little disappointed that the heat of passion had cooled in him.

Perhaps this was exactly what had occurred between Christopher and Cathy at that moment. We were too loyal to the attic world we had decided to enter and respect. If it didn't happen there and then, it wouldn't happen here and now.

"I gotta go," he said. "I have to do something before we have dinner with my sister and her boyfriend later."

"Oh?"

"I've got to see my father at the Mercedes dealership. He wants me to start working weekends there. Until now, I've done a good job of avoiding it."

"How are you going to get out of it now, assuming you still want to?"

"Oh, I want to. I don't want to have anything to do with his dealerships, and we go around and around about it at least once a week. I'm going to claim that schoolwork demands my free time. I'm failing math."

"But you're not."

"I deliberately failed two important tests this quarter. I have the exams in the car to show him. I can't fail math and graduate. Solution? Being tutored by the girl who's mostly likely to be valedictorian."

"He's going to believe that?"

"Maybe he won't believe it, but he'll put up with it. He has enough grief coming from my mother and her complaints about Darlena this week."

We rearranged the attic, and he put his wig and my scarf in the same trunk before leaving. I followed him down to the front door, thinking more about what he had said. These days, we were thinking more about Cathy and Christopher than about ourselves. I was afraid of losing a grip on reality.

"What do you want to do, to be, Kane, if you don't want to take over your father's car dealership empire?" I asked him before he stepped out.

He smiled. "Empire? Yeah, that's what it is. I don't particularly feel like anyone's emperor, though. Parents often think that if they've built something, you should be grateful and become part of it, but what about building something yourself, for yourself?"

"So what do you want to build for yourself?"

I could easily predict I'd get that Kane Hill shrug and smile. "I don't know." He stopped smiling. "Maybe I should think seriously about becoming a doctor," he said. "Like Christopher."

I closed my mouth when he leaned in to kiss me. "You're not serious enough for that," I said.

He shrugged. "Maybe I'll get serious. I'll return about six thirty, okay? We'll meet them at the restaurant." He started for his car. "Let me know what you want to do about going to Tina's party afterward. We'll do whatever you want," he called back before he got into his car.

After he left, I thought about what I would do with the rest of my day and decided to go pay my father a visit at the site. We hadn't spent that much time together this week. Maybe it was also because Kane had gone off to spend time with his father, too, and that reminded me that I should spend time with mine. I put myself together quickly and headed for the Foxworth property.

The deeper we got into the diary, the more intense were my feelings of tension whenever I approached the property now. It was as if I was returning to a place where I really had spent a great deal of time, unhappily and tragically. Something in me constricted in fear and disgust with every mile I drew closer. Even in broad daylight, I anticipated seeing ghosts, hearing voices, crying, and pleas for freedom.

It was my father who put the idea into my head that places, especially houses, took on the identities of those who lived there. "After all," he'd said, "wasn't that a prime reason why whoever bought someone else's home wanted to redo so much of it? It's like not wanting to wear someone else's clothes. Lucky for guys like me who rip down the old and rebuild the new."

How many people in construction thought so deeply about their work as my father did? No wonder he had even deeper feelings about Foxworth Hall.

When I got up there, I realized it was a little warmer than it had been. It was mostly sunny, with just a slight breeze from the south. I knew my father wanted to get as much of the exterior work done as possible before winter came rushing in full-blown on what he called "the skirts of the dropping jet stream." I'd told him that from the way he could predict the weather, he could have just as easily been a farmer. "When I retire, that's what I'll do," he'd replied.

I was surprised to see just how far along he and his team had gotten with the construction of the new house. Everything unusable from the restored Foxworth Hall had been hauled away. The part of the old foundation that was visible and utilized was freshly painted with an off-white waterproof material. The framing of the two stories was completed, with the upstairs floor laid. It was easy to envision it now even without having seen the plans.

Behind it and to the right, two bulldozers continued to expand the grounds by driving out the overgrowth and cutting back the forest of birch, maple, and oak saplings. I could see that the plans for this new property created what was going to be an even larger and more elaborate landscaping than what had been done for the development of the original and the restored Foxworth Hall. The bulldozers had already moved and flattened much of the ground. Footings for fountains and the setting of tile or cement pathways was to follow. The scent of fresh earth permeated the air. What had once been more like a rotting corpse of a property now had the look of something fresh and new, full of promise and potential beauty.

My father and Todd were standing back and observing the crew constructing the pool, which looked like it would be at least as long and as wide as the one in our school. Todd had his arms folded across his chest the way my father had his. If he could, he'd walk in my father's footsteps all day, I thought. He saw me first and nudged my father to turn my way as I drove up and parked. They both watched me approach.

"What's up?" Dad asked. I think ever since my mother took ill and died, every time something or someone surprised him, his first reaction was always to tighten up and prepare himself for some sort of bad news. Running through his mind was surely that someone had called the house with some.

"I thought I'd come up to see if you've been working as hard as you've said or just jawin' up a sweat," I replied. It was his favorite way to kid fellow construction workers.

With relief, his face quickly softened into a broad smile. He looked past me at my car. "By yourself?" he asked, even though it was quite obvious. It was his way of asking where Kane Hill was.

"Yes. Kane has a meeting with his father, and I wanted to see what was already done up here."

"Well, you must be bored," Todd said.

"Don't you think your work is exciting?" I fired back, and he shook his head and looked to my father to save him.

"Todd's good at holding in his feelings," my father said, and Todd laughed. My father studied me a moment and nodded to himself, thinking. "Come on," he said. "Since you came here, I'll show you something."

He put his arm around my shoulders and walked me back toward the house. I was a little nervous. The last time he had brought me to the remains of the Hall, we'd discovered Christopher's diary. Had he found something else to do with the Foxworths?

"Careful," he said, as we stepped through the front door framing. There were loose wires threaded through boards and lots of nails and sawdust scattered about, which was nothing unusual and didn't surprise me. I had been to many of his building sites, even as a little girl when my mother was alive. We paused in what I knew from the plans was to be the living room.

Two men from many other jobs my father had done were constructing the fieldstone hearth for the fireplace, working meticulously, as if they were creating an artistic masterpiece. It probably would be. The stones were taken from an old fieldstone wall on the property, which, like so many in our area, was constructed in the nineteenth century and had remarkably stood the test of time. From what I understood of Malcolm Foxworth, he wouldn't have wanted those fieldstone walls destroyed. He would have had

Robert Frost's poem "Mending Wall" mounted on his wall and chanted "Good fences make good neighbors."

When I had first approached the rubble and the foundation of the burned-down restored Foxworth Hall on the day we found Christopher's diary, I had seen where the fireplace was, but it was charred, covered with debris, and, although large, otherwise unremarkable standard brick seen in many houses. It was one of the things left from the original mansion. Now the stone floor within had been scrubbed clean. It was clear to me that the guts of the original fireplace were still there, but the fieldstone replaced the bricks, and its design ensured that it would be wider and more elaborate.

The men paused and turned to us.

"You remember my daughter, Kristin, don't you, Butch?" my father asked the older of the two. I remembered now that Butch Wilson worked with his younger brother Tommy. They were master stone craftsmen, specializing in fireplaces, but did lots of other stonework around homes. I didn't think my father had ever worked on a project that required stonework without them, as long as I could remember. Strangely, they both had that flaxen-blond hair that distinguished the Dollanganger children.

"Sure. Growing faster than a radish. She's looking more and more like your wife," Butch said.

"Lucky her," Tommy added, smiling impishly.

My father laughed. "You won't get any argument about that from me," he said. He urged me on to approach the fireplace. "I wanted to show her what you found."

The two stood up and moved back. Butch nodded at the stone floor of the fireplace.

"Check it out," my father said. I knelt down and looked closely. At first, I saw nothing, but when I leaned in closer, I saw the initials *CF*, a heart, and then another *CF*, all a bit crudely engraved in the stone. I reached in and touched it and then looked up at my father. I was surprised that he wanted me to see it. He knew that I knew what it meant. It was obvious Butch and Tommy didn't.

"So?" Tommy asked. "Your father says he can't make head nor tail of it."

"It's got something to do with the nutty family who lived here," Butch said.

I looked at my father. Did he want me to tell them? Was he testing me to see how much I really had learned from reading Christopher's diary? He was stone-faced. After a moment, he stepped closer and nodded at the stone.

"Butch thinks the devil might have engraved it there," he told me. "Butch's grandfather worked on the construction of the original Foxworth Hall."

"That's right, and he never had a nice word to say about the Foxworths, either. The old man counted every minute my grandfather worked here and didn't pay him a nickel over the hourly wage. He put in this hearthstone with the old man or his wife looking over his shoulder the whole time. Neither would have tolerated this defaming of it," he said, nodding at the initials. "If he had seen it, he'd have had my grandfather back to grind it out, unless he was told to leave it."

"Who would tell him that?" I asked, curious to hear what else he knew.

"Satan, who else?" Butch said, and Tommy nodded.

I looked at my father. He still wasn't smiling. He nodded at me, turned, and started out. I glanced at Butch and Tommy and saw that they really believed what they were saying. Afterward, when they told friends what they had found here, they'd surely add to the Halloween image of what had gone on at Foxworth Hall years ago.

I caught up with my father. "Why didn't they use a new hearthstone instead of the one from the original mansion, Dad?"

"The owner wanted it kept," he said. He stood there watching my reaction. "At least, who I think is the owner."

"But did he know what was carved into the stone?"

"Maybe. You know whose initials they are, don't you?"

"Christopher Foxworth and Corrine Foxworth," I replied.

He nodded and kept walking toward Todd.

"They changed their name," I said. "At least, Christopher did."

"And why did he do that?"

"They didn't want anyone to know that they were related."

"Have you finished reading that diary, Kristin?"

"No."

"I want you to promise me you'll get rid of it when you do."

"Why, Dad? You don't believe what they said, do you? You don't really believe the devil was in that house?"

"In one way or another, maybe he was and moved right back in when it was previously restored," he replied. "Whatever. The less we have to do with what went on there, the better off we'll be." He looked back at the structure. "Something in me didn't want me to take this job, but the money's so good I couldn't refuse. It'll pay for your entire college education."

"Then that's the way to look at it, Dad. Something good can come from it. Period, end of sentence," I said.

I was expecting him to look upset with me because of how firmly I said it, sounding like I was the one giving the orders in this family. Maybe he'd even get very angry and finally show it, I thought, but instead, he looked amazed and then smiled. It threw me off.

"What?" I asked.

"That was exactly how your mother would put it when she wanted to end a discussion. 'Period, end of sentence,'" he said.

He walked off, shaking his head, and left me standing there a little amazed myself. I couldn't say where the words often came from, words I didn't recall hearing my mother say, or anyone else, for that matter. They just came. Worried that he was taking this all too seriously, I watched him for a few moments, but he got right back into his work. I was tempted to leave, but I didn't. Instead, I started to walk around the developing house, now pausing when I reached the rear to look up at how high I envisioned it had been once from the pictures and drawings I had seen.

But I also imagined Christopher and Cathy lowering themselves out of the attic on their sheet ladder for their swim that night. Now that the grounds were cleared, I had a better sense of what it must have been like, the distance they had to travel, constantly terrified that they'd be seen. I could almost see them, disappearing like ghosts into the protection of the trees. I looked toward the lake before starting around to return to look closer at the pool being constructed.

"Isn't it very big?" I asked Todd. My father was talking to one of the workers.

"Biggest I've seen at a private house. You should have been here when they started digging the hole for the pool," he added.

"Why?" I had been to many of my father's job sites and enjoyed seeing how he made something out of nothing or turned a pig into a princess, but I wasn't terribly excited about watching the actual work, especially the tedious work of digging a hole for a pool.

"They kept looking for the skeleton of a child,"

he said. "Every time they hit a stone or saw some tree roots, they paused, thinking they had found some bones." He laughed.

My father turned and looked at us, his face full of questions. He walked over to us, expecting me to tell him why Todd was laughing and I wasn't.

"I've got to go home," I said. "To get ready for dinner with Kane's sister and her boyfriend."

"Oh, right. What time are you going?"

"Six thirty."

"Right. I should be back by six. See you before you leave."

"Okay," I said.

I looked at the structure, the grounds, the pool construction, the place on the property where there would be a tennis court, and imagined all of it from the landscape plans I had seen on my father's desk. There were to be fountains and walkways, gardens and ponds. It was as if whoever was behind this really wanted to develop a property that would erase practically all memory of what it had been. I knew that was the reason my father was aboard so fast.

"It will be something, Dad. You'll be proud of it. No one will think of it as Foxworth Hall anymore."

He smiled, nodded, and returned to the work. I headed for my car. I didn't regret taking the ride over to see my father and what had been done, but I couldn't shake off this dark feeling of dread that had come over me. Maybe it was that overworked imagination of mine, but suddenly, there were more clouds, shadows grew deeper and longer, and the mountains in the distance looked higher and reminded me of clutches of people who had hoisted their shoulders as if they all had experienced the same sudden chill because something had frightened them. It filled me with a strange sense of foreboding.

I had asked myself many times since my father opened that metal box and handed me the leather-bound book if I should continue to read it. My father's displeasure about that notwithstanding, I had my own hesitations and cautions now. Kane would laugh at me if I even mentioned the idea that the devil had been in that house and maybe had invaded Christopher's diary. Yet look at how it was affecting the two of us already.

Ever since I had begun to read the diary, everything I looked at, every laugh I heard coming from my friends, and almost every comment any of them made seemed to reach me through the prism of Foxworth Hall's attic. In the morning, it was like waking up in two bodies, Cathy's and mine, and carrying her inside me through the day. Finally, she could be released up in my attic as soon as Kane had begun to read. Was I possessed? Was Kane? How would it end?

Dressing and preparing to go out for dinner took my mind off these bleak and dismal thoughts. Somehow, because we were going to be double-dating with college-age people, this date was extra special. I wanted to look my best, dress up, and wear the jewelry that my father had given me, jewelry that was my mother's. In the back of my mind was the idea that we should look older, more mature. I would never tell Kane that; he would laugh for sure.

I was going down the stairs when my father arrived. He stood back and watched me descend, as if I was making some dramatic entrance in a scene in a movie or on a stage.

"Excuse me," he said when I stood before him, "but do you know where my daughter might be?"

"Very funny, Dad. I look all right?"

"All right? That's not half the way I'd put it."

I saw his eyes go to my mother's necklace.

"How proud she'd be," he said, touching it and then drawing his hand back quickly.

I leaned forward and kissed him on the cheek. "I don't believe you. Fathers are supposed to exaggerate."

"I'm not exaggerating. Blow something up bigger than it really is, and it will burst in your face someday."

"Okay, Dad," I said with the tone of someone who had heard that a thousand times, probably because I had.

"Where do I have to take you to get you to dress like this for me?" he asked.

"Anywhere but Charley's."

"Right. Well, I've got to go shower and dress. I'm going out to dinner tonight, too."

"You are? With whom? Where?" I asked in shotgun fashion.

"The Johnsons again. Tiramisu."

"Well, you always say that's the best Italian food in Charlottesville."

"Right, but I'm a little suspicious about the invitation this time."

"Why?"

"Something about a good friend of his wife's mother they want me to meet. Supposedly a professional home decorator, and this is just to—how did he put it?—marry it well to the architecture. Note the word 'marry.'"

"Don't be so suspicious. Maybe that's all there is to it."

He smirked. "I wasn't born yesterday," he said. "You have a great time." He hugged me and started for the stairs.

"You, too," I called after him. He nodded and continued up.

Actually, I was surprised he had agreed to go out. He was relentless about avoiding setup dates. What had suddenly changed him? I didn't think I had to look too hard for the answer. It surely had started when he had heard Kane and me in the shower. How many times this year had he heard someone say that I would soon be leaving the nest? I had filled out college applications, and it wouldn't be long before I would begin to get responses. One day, he and I would discuss my choices, but most likely, any of them would involve my leaving home and returning only on holidays.

I knew it was difficult enough for parents of an only child to watch him or her go off to college or to the armed forces or to a job that took him or her out of the house, but at least those parents had each other. I had even heard some say it gave them a second honeymoon. For my father, my leaving would only add the memory of a second pair of footsteps to the ones he heard after my mother's death. He would sit at the breakfast and dinner table alone all week. He surely had thought about it often, but in his way, he had put it aside or ignored it.

And then here I came along and demonstrated how fast I was maturing, how independent I was becoming, and how quickly I was leaving behind the little girl he knew and becoming the woman I was supposed to be. Not that showering with a boyfriend was exactly that. It just made it clear that I wasn't thinking only about lollipops and dolls anymore.

The sound of Kane's horn sent a little shock through me because I was so deep in thought. He had gotten out of his car and was on his way to my front door when I opened it to step out.

"I see your dad's home. Shouldn't I say hello?"

"He went up to get dressed. He has a dinner . . . appointment," I said, rather than *date*. Would that word "date" always get stuck in my throat when it applied to him?

"Okay," he said, unable to keep the relief from washing over his face. He stepped back abruptly and paused, finally looking at me. "Holy smokes," he said, a smile curling his lips with delight. "You look fantastic."

"Why should that surprise you?" I teased, spinning around like a fashion model.

He did look very handsome himself, wearing a fitted light blue seersucker sport coat, a rose-pink shirt, and a black tie, with a dark blue pair of slacks and black laced shoes. I saw he was also wearing a much more expensive-looking watch than he usually wore. His smile broadened.

"Well?" I asked.

"I only meant . . ."

"You're very handsome tonight, Kane. You almost look like that emperor of car dealerships."

"Huh?"

It was my turn to laugh.

"Wise-ass." He held out his arm and escorted me to the passenger side of a black S-class Mercedes. It looked brand-new.

"What's this car?"

"Demonstrator my father loaned me for tonight," he said. And then he added, "A bribe."

The car had that brand-new car scent and soft leather seats with expensive-looking woodwork. He got in, looking very taken with himself, very unlike the Kane Hill I was used to seeing. Maybe in the end, despite your rebellious ways and thoughts, your heritage exerts itself, I thought.

"Is the bribe working?" I asked.

"It is tonight," he said, instantly returning to that offbeat smile that annoyed some but also could be enchanting. "Although the pressure's off me working weekends at one of the dealerships until I get my math grades up. Plan A is successful. For now."

"What's plan B?"

"Running away from home. Who knows?"

We drove off. I looked back at the house and wondered if my father would use my car or take his truck tonight. He had never bought himself a new car after my mother died. I couldn't imagine him going on a date in his truck, not that he would go out with any woman who would think it beneath her to ride in his truck. It was just that whether he said so or not, I knew that he always saw my mother beside him in that truck.

"So I didn't say anything to Darlena about Foxworth, the story, anything," Kane began, "but apparently, soon after she and Julio had arrived, my mother mentioned that I was seeing you, and then there was some talk about what your father's doing, so she asked me about it tonight before I headed out to pick you up."

"Asked about what?" A little tremor moved through my body in anticipation. From the day I had revealed what the book under my pillow was, I had dreaded the possibility that other people would find out and that my father would be very upset, especially now when he was working on the property.

"The construction of a new building at Foxworth."

"Oh," I said, a little relieved.

"But then she told Julio the high points of the story, which we know now was mostly developed through rumors and legends. I didn't say a word," he added quickly, "but like most everyone who knows about your family, she mentioned that you were a distant cousin of Malcolm Foxworth."

"Great. He'll be looking at me expecting some sort of weirdness or madness."

"Just don't eat all your food with only a knife," he said.

I poked him in the shoulder. "It's not funny."

"Okay, okay. Don't worry about it. As soon as he sees how charming and beautiful you are, any such thought will die a quick death."

We arrived at La Reserve before his sister and her boyfriend, but the hostess took us to the booth they had reserved. I had never been to this restaurant and was surprised at how small it was compared with the size of its reputation. Perhaps that was why it was so expensive and why a dinner reservation usually had to be booked well in advance—maybe not for the Hills, but for most people. The maître d' recognized Kane, just as the maître d' at the River House had when he took me there on our first formal date.

"I haven't been to France," Kane said after we were seated, "but my mother told me this is very much like a good restaurant in Paris." He leaned over. "Both Darlena and Julio can drink. Maybe we can have a taste of champagne. Darlena loves champagne."

"You can have a taste. I can have a glass," I teased, and he laughed.

Although my father and I didn't often go to fancy restaurants, like most people who could manage it, we did so on occasion. He told me my mother could be comfortable in any setting. A restaurant like La Reserve or the River House did not intimidate her. "She looked like she belonged wherever we went," he'd recalled, his own precious memories streaming before him. "I used to call her my chameleon, because she could just blend in. Not that she wouldn't be noticed," he'd added quickly. "She was too beautiful not to be noticed."

The way he clung to anything that reminded him of my mother always impressed me. He was still sacrificing for her, thinking first of her and not himself. It occurred to me that this was what was missing from Christopher's descriptions of his mother. If she talked about his father, it was only to explain the situation they were now in, how their romance and marriage had put them in this place, but she didn't keep his memory as close to her heart as my father kept my mother's memory. If she mentioned Christopher Sr., it seemed clear to me that she did it to manipulate Christopher Jr. more. And apparently, she was already having a serious new romance at the point we'd read to in the diary.

Would Christopher Sr., even for one minute, tolerate what she was putting their children through now? That was a question I wondered if Christopher Jr. would be able to answer for me, for us, even for himself.

I felt Kane's hand take mine, and I snapped out of my reverie.

"Where'd you go?" he asked. "I finally realized I was talking to myself." I leaned forward to tell him my thoughts, but he interrupted me. "Here they are."

I turned to see Darlena and Julio enter the restaurant and start in our direction. I hadn't seen his sister for a long time, but my memory of her was that she was very pretty. She looked taller and more elegantly beautiful and graceful now, her soft chestnut-brown hair floating over her shoulders, a stylish sweep of strands just inches from her right eye. The chandeliers captured the dazzle of her unique amber eyes. She had a svelte Nicole Kidman figure enhanced by her form-fitting half-sleeved black dress with a lace bodice.

Julio looked a little more than six feet tall. He had a dancer's physique and seemed less comfortable in his dark blue suit. His ebony hair had a silky sheen. His more caramel complexion made his black-marble eyes stand out. I thought he was quite handsome but a little more rugged-looking than a typical male model.

Kane stood to greet his sister. Her face seemed to explode into a bright smile of delight. They kissed each other's cheeks as if they had not just been together in their home but instead hadn't seen each other for years. Julio looked awkward for a moment in the shadow of Kane and Darlena's dramatic greeting, and then he rushed to introduce himself to me. I felt calluses on his palms and thought of my father's hands. Darlena slid in beside me, and Julio sat across from her.

"You look so grown-up, Kristin," Darlena said. "I love your dress."

"Thank you. You look more beautiful than ever, Darlena."

"I don't think I've seen you since . . . since when?" she asked Kane.

"Who knows?" he replied. "Probably before you started college."

"No kidding. That's true. How's your father?" she asked me. "I do remember seeing him a few times during the summer. He was always so nice to me. He always reminded me of a Southern gentleman out of some romance novel. I bet he makes every one of your friends feel special."

"In his way," I replied. "I can tell you he always makes me feel special."

She held her smile, but her eyes were full of questions, surely about what it was like to live without a mother or to have a father whose wife had died so unexpectedly. I felt the urge to tell her we were fine.

"My dad's in construction, too," Julio said, even though no one had mentioned what my father did. "He builds modular houses for a national company. It's dull factory work. He'd rather be doing what your father does," he added quickly. "I work with him sometimes, and I know I'd rather be doing that."

"I'd rather be in Philadelphia," Kane said.

"Pardon?" Julio said.

"Nothing," Darlena said. "He's just being a wise-ass."

"*Moi?*" Kane said, pretending outrage.

"What's it mean?" Julio asked.

"It's something my father loves to say. It's on W. C. Fields's tombstone," Darlena explained. Julio still didn't understand. His quizzical smile looked frozen on his face. Darlena touched his hand, obviously a gesture meant to comfort him. "It's silly. Fields just wanted everyone to know he'd rather be anywhere than dead."

"Oh." He looked at Kane, who shrugged.

The waiter approached, and just as Kane had predicted, Darlena ordered a bottle of champagne. The waiter looked at Kane and me suspiciously, but he didn't say anything.

Darlena giggled. "We're on Daddy's account tonight," she said, smiling like a child told she could have anything in the store. "He told us on our way out, so go for broke."

Julio smirked, seeming embarrassed to have Darlena and Kane's father paying for him. "I told your father this was supposed to be my treat," he said. He looked like he was saying it more for my benefit.

"Don't make it harder for my father to sound like a big shot," Darlena joked, but he still didn't look happy about it.

I started to ask them both questions about college to get him more relaxed and talkative. Every once in a while, I glanced at Kane and saw a proud look on his face because I was carrying the conversation. The champagne came. The waiter brought only two glasses for it. We then ordered, and when he left, Darlena poured some champagne into Kane's water glass and some into mine.

"Let's toast to something different," she said,

holding up her glass. We all raised ours. "To Kristin's father successfully building a beautiful new home to replace the Halloween house."

I looked at Kane. His eyes darkened as if anger had risen into his face from some dark place inside him. Had he told his sister not to mention Foxworth Hall at all? Or had he fallen into his Christopher Dollanganger state of mind and begun to resent anyone wishing the story about him and his siblings could be erased as easily as replacing a building and changing the details of a property?

I saw the way Julio was looking at me, waiting for my reaction.

"If anyone can do it," I said, without any sign of emotion, "my father can."

Kane seemed to relax. One crisis passed, I thought. What would come next?

Nothing more about the original Foxworth Hall or the story of the children was mentioned for the remainder of the dinner, but that didn't mean it was out of my mind. Despite being intrigued by Julio and Darlena, I found myself drawn continually to Kane, to the way he talked and held himself. Something had changed in him with Darlena's toast. It wasn't simply being in a formal setting and being dressed up. He really didn't sound like himself. He was so careful about his choice of words, so thoughtful about everything he said, and at times, he appeared older than Julio or Darlena. He corrected Darlena about the history of the city, but not in his usual offhanded or casual way that suggested indifference. He was more condescending, which really surprised me. I glanced at Darlena. She seemed to be getting upset with him and the way he was going on about the degeneration of some of the city neighborhoods and criticizing their father's regular car customers and the salespeople who worked for him.

"My brother didn't always sound like my mother," Darlena said. "It wasn't that long ago that I was the one changing his diapers," she told Julio, after Kane had challenged Julio on his view of the economy. "And when he had a bad nightmare, he didn't run to our mother. He ran to me."

Kane's face reddened a little. He shot a look my way and started to protest that she was exaggerating, but she was on a roll, I thought, out to get revenge or knock him down a peg or two.

"Mother would ask me to bathe him, because he whined and argued about it so much unless I did it. I even had to put out his clothes, because he wouldn't wear what Mother wanted him to wear. I was still telling him how to dress when he was in the sixth grade."

Kane had shrunk a bit but then suddenly recovered his superior tone. "Why don't you mention how I had to lie for you when you snuck Ken Taylor into your room for the night after the senior prom?" He turned to Julio. "My parents heard a male voice, and she told them I had been in her room at two in the morning. To protect her, I had to pretend I had gotten into my father's liquor and gotten sick because her boyfriend threw up in her bathroom."

Julio's eyes widened.

"That's not the worst of it," Kane continued.

"Okay, okay," Darlena said, holding up her hands. "Truce."

Kane smiled at me in victory, but I didn't smile back. He had told me very little about his relationship with Darlena. The way he talked about his home life most of the time made it sound as if he were an only child, too. Now I wondered how close he really had been to Darlena during those earlier years. How close were they to each other now, despite this banter between them?

For the first time, I wondered if he could appreciate Christopher's diary more than I could because he had a sibling and I was an only child. The way they were both talking about their mother also raised a new red flag in my mind. Kane always made fun of his mother. He was almost indifferent to her, but from the way they were talking about her now, it was as if they were as separated from their parents as the Dollangangers had been. His mother seemed to delegate her role as Kane's mother to Darlena and then to whoever would take on one responsibility or another while she pursued her own social objectives.

That's what made what happened in the original Foxworth Hall attic so fascinating to so many young people like us, I suddenly thought. In various degrees, parents ignored their children and looked for ways to avoid their problems and needs. From the sound of it, Mrs. Hill was more of a cousin to Corrine Foxworth than I or my mother was.

Maybe to bring some relief to the table, Julio began asking me more questions. Kane had told them I was in the running for class valedictorian. Julio revealed that he had been his high school class valedictorian. Darlena apparently hadn't known that.

"Class valedictorian, and you didn't know W. C. Fields's famous tombstone?" Kane asked.

"Becoming valedictorian doesn't mean you know trivia, Kane," Darlena said, coming quickly to Julio's defense.

Kane pursed his lips with annoyance and sat back.

Julio and I talked about our favorite subjects, and he described his interest in an international law career.

I saw that Kane was losing interest. Suddenly, he burst out, "Kristin and I have a party to go to. We'll skip dessert, but you two enjoy."

He saw the surprise on my face.

"Right?" he asked, more or less demanded.

"Yes, not that I'm so crazy about the person giving the party."

"Yeah, but we'll ignore her like we always do," he said.

"*I* always do," I corrected.

"Whatever you want," Darlena said. "We enjoyed seeing you, Kristin. I'm sure we'll see more of you."

"You will," Kane said, punching his words at her.

"Good," she said, with just as much defiance in her voice. How quickly they had bounced from being loving brother and sister to competitive siblings.

Kane rose and Darlena and Julio stood to hug and kiss us good-bye. Kane took my hand, hardly giving me a chance to thank them for including me in their dinner. I felt like he was rushing us out of the restaurant.

"Sorry," he said when we had stepped out and were waiting for the valet to bring the car. "I didn't expect it to be so boring."

"It wasn't."

He looked at me like I was joking. "I haven't had much time with Julio except for that stuffy, dreadful dinner my mother arranged at gunpoint," he said. "Thank God we have more people at our Thanksgiving dinner. He's not what I imagined my sister would bring home, and not because he's half Latino or anything. He's just too . . ."

"Too what?"

"Full of himself," he said. "Compensating for an inferiority complex. It gets tired."

"Are you serious?"

"Absolutely. I can see it clearly," he replied, with uncharacteristic arrogance.

The car arrived, and we got in.

"Are we really going to Tina's party?"

"I can't take you to my house, and we can't go up to your attic, because your father's probably home or on his way," he said. "It's still early."

I sat back like someone resigned to a fate.

"We'll have a few laughs and leave," he decided. "Okay?"

"Whatever," I said.

We were both quiet during the drive to Tina Kennedy's home. How complicated the world had suddenly become. When you're very young, everything seems so simple, even what is good and what is bad. Too much candy is bad for you. Being clean and neat is good for you. Policemen are good. Criminals are bad. Not looking both ways when crossing is bad. Waiting for the green light is good. Most important, parents love their children; children love their parents. Grandparents are loving and kind, as are uncles and aunts. It's all so simple. On your birthday, people who love you make you feel special. You get and give presents on Christmas. You wish one another love and happiness on New Year's Eve.

You are told that someday you will be old enough to drive and stay out later, and someday you'll fall in love, and you'll marry and have children. Everything ahead of you looks good and wonderful. Yes, people get angry at each other, but those who love each other apologize and are even nicer to each other afterward. Everything in the world seems organized; everything works the way it is supposed to work.

And then suddenly, one day, yes becomes maybe, and maybe becomes no. Black is also gray at times, and white might really be black beneath. Smiles are not always true. Sometimes they are empty, false. The lights are on in the houses you pass, but the people inside are cloaked in darkness. Nothing you hear, nothing you see, is necessarily true.

Getting older means learning how to leave with doubt and how to get home again.

In those years when they were shut up together in the attic, the Dollanganger children were rushed out of their childhood. Gradually, they had lost their chance to dream. What a horrible thing to do to your own children, I thought. Reading about it, reliving it, was making both Kane and me lose what little childhood faith we had left. I suspected now that this was truer for Kane.

What worried me the most was that by the time we finished the diary, we might not know who we were.

When we arrived at Tina's, we could see the party was in full swing and quite unlike the party Kane had had at his home recently. Beer and other alcoholic drinks were in plain sight. The music was so loud you had to shout to be heard by someone standing beside you. A small group was already smoking weed in a room off the living room. How was Tina going to get away with all this once her parents returned?

The way we were dressed drew everyone's attention. Kane's friends began to tease him. Kyra and Suzette had nice things to say about my dress, but most of the other girls were smirking at me with the expression that says, "Who does she think she is?" They didn't know we had gone to dinner before we had come to the party. Tina's comment was that she would gladly give me something of hers to wear so I wouldn't look so stiff and out of place. She looked well into a buzz of some sort, slurring some of her words. I was anticipating her pursuit of Kane.

When I looked at him, he seemed oblivious to everything going on around us. He just stood there like a disgusted chaperone, turning down offers of beer and booze and declining an invitation to smoke some pot. He brushed everyone off abruptly. Even I was surprised at the way he was ignoring his buddies. I saw the surprised and disgusted looks on their faces. When Tina put her hands on his arm, he pulled away from her so abruptly everyone around them stopped talking and drinking. I didn't hear what he said, but whatever it was, it shocked her.

"What's with Kane?" Suzette asked me.

"Nothing. Why?"

"He looks like he lost his best friend or something," Kyra said. "Usually, he's the life of the party."

"Maybe he's just a little tired."

"From what?" Suzette asked, her eyes widening with some sexual suggestion.

"I don't kiss and tell," I replied, and the girls laughed. Tina was standing nearby, eavesdropping, so I spoke louder.

They asked where we had gone to dinner, and I described it and the restaurant. Kyra was the only one who had been there, with her parents on an anniversary. Of course, they wanted to know about Darlena's boyfriend and what she was like, too. While I talked to my girlfriends, I saw Kane circle the living room, gazing at everyone, the couples dancing, observing like someone researching a primitive tribe, paying only half attention to anything anyone said to him, and then planting himself in a corner of the living room and sipping a soft drink. He stood back, looking aloof.

Tina was off to my right, holding court with some

of her closer friends, complaining about Kane, and looking at me with darts in her eyes. What could he possibly have said to her? I didn't have to wait long to find out. She came toward me with her friends. I braced myself.

"I don't know . . . I mean, we don't know what you've done to Kane Hill, but he's more of a snob than ever."

"That's lame. I didn't think he was ever a snob," I replied coolly. I looked at my girlfriends. "Did any of you?"

"Of course not," Suzette said. "He's anything but that." The girls around us seconded it with "Absolutely" and "For sure," nodding their heads.

Tina could see she was outnumbered. "He's ruining my party," she whined.

I looked at him across the way, still standing in a corner, looking so defiant that no one approached him. "You mean, it wasn't ruined before we got here?" I asked.

Even her friends broke out in smiles, and a few laughed.

"Anytime you want to leave is fine with me," Tina said, and marched off.

"Me, too, actually," I muttered. I made my way across the living room to Kane. "What are you doing?" I asked.

"Opening my eyes," he said. "I never realized how juvenile some of our friends are."

"Are they?"

He looked at me with a smirk instead of that

charming offbeat smile I had come to cherish. "Christopher Dollanganger at ten was more mature."

"But was he happy? Could he ever be?"

"I guess we'll find out."

I didn't want to continue talking about the Dollangangers. Even with the music blaring, I was afraid of being overheard. "What did you say to Tina Kennedy? Our quick departure won't break her heart."

He finally smiled. "I merely told her that her multiple orgasms were embarrassing me. And I added something else that had to do with her physiology."

"Why did we come here, Kane? You're not even trying to enjoy this party."

"You don't want me to get into things, drink and then drive, or smoke that crap and talk about some new violent video game or about which one of these girls is the easiest, do you?"

"Then let's go," I said, almost shouting. "I didn't want to come here."

He nodded and started around the living room, avoiding anyone who wanted to speak to him. I followed, and just before we exited, I looked back at my girlfriends. Almost all of them lifted their shoulders and raised their hands, palms up. What could I tell them that would help them understand? That everyone gets in and out of a mood, and Kane was just in a dark one? It would pass, just like it did for them? That was all I could think of saying, and I knew it would be what I would repeat when they called or saw me. I smiled and nodded. Only Suzette smiled back. Everyone else continued to look confused.

The cool night air was a relief. My ears were ring-ing when I got into the car. Without speaking, Kane started the engine and drove us away as if we were fleeing a bank robbery. He slowed down at the corner.

"I'm sorry," he said. "I thought we'd amuse our-selves for a while, but I guess I was just not in the mood."

"Exactly how I would put it," I said.

"Let's face it, Kristin. You and I are so far above all that now."

"Above what, Kane? A party with the only friends we have?"

"That sort of party."

Maybe he was right, I thought. I should be happy that he felt this way. It wasn't a party my father would approve of me attending. Someone could easily get into serious trouble driving later on, and Tina's parents would be in equally big trouble. Everything he was saying was right, and yet there was something about it that disturbed me. It was as if he were being too adult. No wonder Tina had called him snobby. People who were as wealthy as Kane's family were expected to be snobby. Their friends were all well-to-do. If they mingled with people who had less, it was usually at some event at school.

When we arrived on my street, he slowed down and suddenly pulled to the curb when my house came into view.

"What are we doing?" I asked. He was just looking up in the direction of my attic.

"I so looked forward to going up there with you this week," he said, still looking at the attic and not at me. "It really has become special for us, hasn't it?" he asked, turning to me.

"Yes."

He smiled. "I'm glad you think of it the same way. I'll probably be sorry when we reach the end of the diary."

I didn't know what to say. Sorry when we reached the end of the diary? He looked like he really meant it. "I don't know how I'll feel then, Kane. What I do know is not to expect a happy ending."

"Yes, but we're there. We're part of them in a way no one else is, right?"

"I suppose. Yes."

"Maybe when we're alone like this, we should call each other Christopher and Cathy."

"What?"

"I'm just kidding," he said quickly, then shifted into drive and turned into my driveway. My father's truck was there. I could tell from where it was parked that he had used it and not my car to go to his dinner. "Sorry this wasn't the greatest night," Kane said.

"I enjoyed the dinner, Kane. I really did. I like your sister, and I liked Julio, too. I think you're being a little too hard on him."

"Yeah, maybe. We'll do it again, but just ourselves one night. I like dressing up for you."

He leaned forward to kiss me. It wasn't a bad kiss; it was just different. I could feel him holding back, and

I thought that maybe he didn't want to get too passionate in my driveway. He opened his car door and hurried around to open mine.

"M'lady," he said, holding out his arm. We walked up to the front door together. "Any way we can get together in the attic tomorrow?" he asked as soon as we got there.

"I don't think so. I have to do some housework in the morning and then go with my father and get all our shopping done for Thanksgiving dinner and our regular week's food. We'll probably do some pre-Christmas shopping, too. Dad likes me to help him pick out gifts for Todd's children and his wife and something for my aunt Barbara. We'll have lunch out, and he'll want to make us dinner. He hasn't for a while. I need to spend some quality time with him."

I could feel his disappointment. Then he burst into more of a Kane Hill smile. "Well, only two and a half days left of school before the Thanksgiving break. I bet we finish the diary by a week from tomorrow, anyway."

"Maybe," I said.

He kissed me again, softer but quicker, and then headed to his car. Before he got in, he paused and looked up at the attic. He didn't look back at me. He got in and backed out. Suddenly, I felt very cold and hurried into the house.

I was surprised my father wasn't waiting up for me. The television wasn't on, and there was only a small lamp lit in the living room and a nightlight on in the kitchen. I turned off everything I had to and started up the stairs. He came out of his room in his robe just as I turned toward my room.

"Hey. I was just going down to wait for you," he said.

"Oh. I turned everything off."

"That's all right. You won't have to wake me up to go to sleep. How was your dinner?"

"Very impressive. I had something called coq au vin."

He raised his eyebrows. "I haven't had that for years. It's going to get so I'll have to study up on some recipes to impress you."

"I doubt it. How was your dinner?"

"The steak was a little overcooked."

"I didn't mean the food. Was it a business dinner or what?"

"Business dinner," he said. "As it turns out, the decorator is married." He shrugged. "Which was fine with me. I guess I'm just a little . . ."

"Paranoid," I filled in, and he smiled. "Anyway, Mrs. Osterhouse will be happy to hear it," I added, and he shook his head.

"Good night, Kristin," he sang, and headed back to his bedroom.

"*Bonne nuit*," I said, mimicking the maître d' at La Reserve.

He glanced back, smiled again, and went into his room.

I meant what I had told Kane. I wanted my Sunday to be full of quality time with my father. To do that,

I had to put Christopher's diary and Foxworth Hall out of my mind. And to do *that*, I had to put Kane out of my mind, too. With my vague answers, I thwarted my father's questions at breakfast about my dinner date, and he changed the subject quickly. One thing we were both good at was reading each other's moods.

Sometimes I thought we could blindfold ourselves and move through our house all day without bumping into each other. We were very good at anticipating each other's needs. I was confident that this was true to some degree for all my friends and their parents, but not to the extent that it was for my father and me. It wasn't only because I was an only child. My mother was no longer with us. He had no one else to command his interest and attention, and neither did I. Once we were both home, our world revolved around only each other. How were our days? What had made us happy, and what had made us sad? Sometimes the most trivial things became headline news. We worked at making each other laugh and often talked until I retreated to do my homework. It was as if from the day my mother passed away, we were both afraid of silence.

We began this Sunday morning like all others, by doing our weekly cleaning of the house. My father always took the kitchen, because "it's a battleground I've known," he said, referring to his earlier days working in the diner. While he went at the floor, stove, grill, and refrigerator, I vacuumed the living room, polished furniture, and went over the windows. Both of us did laundry, but he was better at folding everything, because he did it so long in the navy and when he was a bachelor. The bottom line was that we had become an efficient two-man team and could do this house by midday. We would go off to lunch to reward ourselves.

Midway through my work, the phone began to ring. The first call was from Suzette. I had anticipated it, of course, and gave her my planned response about Kane's behavior at the party. I knew she didn't buy it, but I deflected any more questions and told her I had to get back to my housework because my father and I had plans for the day.

The last thing she said made me nervous. "You didn't used to be this secretive, Kristin. Something's changed you."

Of course I protested and then promised to talk to her more the first chance I got.

Kane's call came not five minutes afterward. My father popped his head into the living room and chanted, "Busy, busy." I grimaced, and he laughed.

"Both my sister and Julio think you're great," Kane began. "I took your advice and apologized to him for my behavior. He's not so bad, and my sister needs an ally in this house, anyway."

"Good."

"So your day is still full?"

"To the brim. I've got to get back to my vacuuming, or I'll be too far behind to do what we have to do."

"Tomorrow afternoon, then?"

"Yes. Oh, and I'll meet you at school, Kane."

"Why?"

"I just think it's better if you don't pick me up every morning."

"Better?"

"Trust me," I said.

"Okay," he said, obviously upset. "Have a good time."

"Thanks," I said. Later, when I had a chance, I would explain to him that it would help me keep everything secret if I didn't look like I was spending every free breathing moment with him. My father knew I was still reading Christopher's diary. It would only be natural for him to suspect that Kane knew about it if he was with me whenever I was free to do it.

The phone rang again, but I didn't answer it. It was Kyra, and I knew she would have the same questions and the same reactions to my answers as Suzette did. Most likely, Suzette had already called her to complain about me, and she had volunteered to see where she could get with me. We were always curious about each other, but this curiosity about Kane and me was becoming irritating. Probably unfairly so, but I couldn't help it. Besides, the calls were slowing me up. When I finally put away the vacuum cleaner, I saw my father waiting at the foot of the stairs. I had the feeling he had been watching me for a while.

"What?" I asked.

"Maybe we should do the attic," he said. "We haven't for some time."

There's some truth to the advice that if you want

to get away from a lie, you should tell a half-truth. It reduces the chances of your being doubted and gives your troubled conscience some relief, not that it was something I had to do too often. If it was ever necessary, however, it was right now.

"Oh, I've done that this week," I said. "I even did the windows."

He simply stared at me for a moment. My heart was starting to race. Was this it? Was this the moment I confessed? I had full intentions to do so after Kane and I had finished the diary. I often thought about how I would do it. I even considered first turning the diary over to him to do with it what he wished and then revealing what Kane and I had done. I dreaded the look on his face that I knew would come. One reaction I feared was his telling me that now he had no choice. He couldn't get rid of it. If it got out into the community that we'd had such a document and had destroyed it, the horrid rumors would multiply tenfold. It wouldn't matter how much I assured him that Kane would keep it a secret. Kane could come over and make the pledge in person. My father would say, "The genie is out of the bottle."

I heard it often in dreams.

To my surprise, this time, he smiled.

"I should have figured you would do that," he said. I knew that in his mind, I had done it solely because of my mother's things in the antique wardrobe.

Guilt made my shoulders sag, but once again, he misinterpreted my reaction. Now he felt sorry for bringing on a moment of sadness.

"C'mon. Let's go get some lunch. You drive," he added, which surprised me.

"We're not going in Black Beauty?" He was never comfortable with me driving his truck. He said it was a one-man horse.

"No. What's the point in having a built-in chauffeur if I don't use her?"

"Don't make me nervous," I warned, and we started for the garage. "Charley's?" I asked when I started the car.

"No. I need a day off from those guys. Take me someplace new."

I wanted to avoid any of the places my friends might go to, so I drove us to a restaurant I recalled Mrs. Osterhouse mentioning once. My father was quite surprised but also looked a little pleased.

"You've been to the Dew Drop Inn? I thought it was only for members of the AARP. It's the only place that serves prune juice in warm water," he joked.

"Never, but I thought you'd appreciate the peace and quiet."

Still smiling, he shrugged. When we entered, he probably immediately thought that I had planned it. There was Mrs. Osterhouse with one of her neighbors, Lilly Taylor, seated at a corner table. She had obviously had her burgundy hair cut and styled over the weekend. I had to admit to myself that she looked much more attractive than usual, even younger. Perhaps unfairly, I never liked to think of Mrs. Osterhouse as being a pretty woman, but she did have extraordinary Irish green eyes, which made sense since her maiden name was O'Brian. Actually, I didn't know all that much about her. From the moment I had sensed her feelings for my father and her sometimes not-so-subtle pursuit of him, a wall dropped between me and her. No matter how sweet she was to me, and she was, I couldn't help being cold and formal with her. If I told Kane any of this, he would surely accuse me of having an Electra complex.

I couldn't help my feelings toward her, but I knew they were wrong. After all, she had lost her husband when he was only in his early forties, when he was killed in a terrible car accident on the interstate during a freak storm in April that year. I should have been thinking of her when I had read Christopher's description of their learning about his father's rather weird car accident. It had been more than five years for Mrs. Osterhouse. I knew she had tried dating again but hadn't found anyone in whom to invest her love and energy—until she began working for my father, that is.

He looked at me, and I shook my head.

The Dew Drop Inn was a modest restaurant with the capacity for about fifty patrons. It was done in a light oak, with a half dozen booths on both sides and a dozen tables in the center. The far wall consisted of a large fieldstone fireplace that I imagined was built by the Wilsons. It was lit with four or five chunks of hard oak firewood. The scent of it was not overpowering but did add authenticity, along with the antique pots and pewter farm implements hanging on walls and the paintings capturing colonial Virginia in villages and farms.

We crossed to say hello to Mrs. Osterhouse. She had been after me for years to call her Laura, but I was reluctant, sensing that the moment I did so, I would open the door to more intimacy and, in my young girl's mind, maybe signal to my father that he had my permission to pursue a romantic relationship. I realized how foolish and even selfish that was now, but I still hadn't called her Laura once.

She introduced me to Mrs. Taylor. My father knew her from the First National Bank, where she worked as VP of commercial loans.

"Looking forward to Thanksgiving, Kristin?" Mrs. Osterhouse asked. "I am," she added, before I could reply. "I still don't know your father's secret to making that turkey moister than any I've ever eaten."

"Yes," I said. "He has a few cooking and baking secrets he won't reveal. I think he gets up in the middle of the night when I'm asleep and does things."

Both women laughed.

"It's all very simple once the turkey and I come to an understanding," my father said, and the women laughed again.

I was afraid they would ask us to join them, so I turned to the hostess and nodded at the booth behind them. She set the menus down. My father added some small talk about the weather and then followed me to the booth. He looked at me over the menu.

"Just a coincidence," I said to those suspicious eyes.

He shook his head. We'd had this discussion a few times. He didn't believe in coincidence. He always said, "If you didn't plan it, someone else did. Someone behind you or above you."

Maybe he was right, I thought. Maybe everything happens for a reason, even the fate of the Dollanganger children. What's often difficult is discovering what that reason is, especially if it's something tragic or sad.

We enjoyed our lunch, and as usual, when my father felt relaxed and comfortable, he talked about his own youth more and revealed more about our family. Inevitably, our conversation worked around to my mother and some new memories of her that he wanted to share. It was therapeutic for both of us to think of her in happier times. We had finally reached that point where we could do so and not feel all broken up inside and cast ourselves into the darkness for the remainder of the day.

Mrs. Osterhouse and her friend left before we did. She paused to talk to us a little more about Thanksgiving. I could see how much she really was looking forward to it, and I felt guiltier about making it seem so matter-of-fact. Before she turned to leave, I told her I was really looking forward to it, too, even to overeating. I saw the way her eyes warmed. Her smile was full of gratitude, and when I glanced at my father, I saw that he was happy I had broken the ice just a little.

And then, I don't know why, but I suddenly had the feeling that he might have broken that ice a while ago.

I said nothing about it. After lunch, we went to do

our shopping. Aside from the care and interest he always took with groceries, he was not fond of shopping for anything else. He really did depend on me for help with the gifts and navigating the department stores. He confessed that my mother had never liked going shopping with him.

"I've always been an in-and-out guy," he told me. "I'd go for what I needed, get it, and leave, whereas she'd want to look at everything, spend time studying new things, even though at the end of the day, she left with what we had come for."

We carried our laughter home with our groceries. I saw that I had more messages on my cell phone from girlfriends, but I didn't call anyone back. I knew I'd be repeating the same things, and I thought I might do better dealing with it at school. I spent my time doing homework and studying for some quizzes I knew were coming. Teachers always hit us with something a day or two before we broke for a holiday.

In the morning, my father didn't say anything when I indicated that I was driving myself to school, but I could see he was more than a little curious about it. On my way, I debated suggesting to Kane that we put off any more diary reading until after Thanksgiving, but as soon as we met, it didn't take me long to realize that if I did that, he would be more than seriously disappointed; he might even be very angry. I didn't know where that would take us. Ironically, the diary had become the glue that bound us in our relationship now. It frightened me a little to think of it that way.

What would happen to us when we closed it on the last page?

I knew my girlfriends were still dissatisfied with my explanations for Kane's behavior at Tina's party. She was still complaining about it as loudly as she could. I saw that Kane's buddies were a little put out with him, too, but he didn't seem to care. He was with me every possible free moment, anyway.

Even though I had driven myself to school, he waited for me in the parking lot. He had rejected any invitations or activities for after school and actually led the way to my house. I fell behind him, because I wasn't going to break the speed limit.

"You're lucky," I told him after I got out of my car. "They really watch that street this time of day."

"Yeah, I forgot," he said. He looked at his watch. "We've only got a few hours, probably, right?"

"Right," I said, even though I knew my father would push his day later. I led him into the house.

While I got us something to drink, Kane went up to arrange the attic. This time, he asked if he could get the diary, too. I could see how anxious he was to get started. It bothered me, but I didn't say anything. He put on the wig and handed me the scarf. I took it, but I didn't put it on.

"You don't want to put it on?" he asked, surprised.

"Not yet," I said. "Let's just get into it."

"Okay," he said, and opened the diary slowly, looking like someone who was about to enjoy one of the most delicious things in his life.

I never thought I would use my medical knowledge to save the life of a mouse, especially since we were trying to rid the attic of them, but one morning, Cory woke us all with his screams from the attic, and as usual, if Cory or Carrie screamed or cried, the other automatically did, too. Cathy and I rushed up to see what was wrong. Cory was pointing at a mouse that had its left forepaw caught in a trap. It disturbed Cory so much I had to work it loose, and then Cathy worked beside me like a surgical nurse while I cleaned it up and created a tiny bandage and splint. I felt foolish, but Cory and Carrie were so pleased. Cory had a pet.

In the middle of it all, our grandmother arrived with a basket of food. She saw the mouse and loomed over us silently, looking like she was adding up all our violations. I pretended not to even notice her, just to irritate her. I went up to the attic, found an old birdcage, and brought it down to fix up a home for Cory's pet mouse, doing it all right in front of our grandmother. When she realized we were going to keep a mouse for Cory, she finally spoke up, telling us it was a pet that fit us.

Ironically, that little mouse did become a delightful pet for us all, and although I would never admit it, it kept us from thinking of how dreadful everything had become that we would find delight in a creature we were otherwise killing by the dozens. Maybe Grandmother Olivia was right. Maybe we were no better than a small trapped creature locked away in a world with spiders and other crawlers. We had to continually remind ourselves who we were and what we were in order to hold on to any self-pride at all.

Cathy was always good at reminding me how much time had passed. If I tried to ignore anything, it was that, how long we had been locked away, and how long it had been since Momma had come to see us. At the moment, Cathy pointed out that we had been here almost two and a half years.

When you spend so much time so close to each other the way Cathy and I had for that long, you get so you can tell each other things without speaking a word, and I don't mean through sign language, either. It was more what we said when we merely looked at each other.

What struck me most about Cathy one day was how much she had developed physically. Her breasts had filled out, and the curves in her waist and hips revealed that she had crossed that line between little girl and young teenage girl, who surely, if she was in school, would be attracting the interest of older boys. Thinking that helped me justify my own new way of looking at her every time I could catch her undressed or half-dressed.

Most boys my age would have these feelings, I thought, this interest. Repeatedly, I told myself not to hate myself for it. Sometimes when I looked at her and felt the rush in my blood and the hardness growing in my penis, I deliberately poked myself with something sharp. The pain distracted me for the moment, but it didn't end what I was feeling.

And then there was that look on Cathy's face when she caught me looking at her or I caught her looking at me when I was undressed. Why shouldn't she have that look? I asked myself. Girls mature faster than boys. That's why they favor boys older than them most of the time. She had entered that realm of titillation. I saw her nipples harden. I caught her touching herself, thinking about herself and the sensations she was experiencing. I even heard her moan occasionally at night when she thought I was fast asleep.

Finally, one day while the twins were napping, wrapped in each other's arms to comfort themselves, Cathy paused in her dance routine and flopped down next to me. I had been reading an article in an old newspaper that had been used to wrap something. The article was about the spread of the Spanish flu after the First World War.

For a few moments, she didn't say anything, but I could see out of the corner of my eye that she was working up to asking me something. Finally, I lowered the newspaper.

"What are you thinking?" I asked.

"I was wondering if you thought we were growing normally. I don't mean being with others our age and all that. I mean . . . our bodies."

"I think we are," I said. "Despite everything.

All the cells in our bodies have these built-in messages, orders, and things happen automatically."

"Do you think my breasts should be bigger by now?"

"No, they're fine," I said quickly. I didn't want to reveal how often I had gazed upon them.

"There was this girl in the seventh grade I remember, Linda Swanson, who was bigger than Momma."

"That happens sometimes. It's called precocious puberty," I told her. I had read about it recently because I had wondered about us both either maturing too quickly or not quickly enough.

I could see she had many more questions to ask, probably mostly about herself, but she was too shy and too embarrassed.

"Nothing you're going through is unnatural," I said firmly. "I've read a great deal about it."

She nodded, looking a little relieved, but when her gaze went to the twins, her chin began to tremble. "I've been measuring them, and I want you to do it, too, Christopher. You and I have grown, as you say, normally, but they're too small. Their heads look too big."

This wasn't something I had not thought about myself. I was always hesitant about bringing up negative or sad things to her. Like a firecracker, she would go off ranting and raving about Momma and our grandmother, and I would have trouble calming her down. It was only when I told her she was frightening the twins that she eased up.

I nodded. "We'll study them," I promised.

We began to measure their growth daily. Cathy was right. They looked stunted and always too fragile. I thought what they needed was sunshine. We tried to get them out and on the roof when it was safe, but they fought us. Strangely, they had become terrified of leaving their confined world. Their resistance and their screams forced us to give up. We could attract attention, and who knows what our grandmother would do to us then?

Cathy was very upset about it. She cried continually. They were going to become dwarfs. They'd soon die. They'd be freaks. On and on, she predicted one horror after another for our little brother and sister. We couldn't force them to eat more than they would, and lately, they were reluctant to do anything physical. In small ways, they were dying. Cathy was right, I thought. I was growing desperate about it, and then finally, one day, the door opened. We all looked up, and there was Momma.

I should say she burst in, more bubbly and happier than we had seen her since we had come here. Of course, she went on and on about how happy she was to see us and how often she had thought about us. I stood there listening, and I'm sure I looked like someone who was listening to a woman who had gone mad. Finally, I was able to speak, and I told her in a calm voice how wrong she had been to leave us for so long, no matter what her reasons could possibly be.

The smile on her face, which I would have to admit looked more false and empty than any smile she had ever given us, disappeared instantly. Her eyes narrowed, and that little ripple of anger I had seen too often since we were brought here revealed itself in her tightened lips. I always believed I could read her better than anyone, even our father, maybe especially our father.

"You sound different," she said cautiously. "Did anything go seriously wrong?" Perhaps the casual way she asked that question shocked me the most.

"Did anything go wrong!"

I couldn't help myself. A dam had broken. Cathy's rants had nothing on the one I delivered, crying out about all that had happened to us since she was last here, how we had grown and matured but how the twins had not. Before she could flood us with presents and promises, I made it clear to her that nothing she could give us now but our freedom would matter. We had outgrown this place, outgrown our childish bodies. We wanted to be our own ages, doing things people our own ages did. Already, I told her, she had taken away what we should have had just like any other young person, and we could never get it back.

I had never spoken to her as sharply and as

truthfully as this. All her false walls crumbled. The shock on her face was stunning. Even Cathy, who was apt never to give her any credibility, looked genuinely surprised and impressed. Could we give her the benefit of the doubt, believe this new face? She looked like she would die on the spot if I no longer loved her.

I didn't want to do it, but I felt myself retreat a little. I told her that of course, I loved her. I made it clear that it wasn't easy to love her now. I reviewed everything she had told us, especially how a few days had turned out to be weeks and then months and now years, all this time waiting for an old man to die, an old man who was supposed to have been so sick he wouldn't last hours, let alone years. We had endured all this to inherit a fortune with her.

I gave her an ultimatum. Turn over the key to the room, and let us go far away. She could send us whatever money she wanted, if she wanted. If she didn't and she wanted us out of her life so she could inherit her father's fortune, so be it. We simply had to be set free. She had no other choice. We would stand for nothing less. I glanced at Cathy. She looked shocked at my determination, but I wasn't going to play the fool any longer. I had to make our mother understand that we had come to the end of our hope and our tolerance.

She stared at me for a few moments silently and then gave Cathy a most hateful look. Did she think my younger sister had turned me against her and that was it, the only reason I had spoken to her this way?

Cathy leaped up and joined in now, pointing out the condition of the twins and screaming at her for permitting it all to happen. I didn't interrupt her. Everything she was saying was painfully true. I looked to Momma, hoping she would see it all and break down with regret and apologies, but our attack on her seemed to only strengthen her resolve and self-pity. I was so disappointed.

This was all my fault, I thought. I had given in to Momma too easily, defended her too often, and believed in her too much. Cathy and the twins should hate me just as much as I hated myself at this moment.

In a slow, mean tone of voice, Momma defended herself, giving herself credit for keeping us alive and not in the streets begging. She repeated all the efforts and work she had put into this plan and then told us her father was so sick now that he couldn't even be placed in a wheelchair. We were so close. He would die any day, and she would immediately come to us and free us to join her in the fortune she was to inherit. Every dream and plan we had would come true.

Neither Cathy nor I reacted. How often had we heard this? And yet I couldn't help but wonder if this time, it might be true. I held back my comments, and I didn't apologize. And then, suddenly, she went into a tantrum that rivaled any Cathy had performed. In fact, she looked just like Cathy, pounding the pillows on the bed and crying about how heartless and ungrateful we were. She wailed and looked like she would tear out her hair.

I couldn't help it. She was the only one left who would love us. Maybe she had permitted all the terrible things to happen to us, but she was dependent on her mother, too. She had been just as lost as we were. I looked at Cathy. She was feeling terrible for her. Together we approached her, and both of us pleaded for her to forgive us for our outbursts. The twins looked stunned and lost in the midst of all this. I felt terrible for them.

Momma calmed down, but she didn't look forgiving. She then described the gifts she had gotten for us, how she had thought of each of us and what we would appreciate the most. For me, it was a new set of encyclopedias ordered for my upcoming birthday, bound in leather and gold and with my name and the date engraved on them. I looked at Cathy and realized she was back to being very angry. Momma had talked about my gift, how much she would spend on me, but did not say anything to Cathy or the twins about theirs.

Momma looked at Cathy, and something she saw in her face brought back her rage. She went to the door quickly and turned on us, berating us for how we had treated her. Then she said a shocking thing: Until we really thought about how we had hurt her, she would not return. She left. I was stunned.

How would she know if we were sorry, if she planned never to return until we were? It was illogical.

Cathy looked at me and then at the twins, who came rushing up to her, embracing her. She glared.

"She never even kissed them," she said.

Kane lowered the diary.

"She sure knows how to play them," Kane said. "I'm disappointed in Christopher, falling for that act and asking her to forgive them. See? You can be pretty smart, book-smart, but it doesn't do you any good if you're an emotional cripple." He stood up.

"I wouldn't go that far, Kane. You once said it. He wants to believe her so much, loves her so much, that he lies to himself."

He stood by the window with his back to me. "Your parents ever lie to you?" he asked, still not turning around. Then, after a second or so, he did. "I don't mean little white lies to get you to do things when you were younger or telling you there's a Santa Claus or something. I mean a real lie, a serious lie."

"No. I can't even imagine it happening," I said.

"Mine did. Big-time." He looked down and then walked back to his chair. I thought he wasn't going to say any more about it, but he looked at me and said, "I've never told anyone."

"You don't have to tell me," I said. I was caught between my curiosity and my desire not to hear anything unpleasant to add to what we were reading together. I felt overwhelmed with sadness and anger as it was.

"I never knew anyone I wanted to tell it to," he said. He glanced at the diary. "Maybe when you open up someone else's secrets, your own pour out whether you like it or not."

"Kane . . ."

"No, it's all right. It's supposed to be good to get things out, things that have been eating away at you for a long time, right? Don't all psychologists tell people that? Revelation therapy."

I stared at him, waiting. Seeing how determined he was, I didn't want to stop him and make him feel any worse about whatever it was he was going to tell me.

"How come your parents never had another child? I mean, you were about eight when your mother died. Her death didn't have anything to do with her being pregnant or anything, did it?"

"No. My mother had a bad miscarriage when I was four, and the result made it difficult, if not impossible, for her to have another child."

"But they wanted one, right?"

"Yes, very much. My father once told me they were toying with adopting."

He nodded, looked away and then back at me.

"After my parents had my sister, my mother didn't want any more children."

"Oh, so you were an accident?" I asked. A few of our classmates had revealed that they had been, but that didn't seem to have made much of a difference in their lives. I imagined no one liked to be thought of as an accident, but if the end result was being loved just as much as a planned child, what difference did it make in the end?

"I wish," he said.

I shook my head. "I don't understand. You're not adopted, are you?"

"Hardly. I'm really more like my mother than I care to admit and even more like my father at times, even though he acts as if I had been left on his doorstep. No, for years, I knew nothing, of course. I was too young to understand, anyway. My parents always made it seem like everything that happened was as normal as it was for any couple. My mother became pregnant, and I was born, and lucky for them, I was a boy. My father wanted a boy to carry on the Hill empire."

"So? Where's the lie?"

"The lie was that my mother wanted me. She was very upset at how long it took her to regain what she called only ninety percent of her beautiful figure after Darlena was born. Motherhood was an annoyance. Both Darlena and I had nannies up the wazoo. My parents battled for some time over having another child. Finally, my father bought me. That's the truth, even though I was actually never told it by either of them. Darlena overheard a conversation, an argument between them."

"Bought you?"

"He gave my mother five hundred thousand dollars for her own personal account if she agreed to get pregnant. So here I am, the five-hundred-thousand-dollar baby. Of course, considering inflation and all, I might not be worth that now."

"I'm sorry," was all I could think to say. What child would want to learn that his mother was bribed into having him? Once he learned that, what sort of relationship would he have with his mother? Every time she got angry at him, his mother's eyes would reveal how much she really didn't want to have a child.

And would the child ever do anything that made her regret her resistance, make her proud to have had that child? It was horrible enough being with friends who couldn't care less if you were there, but being with a mother who never really wanted you had to be very difficult, especially while you were growing up and you saw how loving other mothers were with their children.

Suddenly, I understood so much more about Kane. His indifference, the way he made so much in his life seem trivial, that shrug and offbeat smile, his otherwise cool casualness about all that happened to him and around him, which had made him so attractive to so many, seeing him as the calm rebel—it was all really his cry for help and attention. He never took himself very seriously, because he believed there was nothing serious about him. If his mother wasn't so into herself, she wouldn't have taken the offer, and he would never have been born.

Afterward, he was merely an obligation. She solved ninety percent of that by hiring nannies and by permitting his sister or assigning to her so much responsibility for him when he was young. No wonder that closeness had developed.

"I appreciate that you trust me enough to tell me that, Kane," I said.

"You trusted me with this," he said, lifting the diary. "Revealing what we consider secret about ourselves draws us closer. My parents keep secrets from each other. Most of the time, they lie to each other."

"I'm sorry," I said.

"I'm used to it by now. And you know something? So are they. They're comfortable with it. Reality and truth are painful. So when I told you that Christopher might be lying to himself or refusing to believe his mother was lying, I was talking about myself, you see. My mother makes a great show of caring for me in front of friends, and I soak it up."

"Surely she still cares about you now," I offered.

"Yes, but not to the extent she pretends to care. You know yourself; you can sense that. I let her toss her loving smiles at me, kiss me supposedly affectionately, ask me the questions parents are supposed to ask their children about school or their after-school activities, friends, girls, any of it, and I give her satisfactory answers most of the time so that we both pass the test, especially in front of other people, but . . . my mother never came to comfort me when I had a bad dream. I had a nanny or Darlena for that, and once, when I had a cold close to pneumonia, she simply hired a private nurse."

I waited silently to hear whatever else he had to reveal, but he suddenly put up his hands.

"Hey," he said. "Don't feel sorry for me now. I'm over it. I have come to a comfortable acceptance, a truce with my own feelings. I'm fine. Really. I'm fine."

I could see his eyes were brimming with tears. I rose, walked over to him, knelt down, and kissed him softly. "Of course you are," I said, and he smiled.

"Okay. Now I am," he said. He looked at the diary. "A little more?"

"Just a little," I told him, and returned to the sofa bed.

The afternoon sun was struggling to keep twilight at bay. Back at Foxworth, my father was probably about to organize the cleanup, putting away tools, evaluating what was done and what would be done next, and thinking about coming home. A quick thought about my homework passed by me. I knew what I had to do and how long it would take.

When I looked at Kane, now preparing to continue, I realized how much more he had to share with the Dollanganger kids than I did, despite their being distant cousins of mine. Just like Cathy had faced and was forcing Christopher to face the reality about his mother, Kane's sister had brought the reality about their mother home to him. Neither he nor Christopher wanted to believe or accept any of it. What could be stronger than a mother's love for her child and the child's love for her? Shatter that, and what was left? So wounded in your heart, how could you find the power of love for someone else there later on? Would you doubt anyone who expressed it for you? Would you be afraid to believe?

Whom could you trust?

It suddenly occurred to me, came to me like an electric shock—that quick, that stinging, that true.

There was only one person whose love Christopher could ever trust.

Cathy.

She was the only one left.

Momma had left us many gifts, gifts to buy us off, to make us forget how she had deserted us. What surprised me most about the gifts for Cathy and me were how they revealed what she saw in and thought of us. It was as if in her mind, we were exactly as young as we had been the day we were brought to Foxworth Hall. Maybe that was her way of forgetting all that had happened to us since. With a pile of gifts, she could swipe away the torture, the starvation, the punishments, and the lack of sun and exercise we had endured. She could make herself feel better about what she had done if we would indulge in these gifts of candy and games and new clothing. Oh, we would forgive her.

Cathy refused to accept it. She looked as defiant as ever. She didn't understand that if I joined her and kept up our defiance and anger, the twins would suffer the worst. I bawled her out for her self-pity, and she ran up to the attic. I thought I would let her stew in her own juices for a while, and I didn't go after her. I played with the twins. I could hear the music upstairs and her dancing. Good, I thought. At least she was getting it out of her system. I thought she would come down for dinner finally, but she didn't. I put aside food for her. Still, she didn't return. Finally, I went up to see what she was doing. I found her lying out on the roof. She was in her ballerina costume, so I knew she had to be cold. I brought her a woolen jacket, spread it over her, and lay down beside her. I knew she had to wind down from her fury herself. No words I could say now would matter.

"I almost jumped," she said.

"What?"

"I was going to jump off this roof. I would have, too, but I realized Momma probably wouldn't care, and they'd probably say some crazy girl came here, climbed up, and jumped."

"Of course she'd care," I said. "No matter what, you're still her daughter."

"Right, sure. Then I thought, what if I was just injured but so badly that I couldn't dance?"

"Very likely," I told her.

"Then I thought I would live to someday trap

and torture our grandmother and mother just like they've done to us."

"Oh, Cathy, it doesn't do any good to think these terrible thoughts. You'll end up with a sour-looking face forever, and the acid of hate will eat you up inside."

She looked at me and snuggled closer. I put my arm around her, and we both gazed up at the stars. I told her I had saved her some dinner and some candy, which I knew she wanted, even though she pretended not to.

"Don't ever wish yourself dead," I told her. "No matter what, we must think about surviving."

I told her we'd get out someday soon, and the twins would need her to be their mother. She laughed about our mother, but bitterly, and I told her the truth. I told her I knew our mother would always think of herself first and us second, but that was all right, because I would always look after her. She started to cry and told me she was sorry she had all those bad thoughts and she wouldn't think about death anymore. She pleaded with me to do something.

"Remember what Daddy told us often," she said. "God helps those who help themselves."

"I'll think about it," I said. "But she might be telling us the truth this time. We might be close, and any day now, we could all come into that fortune."

She turned away. I kissed her cheek. She closed her eyes.

She's right, a voice inside me said, but another said, What if you ruined everything after all this time and suffering? How would you feel then?

Somehow, some way, I had to find enough strength to go on, strength for all of us.

"No one really knows what these kids suffered up there," Kane said with disgust when he stopped reading. "I mean, all I've ever heard or read was that they were locked away for some time, but how they were treated by their own damn family, the crap they went through, these details . . . it makes me want to throw up."

"Horrible," I said. He looked lost in thought. I glanced at my watch. "We'd better go down. It's getting late, and I have some things I have to do before my father gets home."

He really looked upset enough not to argue about reading a little longer. He nodded, and we organized the attic again. It didn't take long. We hadn't moved much this time. We didn't even open the windows for a little fresh air, because Kane had been so eager to start. He followed me down to my room, and I slipped the diary under my pillow.

"Don't you have a better place to hide it?" he asked. "I mean, if we should lose it now, I think I'd go bonkers not having reached the end."

"It's as safe as anywhere there. We don't have a maid," I said. "I make my own bed, clean my own room."

"I wasn't thinking of that," he said, lowering his gaze to avoid mine.

"Despite how he feels about it, my father would never take it away," I told him. In the beginning, I wasn't so confident, but I was now, now that my father had seen how important it was to me. I wasn't surprised that Kane was skeptical about it, though. His parents would probably break promises as easily as bending straws. "Trust me, Kane."

"Okay."

We went downstairs. He paused at the door, and I could see something else was bothering him. Even though he was looking right at me, he wasn't seeing me. He was too deep in thought. "What are you thinking?" I asked.

"I was wondering . . ."

"What?" I followed quickly when he looked like he was about to change his mind about telling me.

"I hope you don't think less of me because of what I told you up there about my mother, the reason she became pregnant, all of that."

"Why would I think less of you? You didn't do anything wrong. If anything, you're the victim. I think less of your mother and father. I'll say that. I'd even tell them."

He smiled. "I bet you would." He kissed me. It was a thank-you kiss, quick, but a little static electricity snapped, and we both laughed. "I'm a shocking guy," he said.

Just as I opened the door, the house phone rang. "Maybe it's my father," I said.

Kane waited while I went to the phone. It wasn't my father. It was my aunt Barbara.

"Everything's changed. I feel very good," she said. "I'm coming for Thanksgiving. I'll stay until Saturday."

"That's wonderful, Aunt Barbara."

I copied down her flight number and arrival time and told Kane.

He could see how excited and happy I was, but he didn't smile or look happy for me. "She's flying in tomorrow?"

"That's the flight she could get."

"We probably won't get together on Sunday," he said mournfully.

"Oh, you can come over when she's here."

"I don't mean that," he said.

I realized what he meant. I just didn't want to acknowledge it, to confirm that reading the diary was more important than anything else to him now, even just seeing me. For a moment, I had the crazy idea that once we had finished it, he would break up with me.

As weird as it might seem, that idea reminded me of the *Arabian Nights*. A Persian king, shocked to discover that his new bride was unfaithful, had her executed and then began to marry virgins, only to execute each the following day. It went on until he married Scheherazade, who began telling him a story without giving him the end. It went on and on for a thousand and one nights, because as long as she kept from revealing the ending, he didn't execute her. Would Kane and I go on and on for our thousand and one nights and then stop when we reached the ending?

Maybe there was no ending.

"We're not going anywhere, Kane, and neither is that diary. There's no rush. Stop worrying."

"Right. I just hope it doesn't take us as long to finish it as it took them to get out," he said. Then he realized he was being too intense and laughed. "Poor joke. Sorry. Do I pick you up in the morning?"

"No, leave it like it is for now," I told him, which was another thing he didn't want to hear. "Especially with my aunt arriving," I added, to make him feel better about it. "I'm thinking I might need my car after school if I have to pick her up."

"I'd be glad to do that with you."

"I know. I just . . . just want some time alone with her. We don't see each other that often."

"Okay," he said, and started for his car. He looked so tentative, so unsure of himself suddenly. At this moment, at least, he wasn't the Kane Hill everyone was used to seeing. I knew he was still regretting telling me about his parents and him. *It's the magic of the diary*, I thought. *It makes us tell each other secrets we otherwise wouldn't.*

I smiled and waved, and he smiled back. He drove off slowly, looking like he was still in deep thought. I hoped it wasn't so deep that he would drive carelessly.

I felt like my emotions were stuck on a yo-yo. Upstairs in the attic, we were awash in dark, sad, and troubling events, and then, as fast as a yo-yo could come up, my aunt Barbara's phone call raised me to ecstatic happiness. This would be a real Thanksgiving for us after all, with her and my father telling family stories.

I should do something to dress up the house, I thought, make it more festive. We had some Thanksgiving decorations from years past buried in a laundry-room closet. My father wouldn't think of it, but I would create a centerpiece for our table. Perhaps Aunt Barbara would want to help me do that. I knew just where we could get some rustic elements like beeswax candles and gourds and then do a flower arrangement of roses, hydrangeas, some dahlias, and a few sprigs of fall greenery. We hadn't put a pumpkin out this Halloween, but I thought I'd get one now.

I hurried to call my father. I knew how pleased he would be and how, for a while, at least, the holidays would ring true for us again. Even though Todd and his family and Mrs. Osterhouse were here, there were still those moments when everyone else talked about their families and he and I listened with frozen smiles on our faces, afraid to remember too much. I was really excited about this Thanksgiving now.

I knew Kane didn't like it, but the Dollanganger children would have to wait.

They had waited so long. Another pause for another holiday wouldn't matter now.

My father's voice reflected the same joy I felt. He had tried not to show it, but I saw how disappointed he was when Aunt Barbara had told him she wasn't coming. Now I wished that somehow Uncle Tommy could be with us, too. The last time I remembered the four of us together was at my mother's funeral.

"Weddings and funerals," my father told me, "famous for bringing in the strays."

"We have enough food for five more guests, probably," my father said, "but I know she loves that marshmallow sweet potato dish. I wasn't planning on doing it, so we'll have to get the marshmallows later."

"I can pick her up," I said. "She flies in about a half hour after school ends."

"Yes, that might work," he said. "I have a few tricky things to do here before we think about breaking for Thanksgiving. I'll be home soon. I've got those pork chops calling for hungry mouths."

"Yes, I hear them screaming in the refrigerator," I told him, and he laughed.

It was so good to laugh, to feel hopeful and happy. We were getting the Dollanganger children's tragedy almost blow-by-blow from Christopher in his diary, but I still couldn't imagine being shut up without the love of family for so long.

Even a day was too long for me.

Just as it was before most holidays, the excitement was explosive at school. Voices were louder, everyone walked faster, teachers could feel their students chafing at the bit, every bell that rang was drawing us all closer and closer to the one that would open the doors and let us all out, teachers, students, administrators, and janitors, all rushing toward good food and good company. I felt sorry for the building left so deserted and dark behind us. It looked like an orphan.

Just as they were yesterday, my friends and Kane's

were still curious about the way he was behaving. He was so much quieter. His smiles were rarer than his laughter, and even when he was with just me, he seemed somewhere else, his eyes vacant. He didn't want to walk with anyone else or sit at a particular table with his buddies. When I was in the girls' bathroom, Missy Meyer, who was in Kane's English class, made a point of telling me how annoyed Mr. Feldman became when Kane's response to a question was a sharp "I don't know."

"'You should know,' Mr. Feldman told him. He acts like he's angry at everyone for something. What happened to him? Did he have some big fight with his parents or something? Are you two going to break up?"

"No," I said with surgical finality, and washed my hands quickly.

She hovered, persistent. "So what's the matter with him? You must notice it, too."

"Whatever it is, it's personal," I said. "Get on with your life."

I wasn't usually as curt or nasty with the girls in my class, even Tina Kennedy, but I didn't know what else to say or how else to get them off the topic. I was certainly not going to tell them he was disturbed about things he had read in Christopher Dollanganger's diary. However, that thought gave me an idea.

The next time Kane and I were alone and far enough away for anyone else to hear me speak, I told him his behavior was attracting unwanted attention to us both. He seemed genuinely surprised, like someone who was told he was sleepwalking.

"What behavior?"

"I see how you are, Kane, and I know why. Try to do what I do. Now, especially because of the details we've learned, I basically put the diary out of my mind until we go up to my attic. You can't keep thinking about it, ignoring your classwork, ignoring your friends, even ignoring me most of the time."

"I didn't realize . . ."

"You're making me regret reading the diary with you," I said tersely. "Everyone thinks you're sulking about something, and that perks up their curiosity about us."

He nodded. "You're right."

"Pretend if you have to, but don't attract any attention we don't want. It could get back to your parents and then maybe my father."

"Understood." He looked around and then straightened his posture and smiled. "Back to Kane Hill."

"Good."

He did make an effort during the day, and between the last two classes of the day, he spent some time joking with his buddies. At the end of the day, we made plans for when we would see each other over the long holiday weekend. We decided to plan on something for Sunday. Our teachers were merciful this time and didn't assign a great deal to be done before we returned.

I went off to the airport to greet my aunt Barbara. I spotted her instantly as she came through the entrance to the gate. She was an inch or so shorter than my father and had hair just a shade darker than mine. She kept it cropped short around the edges of her ears but held on to her bangs. At forty-one, she still had what my father called "her girlish figure," because she was "Lauren Bacall slim." She had dainty, diminutive features, highlighted by exquisite hazel eyes. Maybe she knew that because most people don't look so directly at you when they speak to you or when you speak to them. My father said she always had that New York arrogance, that look that said, "I can survive well in the city that never sleeps. I can hold my own on subways and on crowded streets. I can deal with the traffic and the noise, so just don't mess with me."

When my father told her all that to her face, she simply replied, "So? Don't mess with me."

There was a part of me that envied her and wanted to be more like her, but there was a stronger part that demanded that I be softer, more demure, closer to how I remember my mother. Aunt Barbara always looked like she had something to prove. I knew about her failed love affairs and thought that a woman like her had to find a man who was so self-confident that he was never threatened by her or one who was so weak he'd permit himself to be broken and trained like some wild horse. Somehow, I thought, Aunt Barbara would not want either kind, and therein lay her doom when it came to romance.

"Look at you!" she screamed, rushing toward me to kiss and embrace me. "You look like you've grown years since I last saw you, Kristin." She held me out at arm's length and loaded her face with suspicion. "Have we—what did you once tell me you called it?—crossed the Rio Grande?"

My face grew so flushed that I thought even the most anxious-to-be-home passengers would pause and look. It was just like my New York aunt to get right to the bottom line. It was why my father had thought of her immediately when he concluded that I had to learn the facts of life quickly. My father said everyone in New York City lived at twice the normal speed. They didn't stroll in New York, he said. "They walk those sidewalks as if they believe the city might roll them up at any moment."

"I'm sorry," Aunt Barbara said immediately. "It's none of my business. You're entitled to your secrets, as entitled as I am to mine." She scrunched up her nose. "When your father's not looking, we'll get drunk, and you'll tell me anyway," she said.

I laughed, but I wondered if I would.

"Speaking of him, how is my Captain Queeg of a brother?" she asked. I picked up her carryon, and we started out of the terminal. I had seen *The Caine Mutiny* and knew that Queeg was the no-nonsense captain who went off the deep end, chasing down missing strawberries and clicking steel balls in his hand.

"He's a pussycat, Aunt Barbara."

"We know that," she said, hugging me, "but never let him know we know."

After we got into my car and started for home, she became more serious, wanting to know how my father really was.

"I've known widowers and widows," she said, "but I've rarely seen any who took the loss as hard. He buried a large part of himself with your mother. If it wasn't for you . . ."

"He's okay. He's strong. Really," I said. "We both are. We know it would wrong her to be anything else."

"That's very wise, Kristin. I'm so proud of you. And you're going to be valedictorian!"

"That's not for sure yet, Aunt Barbara. I'm neck and neck with someone."

"I'm betting on you, but you're already valedictorian in our family," she said. She asked who was coming to Thanksgiving dinner, and I told her about Mrs. Osterhouse.

"I'd like to get to know the woman who thinks she could live with my brother," she joked. "Last time I was here, I put a fork in the wrong slot in the drawer, and he was ready to ship me out."

We both laughed. This was going to happen, I told myself. I was going to be able to step outside the attic for days.

My father arrived a little less than an hour after I had helped Aunt Barbara settle into the guest room, so I knew he was anxious to greet her. The three of us sat in the living room, and I listened to them catch up on their lives and their contact with Uncle Tommy, whom I could see they both really wished was with us. My father decided to take us out for dinner.

His favorite restaurant besides Charley's Diner was a Mediterranean-themed restaurant that emphasized Italian and Spanish cuisine. It had four or five stars on all the Internet sites, and I knew from the start that my father wanted to prove to Aunt Barbara that there were restaurants just as sophisticated in Charlottesville as any in her precious New York. Before the night was over, she had to admit he was right.

He gloated, and she and I covered our smiles and winked to each other when we thought he wasn't looking, but my father was always tuned in to what was going on around him.

"All right," he said. "All right. I know when I'm outnumbered and outgunned."

It was a wonderful first night of my Thanksgiving holiday.

"I'm so glad I could do this," Aunt Barbara told me before we went to sleep.

"So am I," I said, "and so is Dad. Very much."

We hugged, and I went to bed, for the first time in a long time not hearing Christopher Dollanganger whispering beneath my pillow.

The following day was taken up with last-minute shopping for our dinner and Aunt Barbara and me getting the centerpiece and the decorations done. While we were away, Mrs. Osterhouse brought Dad the turkey he had ordered. He liked to brine it for at least one full day. He said it was the secret to perfect juicy turkey. Aunt Barbara confessed that she wasn't much of a cook. She knew how good my father was and told me one of the main reasons she had come was for his dinner. While I drove about, she told me more stories about their youth.

Despite how I wanted to avoid it, it seemed impossible for me now to ever hear stories about brothers and sisters without thinking about Christopher and Cathy. She told me about how protective my father was of her, and I really could appreciate how much she admired him. Perhaps just as much as Cathy admired Christopher.

Years later, could they ever talk about what their lives were like at Foxworth? Did they have horrible flashbacks, wake up at night from images of their living nightmare? Could they comfort each other?

As if she knew what I was thinking, on the way home, Aunt Barbara suddenly said, "So tell me about this diary that was found at Foxworth."

For a moment, I was too stunned to speak. Even though Aunt Barbara was my father's sister, I never suspected that he had revealed it and discussed it with her. First, I was upset that he had done so without telling me, mainly because I believed it was something only he and I shared. I realized immediately how hypocritical being upset because of that was. After all, I had revealed it and was reading it with Kane. Second, I didn't know what he had told her. Could it be that he knew I was reading it with Kane, and this was his way of telling me? Or he suspected it, and this was his way of finding out?

"I didn't know Dad had told you about it," I began. I glanced at her and turned back to watch where I was driving. We were almost home.

"He's worried about your reading it," she said.

"I know."

"Have you finished reading it?"

"Not yet. I've been busy, and it's not easy to take," I said.

"Exactly why he's worried about it," she said.

"I can handle it."

"Oh, I don't doubt you can, but why bother now? You can't do anything to change what happened. I remember how much it all disturbed your mother. Did you know that at one point, your parents were considering moving from Charlottesville?"

"No. I knew she didn't want to talk about it or hear about it, but I didn't know it had ever been that bad."

"It was. A reporter from the *New York Times* once came to visit your mother. Of course, they were doing a Halloween special, and the story attracted an editor's interest. When your mother refused to talk to him, he went around trying to dig up stuff and implied that your mother knew way more than she had ever revealed, even though she had little or nothing to do with the Foxworth family. That set off people she knew who were after her to confide in them. She lost friends over it."

"Dad never told me about that."

"I'm sure he didn't tell you about the fight he got into, either," she added, and I slowed down.

"What fight?"

"It didn't last long. It was one of those one-punch deals. I forget exactly where they were, an event of some sort, and some woman made a nasty remark about your mother's relationship to the mad Foxworth family. Your father said something to her, and then her husband came at him, and your father floored him. I just happened to talk to them that night. You weren't even born yet," she said. "It was around then that they toyed with moving away. The only reason I'm telling you about it is so you'll understand why your father isn't happy about your having that diary. You haven't told anyone about it, have you?"

I felt my throat tighten up. It was as if my whole body was revolting against even the possibility of my lying, and yet I didn't want to confess to my aunt Barbara and not to my father. That would add pain.

I shook my head.

"How much more do you have to read?"

"Not much."

She was silent.

"Did my father ask you to tell me all this?"

"Sorta," she said.

I pulled into the driveway and pressed the garage door opener.

"Let's just forget about it," she said. "I can see you're old enough to deal with anything like that anyway, and I'll tell him not to worry about you. Okay?"

I nodded.

"I mean it, Kristin. We don't want to insert any darkness into this holiday and our time together." She reached over to squeeze my hand gently.

I nodded again, and we got out and brought everything into the house. I really worked at not showing how disturbed I was, even though I was still trembling a little inside. Right before our dinner, Kane called to tell me how things were going at his house. Relatives had arrived for the next day's Thanksgiving "extravaganza," as he called it.

"Darlena, Julio, and I are going out for Chinese. My mother's not happy about it, but my father said it would be all right. All three of us feel like sailors getting liberty at a port." He laughed. "How's it going there?"

It was on the tip of my tongue to burst out with everything my aunt Barbara had told me and tell him that our reading the diary together would have to end, but I was afraid to do so. His commitment to it and how seriously he was taking it, especially now, convinced me he would take it very badly. I had no idea how that would turn out, but I was positive it would be worse than things were now.

"Everything okay?" he asked after I described my day with my aunt. He could hear some worry in my voice, I was sure.

"Yes," I said quickly. "Say hello to your sister and Julio for me, and have a good Thanksgiving."

"It can't be good without you," he said. Kane wasn't one to layer on smooth talk with me or with anyone else. I knew he sincerely believed what he said. I didn't respond the way most people would and automatically say the same thing.

"Maybe next year, we'll celebrate together," I

suggested, and immediately wondered if people our age really ever thought or talked in terms of the future with each other. In our case, we surely wouldn't be attending the same college. No matter how intense our feelings for each other were at the moment, would they survive time and distance and, maybe more important, socializing with others? Did romances like ours simply thin out until they broke? In the beginning, did we flood every free moment with phone calls and letters and then slowly wind them down, subtly bringing it to an end?

"Sure," Kane said. "As long as your father prepares the dinner."

I had to laugh at that. He would prepare the dinner for sure.

"I'll see you Sunday, right?" Kane said.

"Right. I'll call you with our schedule for the day."

Later that evening, after we had eaten, we sat and talked in the living room, where my father went on about the project at Foxworth and showed Aunt Barbara the plans. Then I went up to my room, intending to go right to sleep. Aunt Barbara surprised me, however, and knocked on my door just after I had gotten into my pajamas.

"Hi."

"Hi," I said, a little surprised.

"I wanted to be sure I didn't disturb you with what I told you in your car earlier," she began.

"It's okay. I'm fine with forgetting about it."

She gazed about my room, smiling at my collection of dolls on a shelf and some of my movie posters, then paused to look at pictures of my mother and my father when they were first married. "I remember their wedding as if it happened yesterday," she said. "We used to worry about your father finding someone who could make him happy. He was always so demanding, expecting so much of people he said he 'invested in.' Then she came along and turned him into a softy."

"He's still a softy, but only with me," I said.

She nodded. "He's really excited about this project. I guess it's the biggest thing he's done."

"Yes."

She paused, looking like she was afraid to say anything more. What more was she going to tell me?

"What, Aunt Barbara?" I asked, smiling.

"I was curious and wondering if you would show me that diary. I don't want to read it all, just look at it."

"Sure," I said, and slipped it out from under my pillow.

She widened her eyes at that. "That's where you keep it?"

"I did the first night and just kept doing it."

I handed it to her, and she took it gingerly, treating it like some historical parchment. I watched her open the cover and skim the first page. "So old, and yet it hasn't been damaged by the weather."

"It was in a metal box," I said.

"He had very nice handwriting, so precise," she said, gazing at the page. "Was he very bright? Can you tell?"

"Oh, yes. Very bright," I said. "He wanted to become a doctor."

"Really? I never paid much attention to what happened to them afterward, after the original fire."

"Their mother ended up in a mental clinic."

"What about them—the children?"

"No one seems to know for sure. Lots of rumors suggesting they changed their names, maybe even left the country. Did my father tell you anything more about the new owner of the property?"

"No. What more is there?"

"Not much. There's a corporation or something involved."

"It's not going to be a hotel or something, is it?"

"No."

She shrugged. "Glad someone is building there."

"Were you ever there?"

"No. I never had any interest, and your mother and father never wanted to show me the property."

She handed the diary back to me. She looked like she wished I had told her to take it and just get rid of it or something.

"I don't really want to know the details," she said. "I see enough horror stories on the daily news as it is. Well, good night. Sweet dreams." She hugged me and left.

I stood there thinking about her and suddenly felt myself become as paranoid about it as Kane had been. She wouldn't come in here and just take it, I thought. But what if she did? What if she took it, and then later both she and my father told me they had decided it was better to bury it again?

Instead of putting it back under my pillow, I shoved it down under some books in a carton at the bottom of my closet, and then I put pairs of shoes and some hangers on top of the box.

It's making me crazy, I thought. But I couldn't stop what we were doing now. Maybe I would find a way to get through it faster with Kane.

No matter what that would mean.

Thanksgiving dinner was as wonderful as I had hoped it would be. Todd Winston and his wife, Lisa, brought their children—Josh, who was ten, and twelve-year-old Brandy, two of the most well-behaved children I knew. Lisa was a fifth-grade teacher, a Charlottesville resident all her life, as was Todd. It was easy to see how both she and Todd had adopted my father to be their children's grandfather. I used to be a little jealous of how much they loved him and how concerned he always was for their welfare, but I was beyond those days when my childish insecurity caused me to envy and dislike any other girl or woman he spoke to in my presence. He was, as Darlena had said, a Southern gentleman, as polite and courteous as Ashley Wilkes in *Gone with the Wind*.

Aunt Barbara and I were both attentive to every comment or look between my father and Mrs. Osterhouse, who was never as insistent that I call her Laura. I suppose I always had resisted because I knew that was the beginning of breaking down a wall I had put up between her and my father, or him and any other woman, for that matter. I caught little things this time that I hadn't seen before. When she touched him while they spoke, he didn't recoil. Occasionally, she whispered something to him, and he smiled. She was at his side as much as she could be, helping in the kitchen, making it possible, as she put it, for me to spend more time with Aunt Barbara. She and I smiled at that.

"She's very attractive," Aunt Barbara whispered. "I usually go by first impressions. I think she adores him."

I looked at the two of them again and for the first time wondered if they had been seeing each other secretly, at least secretly when it came to me. I nodded.

"You're going off to college," Aunt Barbara said. She didn't have to follow it with "He's going to be very lonely." I knew what she meant.

I couldn't help thinking of how Christopher was reacting to his mother finding someone else to love. Our situations were in no way comparable, but I recognized that young children were selfish by nature. They want all the love. It takes time, years, for them to realize that their parents could have enough to go around.

While my father and Laura cleaned up the dishes and silverware after Aunt Barbara, Lisa, and I had helped clear the table, Todd and Lisa and their children sat with us in the living room and asked Aunt Barbara questions about life in New York as if it was truly another country, even another planet. I could see how amused she was and how kind she was with her answers. She made life there seem quite nice, in fact, listing all the advantages, the theaters, the public transportation, and the variety of stores and ethnic neighborhoods.

"Don't be afraid of New York," she told them. "It has a lot to offer, and you can remind yourself that you're returning to your world here."

Lisa looked fascinated.

She and Todd and their children left first. We sat with my father and Laura for a while afterward, and then Aunt Barbara gave me a look to say we should leave them alone for a while. She didn't wink, but I knew what she was saying, so I pretended to be much more tired than I was, and she did the same. We giggled going up the stairs. Actually, I had drunk more wine than ever, and I was a little giddy and a little more tired.

"You want to tell me about your boyfriend?" she asked at my door. "I heard his family is rich and he's good-looking and very popular."

"So you know it all," I said.

Her eyes widened, and then she smiled. "Got it," she said. "I'm going to bed." She leaned in to kiss me. "Your mother would be so proud of you." She walked off to the guest room.

I hadn't meant to shut her down so quickly, but I was afraid that if I began to talk about Kane, I would slip up and reveal what we were doing. Look what was happening to me, I thought. I was afraid to talk about things, afraid to make a mistake. Was it the same for Kane? It never had occurred to me until now that he might, just as I might, slip up and reveal something about reading the diary, perhaps when talking with his sister.

We needed to end this.

The only way to do it was to finish it.

I would be as determined as he was.

Before Aunt Barbara returned to New York, my father took her and me and, to my surprise, Laura Osterhouse to see the work accomplished at Foxworth. We followed him about as he explained the plans and helped us to visualize what would be there. Every once in a while, Aunt Barbara would look at me and with that look acknowledge how determined my father was to erase any exterior resemblance to the Foxworth property that had been there. He detailed the changes in the grounds, the driveway, the lighting, and all the new technology the house would have. This was in no way to be a restoration.

I didn't mention what he had told me about some of the similarities inside, but he did make the point that there would be no real attic in the new house, just a little more than a crawl space for storage. Afterward, we all went to lunch, and later that day, my father and Laura insisted on preparing leftovers. She said she wanted to watch the magic he could do with them, making it all seem like a brand-new meal.

In the morning, my father and I took Aunt Barbara to the airport. He promised her that he would find the time for us to visit her in New York. She rattled on about all the things she would arrange for us to do. I could see how excited the possibility of her brother's visit made her. She vowed to call Uncle Tommy and twist his arm so he would come to New York at the same time. It all seemed fabulous but more like a fantasy to me.

Aunt Barbara held on to me longer when we hugged. "You've done a wonderful job with my brother," she said. "I think it was a case of the daughter bringing up the father. Encourage him to get out more," she added.

I knew what she meant and assured her that I would.

After she left and we were heading home, my father was quieter than usual. How important family was, I thought. How much we would forgive each other to keep our family bonds. It helped me understand why Christopher was so desperate to believe in his mother. I also realized that my father needed more than just me in his life. He had a wide hole in his heart that he had to fill. It was so important to have someone who cared about you and for whom you could care. He would always have me but not in the way he had me now. No one mentions that loneliness doesn't simply mean not having someone else there to be interested in you. It means having no one there for you to devote your time and your energy to protect and comfort. It means not being able to give of yourself and not simply take from others.

No wonder Christopher was clinging so hard to

Cathy and they so easily accepted caring for their little brother and sister. I wished I could say, *See, Dad? Reading the diary isn't all horror and pain for me. It's teaching me something valuable.*

But it wasn't time to say that, not yet, perhaps not ever.

When we got home, my father suggested that he would take Laura Osterhouse and me out to dinner.

"I'm sure you're both tired of leftovers," he said.

"Actually, I'm not," I said. "I know there's enough left. Do you mind terribly if I don't go?" I smiled. "I might invite someone to help me finish off the food."

He looked suspicious for a moment and then laughed. "Okay. I'll leave you to do the warming up."

"I have a few tricks up my sleeve when it comes to those leftovers," I said. "I've spied on you enough."

He nodded and went to call Laura. I hurried up to my room to call Kane. I had no doubt he would rush over the moment he could. We'd eat, but we'd go upstairs and move ahead in the diary, no matter where it took us.

He was there a half hour later.

Just one look at me, and he knew. My father had left. We ate fast, both too anxious, anticipating. Afterward, silently, both our hearts racing with anticipation, we started up the stairway. I had forgotten I had moved the diary.

"Something happen?" he asked quickly when he saw me take it from under the things in my closet.

"No, but I became a little worried after my aunt's questions about it."

He nodded, and we went up to the attic. Again, in a deeper silence than usual, we arranged things, and he took the diary, sat, and began.

After five days had passed without Momma's return, I told Cathy she was punishing us for being ungrateful. At first, she flared up.

"We're being ungrateful? We?"

I explained that Momma was just very sensitive now. We didn't know exactly what she was going through outside of this little bedroom and attic. Look how she had been whipped once.

"She's probably walking on tiptoes, dancing like a ballerina," I said, and Cathy relaxed, nodded, and agreed not to be nasty to Momma whenever she returned.

She didn't come back for another five days, but when she did, we were as sweet and grateful as we could be.

Then Momma dropped her bombshell.

She told us she had married the attorney, Bart Winslow. I could see how excited she was. She raved about all his good qualities and told us he had always been in love with her. I felt a tightness in my chest and in my throat. For a few moments, I couldn't speak. All this had been going on, her romance, her marriage, and her honeymoon, while we lingered here in the tiny bedroom and the attic, waiting, hoping to be free. I glanced at Cathy and shook my head slightly. This wasn't the time for a blowup, but we were both hoping that when she saw Carrie and Cory and how they reacted to her, how strange and aloof they had become, she would realize we must be taken out of here now.

"Does he know about us?" Cathy asked before I could.

"Not yet," she told us. She was waiting for her father to die first, and she assured us that Bart would understand why she had hidden us.

Again, I gave Cathy the look that said, Don't. Don't start a fight.

Afterward, I tried to be as optimistic as I could. Although it pained me to do so, I used logic and reason, telling her it made sense. How could she reveal us to Bart Winslow now while our grandfather was alive?

"But maybe we don't need his money now, Chris," she rightly said. "A lawyer should have enough money to care for us all."

For a moment, I was stuck, and then I said, "Yes, but he's our grandfather's lawyer, and he probably makes most of his money working for him. What do you think our grandfather would do? He'd fire him, and then what would we have gained?"

Reluctantly, she agreed. I was happy I had calmed her, but I was sad, too, because she had been right.

Time, like a dripping icicle, began to wear on and on. Winter was coming again. The attic would soon be too cold for us. Day after day,

Cathy and I cared for the twins and spent our free time reading, lying together on the old mattress near the window, talking about one of the books Momma had brought up from the house library. We were talking more about love now, about what it meant to fall in love with someone. Being so close to her for so long, I could see the dramatic changes, not only in her body but also in the way she was thinking about herself, and yes, about me, wondering about the changes in me. I knew it was wrong to think it and feel it, but what was happening between us whenever we had those conversations was the most thrilling thing right now, something I looked forward to doing, feeling.

She was so cute, so eager to have romance and be loved just like any girl her age, but unlike any girl her age, she was locked away from parties, from flirting, from having crushes and giggling about silly little things. I missed all these things, too, although I would never admit it. I tried to feel sorrier for her than for myself. We laughed and giggled, and I hugged her and kissed her cheeks, and just as suddenly, I felt myself drawn to her even closer. I couldn't stop looking at her, at the way her breasts were forming, at the smooth lines of her neck, the gracefulness of her legs, her thighs.

I saw that she realized how I was looking at her, and I couldn't help but feel the blood rush into my face. I turned away as quickly as I could and then told her that all this talk about romance that we read in books was just silly. She got mad at me and accused me, along with all men, of wanting the same romantic things. She was right, of course. I couldn't stand it and lost myself for a moment, wailing just as she would about all I was missing but, more important, how I had to hold back all my manly feelings because we were forbidden to do this or that by a grandmother who was just waiting to pounce on us. I ranted until she reached out and touched me so lovingly and gently I had to stop.

"I understand," she said. "I know what you're missing, too."

I squinted at her. How could she know? Did she figure it out from all those silly romance stories? She tried to make me feel better, telling me she'd cut my hair and that when we were free, girls would chase after me because I was so handsome. She went for the scissors, and she cut my hair, shaping it like an artist. I was shocked at how well she did. I told her she'd made me look like a prince, Prince Valiant or something. I wanted to cut and reshape her hair. She ran off, and I chased her around the attic until she fell and scratched herself. I went for our kit of bandages and antiseptic. All the while, as I treated her, I could feel her eyes on me. I tried not to look into hers, but it was impossible. I had tears in my eyes. It was my fault. I shouldn't have chased her.

She cupped my face just like Momma often did and drew me to her breast, stroking my hair and telling me it wasn't my fault. I lay there quietly, my lips touching her naked breast. Neither of us spoke. I couldn't resist. I kissed her nipple, and she leaped up, surprised at what was going on inside her, too. I was sure of it. I was surprised when she asked me what happened next between a man and a woman. I assured her that I knew, but I also lied and told her that I didn't think about it, not the way other boys did. She asked me if I thought she was pretty. I had an ache inside me like never before, but I stayed calm. I buttoned her sweater, told her she was pretty, but also told her that brothers don't think of their sisters as girls, just as sisters. Wisely, I think, I decided we should go down to the twins. She followed me, but something had happened. She said she wondered if we had been sinful, as sinful as our grandmother expected us to be.

I didn't want to think of it that way, despite the voices I heard inside me. "If you think it's sinful, it is," I told her sharply, and she didn't ask again.

That night, when we went to bed, I couldn't stop thinking of her breasts, her nipples, the feel of her lips on my face, the softness of her skin, the softness between her thighs. I turned to look at her there in her bed and saw that she was looking at me. I couldn't help smiling at her, and she couldn't help smiling at me.

Kane paused and looked at me. A flush had come into my cheeks that matched his, I was sure. He didn't say anything, and neither did I. He closed the diary softly and came to me, kneeling at first and putting his head against my knees. Slowly, as if all resistance in my legs had evaporated, he nudged them apart and leaned in to kiss the insides of my thighs. I gasped and lay back against the sofa as his lips moved gently from my left to my right thigh, until he kissed me between my legs and kept his lips pressed into me. I felt his hands move up my thighs, his fingers move under the waistband of my panties and slowly edge them down.

"Oh, Kane," I finally said, and he stood and then slipped beside me on the sofa. We were dancing on the edge of the Rio Grande.

"I feel just like Christopher," he said. "I see no other girl but you. I might as well be locked in an attic with you for years and years."

We kissed. I let him undress me, but when he went to undress himself, I put my hand on his. "Not yet," I whispered. "Not yet."

I felt the depth of his disappointment, because I was feeling my own. We lay there, our hearts pounding against each other. He kissed me so passionately I almost surrendered, but I clung to *No, not yet*.

"Why?" he asked.

"Cathy hasn't," I said.

"But . . ." He was going to say *You're not Cathy*, but he didn't. "How do you know she will?" he asked.

"I know." I didn't know. I felt it, and I feared it.

"Whoever you do this with, Kristin, won't care for you as much as I do," he said. "Do you believe me?"

"Yes. I just feel . . . not ready," I said. "Please, understand."

He put his finger on my lips and then kissed me. "I do understand," he said. "But I wish I didn't."

That made me smile. He lowered his head to my breasts and closed his eyes. I ran my fingers through his hair and closed my eyes, too. We nearly fell asleep as we were, but I realized how long we had been in the attic, and I rushed to get dressed as he moved quickly to restore everything to the way it was. We went down to my room. I put the diary under my pillow again.

"What about tomorrow?"

"I don't know. Let me see what my father has planned."

He went into my bathroom and threw cold water on his face. I followed and fixed my hair, and then we went down and sat in the living room, watching television until my father arrived less than twenty minutes later. He looked like he'd had a good time. I pushed aside that little nugget of jealousy quickly.

"Hey, you guys," he said. "How'd she do on the leftovers, Kane?"

"Leftovers? I thought it was all new," he kidded.

My father smiled. "This is one clever young man. He knows what to say to glide over thin ice," he told me.

"How was your dinner?" I asked.

"Very nice. Laura found a new restaurant. Quite

homey, run by an Italian family. They call it Diana's, the family's last name. How was your Thanksgiving dinner, Kane?"

"Bountiful," Kane said.

"Well. I'm sure it was good," my father said, laughing. "I'm going up. I have some errands to run tomorrow."

"On Sunday?" I asked.

"I've got to visit this property just outside of Richmond. There are things about its landscaping that the Johnsons want me to see. I figured you'd be catching up on your homework, so I asked Laura to come along," he said. "We'll have breakfast before I go," he quickly added.

I glanced at Kane. His face was lit with expectation and happiness. My father would be gone most of the day. We could be back in the attic.

"Okay," I said. "Yes, I did leave everything for tomorrow."

"Don't worry, Mr. Masterwood. I'll make sure she gets it done and has a good lunch."

"You'll make sure she gets it done? Now, why does that sound like a contradiction?" my father joked.

Kane laughed, and I forced a smile. *Be still, my jealous heart*, I told myself. *Remember what Aunt Barbara told you, asked you to do. Your father has needs, too.*

"I'd better get going, too," Kane said, standing. "Good night, Mr. Masterwood."

"'Night," Dad said.

I walked Kane to the door. As soon as my father

was out of earshot, Kane seized my hand and said, "Isn't this great? Maybe we can finish the diary tomorrow."

"Maybe," I said.

"Call me the moment he leaves."

"Why do I think you might be hiding outside just to see when he leaves?"

"Very funny." He thought a moment. "Maybe that's not a bad idea."

"It is a bad idea. If he sees you just waiting . . . that early, too . . ."

"Okay, okay. Good night," he said, and kissed me softly, his lips lingering on mine. "Until tomorrow."

I watched him leave. *Until tomorrow.* How many nights did Christopher and Cathy think that? Tomorrow never seemed to come for them. How could they live so long with their mother's promises and not lose all hope? Something was happening to them. It had nothing to do with them getting sick, either. They had nowhere to go to explore and discover their own sexuality but inside themselves. It wasn't going to end well, and I didn't mean only whatever happened to their little brother. I was so tempted now to read ahead, but just like every time since Kane and I had begun to read it together, I feared he would feel betrayed. Somehow, for some reason, it didn't seem like something I could do alone.

Usually, even on Sundays, I'd be up by the time my father rose in the morning, but this Sunday, I slept late, so late that he had to come to my room to wake me. I heard him knock and then peek in.

"Hey, sleeping beauty, I wanted to spend time with you at breakfast. I'm working up your favorite omelet."

"Oh, sorry. What time is it?" I looked at the clock. Dreams, I thought, dreams had kept me sleeping later. They were a mixture of my life and Cathy Dollanganger's. In one dream, my bedroom door opened, and Laura Osterhouse tiptoed in to pour tar on my hair. When I sat up in the dream, she wasn't there. Kane was watching from the doorway. I did wake up, and because the dream was so vivid, I ran my fingers through my hair. Relieved, I went back to sleep.

"I'll be right down," I said, and he left. I did rush to get dressed. I so wanted to spend time with him before he left. He had everything ready, the table set, the oranges squeezed into fresh juice, and fresh bagels on a plate with my favorite ginger jelly.

Suspicion reared its ugly head.

Was he being extra nice to me because he felt guilty about his new, more demonstrable interest in Laura Osterhouse? Or perhaps it wasn't as new as I thought. Perhaps he had been seeing her more than I knew. Was he about to make a life-changing announcement? I watched him closely as he moved about the kitchen.

"You feeling okay?" he asked when I began eating, very slowly, almost as if I had no appetite.

"I'm good," I said. "So what exactly are you going to do today?"

"As it turns out, there's a close example of the

architect's work that I've been encouraged to visit. There's also been a serious modification to the plans."

"What do you mean? What modification?"

"We're going to install an elevator," he said.

"But it's only two levels, right?"

"Right, but if someone can't navigate the stairway, it doesn't matter if it's two, three, or four levels."

"Who's going to live in this house? Don't you know that yet?"

He shook his head.

I paused and sat back. "That's weird, Dad. How can you build a house for someone you don't know? I mean, someone who doesn't watch it going up and make comments? Is it an investment property after all? A house built to sell? Are they asking you for an elevator so it could sell to anyone, even a very elderly person or something? I don't get it."

He shrugged. "I ask and am basically told not to be concerned, just do the work and follow the plans. Hey, workers in car factories don't worry about who will eventually be driving them."

"You're not a factory worker. You're a personal builder," I said, perhaps too sharply.

"What can I do? I'm not walking off the job because I don't know the personal stuff. I'll build the house they want, make sure the landscaping is what they want, and hand over the keys to whomever when the time comes. What happens next is none of my business. I will say, Foxworth will be gone. Maybe people will stop asking us about it."

"You never told me about the fight you had over it," I said.

"Your aunt can gossip like a hen in heat," he said.

"Why didn't you ever tell me about that?"

"Roosters don't gossip."

"Chicken," I said, and he laughed.

"I might not be back for dinner," he revealed. "There's a ribeye in the freezer and some chicken cutlets and—"

"Don't worry about me. Where are you going for dinner?"

"Not sure yet. I figure since I'm close to Richmond, there's an old navy buddy of mine I might meet, he and his wife."

"That's nice," I said.

"If you want me to get back, I can—"

"Dad, just have a good time, will you? I'll be on my own most of the time very soon."

He nodded, and we finished breakfast.

I told him I'd take care of all the cleaning up so he could get going.

"I hope Laura's ready," he muttered. "Been a while since I waited on a woman to get herself ready."

"You've waited for me," I said, and immediately regretted it. "But I know you're as patient as a Venus flytrap."

"I'm afraid she knows that, too," he said. "All right if I take your car?"

"Sure. I've got my own chauffeur now."

So does Laura Osterhouse, I wanted to add, but I didn't. There it was again, that nugget of jealousy bouncing beneath my breasts. I tried to shut it down quickly, smiled, and gave him a hug, wishing him a good trip and a nice time.

"And if you worry about me just once . . ." I warned.

He held up his hands. "Keep that shark out of my water," he said, and walked off.

When I heard the door close behind him, I couldn't stop my eyes from tearing up.

It was all happening quickly, the future. Most of the time, people talked about how sad parents were to see their children grow up and away from them. Maybe there was something wrong with me, but unlike my friends, I wasn't eager to rush into adulthood and get away from everything that tied me to my life as it was now. There was that inevitable conflict of emotions coming on graduation day. We'd party and congratulate one another on cutting the ties that bound us to parental authority and all the rules that made us feel too young. But sometime during that celebrating, we were all sure to pause and feel not only a little sadness about putting away our childhood but also a little more fear than we'd be willing to admit or show. Nevertheless, it would all be there. I was simply anticipating it sooner than my friends, probably because of what I had already lost when my mother died, and where the future would take both my father and me, on different paths to different places.

I was in such deep thought about it that I didn't realize how much time had gone by until the phone rang. It was Kane.

"What's happening?" he asked.

"You can come now," I said.

"I'm on my way," he replied.

I hung up and gazed toward the attic, where I knew Christopher Dollanganger was waiting to finish his story. What would happen after that or because of it was actually somewhat terrifying for all the reasons I had conjured up along the way.

Somehow, despite what my father believed, I was convinced that Foxworth would not be gone.

Not ever.

Kane was here in record time.

"We're going to have all day," I said, revealing my father's plans as we walked up to my room. "No need to rush along."

"Okay. I've put aside all my other important appointments," he kidded.

I thought it was time to tell him about the house. I got out the diary but held on to it and sat on my bed.

"What's up?"

"There's another mystery at work here," I began.

He joined me on the bed. "Really? What?"

"It's about the new house my father is building. Apparently, the man who hired him is not the man who's going to live there. The title to the property is under a trust or something, and the one who is really involved in this turns out to be who we believe was Corrine Dollanganger's psychiatrist when she was taken to that clinic after the fire she caused in the original mansion."

"Your father told you all this?"

"Yes, but he doesn't know much more than that and doesn't care to know."

"The answers to that won't be in the diary, will they?"

"Probably not."

He nodded and then stood. I hesitated. "Something else you want to tell me?"

"No."

He knew what I was thinking. "It won't be the same reading it anywhere else," he said. "It's too . . ."

"Bright and happy down here," I finished for him. He nodded.

"Okay." I rose, and we walked up to the attic.

"I couldn't sleep last night," he said when we had settled in, him on his chair and me on the opened sofa.

"Dreams?"

"Yes, but mine were mostly about you," he said. "Just as I know Christopher's dreams have become mostly about Cathy at this point."

"Would they be about me if we weren't reading the diary?" I asked.

The question threw him for a moment. It was obviously something that hadn't ever occurred to him. He smiled. "Of course. Remember, I was after you before you told me about the diary, Kristin."

"Good answer," I said, and he laughed.

"I will say, however, that my dreams about you are a lot more vivid."

"I hope I'm not undressed in every one of them."

"You must be spying on my dreams."

I lay back and closed my eyes. I was doing that whenever he read now. The words were playing like a movie on the insides of my eyelids.

He took a deep breath and opened the diary, delving into it like a deep-sea diver.

Cathy was constantly talking about her dreams, mostly nightmares involving either our grandmother or our mother. I was having nightmares, too, but I didn't want to harp on them. I knew we couldn't go on like this much longer, and one day soon, I promised her, we would escape, all four of us. The first problem was the key that unlocked the doors, a key I now knew was a master key for most other doors, too. My promise excited Cathy and filled her with renewed hope. I told her we had to keep this plan secret, and to do that, it was best to let Momma believe we appreciated every little thing she was doing for us, buying for us. We even pretended to enjoy her stories about her own happiness.

On one of those occasions, Cathy kept Momma busy, asking her about her parties, her clothes, everything, while I slipped her key into my pocket, went into the bathroom, and pressed it into a bar of soap to get the impression. It took me three days after that to carve a successful hardwood version of it, but I did, and it worked.

But I told Cathy that an opening of the doors wasn't enough. We would need money once we got out, money to travel and live on. There was only one way now to get it, to venture out when

I could. I spent most of the winter pilfering from
Bart Winslow's pants and sometimes his wallet
whenever I found it in their bedroom. I wanted us
to have as much as possible, at least five hundred
dollars. Of course, Cathy was impatient. She
counted and recounted what we had, pressing
me to say it was enough. But it wasn't, and I had
to convince her that it would be worse for us
out there with two little children and no money.
Oddly, our grandmother was taking relatively good
care of us now, always there with the food, even
some dessert, powdered sugar doughnuts. Cathy
was still impatient. Finally, I asked her to come
along on a money mission. I thought she should
see the house, too, in all its grandeur. Our house
in Gladstone would fit at least three times in this
house. I especially wanted her to see our mother's
bedroom.

The truth was, I wanted to see her reaction to
the opulence, the sight of our mother's clothes
and jewelry and that swan bed. I wanted Cathy to
see how well Momma was living with us stashed
away like forgotten old clothes in an attic and a
bedroom one-quarter of the size of hers, and ours
for four of us. Her eyes nearly exploded at the
sight of it. She tested the bed and then went into
the walk-in closet. "There are more clothes here
than in a department store!" she cried. I smiled
to myself and began my search for money, rifling
through drawers, while she explored and then
began to experiment with Momma's makeup, just

the way she had when we lived in Gladstone. I wasn't paying attention to her now. I concentrated on searching every possible place, collecting even small change.

When I turned to her again, she had put on one of Momma's bras and stuffed it with tissues, was wearing high heels, all that makeup, and a ridiculous amount of jewelry, dozens of bracelets and rings. In my mind, it was like someone turning my mother into a cartoon. "Take all that off!" I told her. "You look like a streetwalker. Ridiculous."

Her joy collapsed like a balloon with a hole in it, but she took everything off.

"And put it all back neatly enough so no one will know it was used, Cathy. That's very important."

I didn't notice what she was doing next, but when I turned to her, I saw she was engrossed in a book. I stepped up behind her and looked at what she was reading. It was a book depicting couples having sex, showing a variety of positions, even pictures of multiple people having sex. For a moment, I couldn't breathe or take my eyes from the pages. She turned and looked up at me.

"We've got to get out of here now," I told her, and took the book out of her hands. "Put this where you found it!"

She said nothing, and I said nothing. I took her hand and quickly led her out of the room, through the halls, and back to our small bedroom.

"Chris, that book."

"Don't think about it," I said. "Go take your bath."

She checked on the twins and then went into the bathroom. I sat there, my body still trembling from seeing those vivid and explicit sex pictures. I was unaware of how much variety there was to what I thought was the simple act of intercourse, and those women, with their firm and large breasts, the curves in their waists, and what my father used to call "butts," quickened my heartbeat. I felt myself getting more and more aroused, and when Cathy finally emerged, looking soft, lithe, and graceful, her robe opened just enough for me to see most of her breasts, I quickly turned away and tried counting and multiplying numbers. Then I rose quickly and went into the bathroom to take my bath, but I couldn't help it. I had to relieve myself first. I was afraid I would appear again with my erection still firm, and Cathy would see. Now that she had seen those pictures, she would know exactly what was happening. She was still brushing her hair when I came out. I avoided looking at her until we were both in our beds. She was staring at me strangely. My mind was reeling with images and thoughts. I could simply slip in beside her, just to feel her against me. Maybe . . .

I was arousing myself again.

"Good night," I said quickly. She said good night, and we turned away from each other. Sleep couldn't come fast enough for me this night, I thought.

"Should I tell you how often this has happened to me since we started going together?" Kane asked, pausing.

"No," I said quickly. "Don't talk about it. Just read," I ordered, and he laughed.

"Yes, boss," he said. He stared at me a moment and then opened the diary again.

I had tried to look angry and bossy to keep him from seeing how riled up inside I was, too. Aside from my friend Suzette, who I always believed was the most promiscuous of all of us, none of us openly admitted to being sexually aroused at what we would all consider the most innocent occasions, like simply standing in the hall talking and watching some boys horse around with each other. One might grab at the other's crotch. She would openly admit to having orgasms at that sight and even having them when she went to try on jeans and they were too tight in her crotch. Most of us stared at her with amusement when she said things like this, half believing, but some of us, especially me, wondered if we were missing something by not being as sexually sensitive as she was. I almost asked my aunt Barbara about it, but I hesitated in the end.

Suzette swore that she had overheard her mother and a few of her friends talking about all this, confessing to having orgasms just looking at pictures of male models or something. Kyra told me Suzette's mother was "a bit trampy," but I had never seen her do or heard her say anything I'd consider off-color. As far as I could tell, she was critical of Suzette's loose ways, the sexy clothes she wore, and the late hours she kept whenever she did go out on a date. I told Kyra that, and she just shook her head, confident she was right, and said, "It takes one to know one. Her mother is one."

"But by that logic, you'd be one, too," I told her, and she got mad at me.

When I first began to read the diary by myself, I anticipated discovering secrets about the Foxworth family and what was true and what wasn't about the legend of children being locked in a house attic for years and years, but I had no idea, of course, that it would come to these intense sexual revelations. Surely, no one could know what went on between Christopher Jr. and his sister. Their mother and especially their grandmother would never reveal any of that later on. The truth was that it would be only in this diary that those discoveries would be made.

Boys loved to label girls who were considered more uninhibited, like Suzette, as being nymphomaniacs. Once you had that reputation, it wasn't easy getting washed of it. It would stain you and last throughout your high school life. I knew of girls who had that reputation and then left either for college or some job, and I could only imagine how difficult it was for them to return to live here, especially if they married someone not from here and then returned.

Boys from school who had never left and knew of their reputation would surely smirk and whisper behind a new husband's back. "Who hadn't had your wife when she was in school here?" they might say, and cause terrible fights, even divorces.

How unfair it was for girls. Boys were looked up to, respected, admired, and envied if they achieved the reputation of being good and experienced lovers. They could strut and smile, throw out their chests, and tease young girls, promising to give them the time of their lives and teach them things about sex no one else might, and that would be all right, just perfect, even expected, but if a girl would even suggest such a thing—there went her reputation, maybe for life if she remained here.

Tack onto all that a mere suggestion of something "dirty" happening between a brother and a sister, and both, but especially the sister, had better go pretty far away, maybe even change their names. Now I recalled an occasion once when I was with my father in Charley's, and one of the construction workers was telling jokes about redneck hillbillies. I was only ten and didn't really understand why my father got so upset with him telling the joke in front of me, but now I understood why. The joke was about a hillbilly introducing his wife to someone new. "I'd like you to meet my wife and my sister."

Ha, ha. Lots of laughter followed, but my father had turned on him.

"I have my daughter here," he said. I rarely saw him get that angry. The man slinked away like some rodent and sat in a booth mumbling under his breath. We went home pretty quickly after that, and when I asked my father what had happened, he said, "Someone undressed his stupidity in public," which I didn't quite understand then, either.

"Are you going to listen?" Kane asked, because I was obviously in such deep thought that I looked far away.

"Yes, go ahead," I said petulantly. "Don't worry. I'm listening."

A few days later, I was suddenly taken sick, vomiting and feeling generally weak and nauseated. I knew I couldn't go out and safely sneak around the house to rummage for money, but we desperately needed to get as much as we could as quickly as we could. I didn't like what was happening with the twins now. They were lethargic, sleeping too much, uninterested in everything, with their attention spans even shorter than they were, and they were just not growing the way they should. I told Cathy she had to go alone. She was very worried about me, but I assured her I would be all right. I was going to study up on my symptoms while she was out there. I warned her about not being discovered. Reluctantly, she left without me, but when she returned, I saw immediately that something had disturbed her.

"How much did you find?" I asked.

"Nothing, not a penny," she said.

Something wasn't right, but I was too tired to

pursue her with more questions. She wanted to
stay beside me, holding me, more than usual, but I
warned her that our grandmother could just pop in
on us, so she returned to her bed.

Time went by slowly, and our thoughts about
escape were suffering, because our hunt for money
wasn't producing enough yet. We had to be careful
not to take too much when we did find some, or
else we would arouse suspicions. That's all our
grandmother would have to find out, I explained.
Forget about her whipping us. She would do
something much worse, I was sure. Summer was
here again, and Cathy pointed out that we were
entering our third year. The twins were getting
worse. I was very concerned about their bouts of
nausea, their listlessness, their loss of appetite, and
the stunting of their growth.

"Look," Kane said suddenly, turning the diary so I
could see it. "There's a page blank right here. Weird."

"Maybe he just turned it too quickly. What could
he do once he began writing, that's all."

Kane shook his head. "I don't know," he said.
"Christopher is too much of a perfectionist."

"So what do you think happened?"

"I think he was going to stop."

I froze for a moment. What if Kane was right?
What would make Christopher change his mind about
keeping a diary? What would stop anyone? Was this
why he locked it in that metal box and hid it away,

why he didn't take it with him when he left? And yet he hadn't destroyed it, torn it up, or anything. It was almost as if he wanted someone to find it years later. That was his plan, never anticipating a horrendous fire.

"Maybe we should stop, then, Kane."

"Could you do that?"

"I've always felt that my father knew something more, and that was why he was so concerned about my reading it. This might be it. Some things are better left buried."

"It can't possibly matter now, can it? Malcolm Foxworth and his wife are dead, and Corrine is probably still in the loony bin. If we gave this to the district attorney, he'd file it away somewhere under 'Why waste my time?'"

"I suddenly just had a terrible chill," I said, hugging myself.

He got up quickly and sat beside me, hugging me and rubbing my shoulder and my back, kissing my hair, my forehead, and my cheeks.

"It's not the kind of chill that comes from being in a cold room, Kane. It's the kind of chill that comes from deep inside you."

"Take a deep breath. It'll pass," he said.

"Suddenly, I'm really frightened for both of us," I said.

He smiled. "Kristin, this is just someone's diary. It doesn't burn our fingers to hold it. Nothing terrible has happened to either of us because we're reading it or to anyone we love. There's no such thing as a curse. You're acting like those fools who go up to Foxworth on Halloween and scare each other."

"Because we're reading this diary, you've told me things you've never told anyone else, right?"

"So?"

"There's something about it, something more than it just being a diary about a terrible thing being done to children."

"Whatever you think about it is coming from you, not from the diary. I probably would have told you things about myself anyway, because I trust you and I care more for you than any other girl I've met. Okay, it's magical. It brought us more closely together. I'll give you that but nothing more," he said. "We've got to go on. If I were really Christopher, I'd want you to go on."

I looked into his eyes. Yes, maybe he was right, I thought. I nodded softly. He smiled and kissed me and hugged me again, holding me tightly for a few moments. Then he rose and returned to the chair. I would never look at that chair again without thinking of these days, without hearing his voice, and without envisioning the Dollanganger children. My father was right. Things, furniture, mementos, all do take on a life of their own and become far more than wood, metal, plastic, and paper. Nothing deserves to end up in a junkyard along with other lost memories. I recalled him once saying, "We hold on to things we were given and things we shared with loved ones because we don't want to die."

You die a little more with everything you leave behind, discard, and destroy. That was why he clung so hard to his old truck, why he despised the idea of people building and owning homes as investments. Homes weren't another form of commodity to him. They were filled with family, with the aromas of their favorite foods, with the echo of their laughter and the rumbling of their unhappiness, still damp with their tears. "When someone moves into someone else's home, despite the new paint and even the new appliances, they're putting on someone else's old socks," he told me.

"But can't they make it their own, too?"

"Maybe," he said. "But it gets crowded."

My father, I thought, there was no one like him.

I took a deep breath. So did Kane, and he opened the diary, turned the blank page, and continued.

I couldn't get the book with the sexually explicit pictures out of my mind. Whenever it was time for me to venture out to search for more money, I had to admit to myself that I was drawn to look at that book almost as much as I was drawn to look for the money we needed for our escape. I confessed that to Cathy, and then I described what had nearly happened on my latest visit to Momma's bedroom and what I had overheard. It wasn't until I described it to her that I realized what she had done and how close to revealing us she had come.

I was looking at the book when I heard voices and realized it was our mother and her new

husband. I had no time to slip out, so I went into
our mother's closet and crouched. While I was
in there, I heard Bart Winslow complain about
missing money. He was blaming it on the servants,
but Momma wasn't very interested. They argued
about going to a play, and fortunately for me,
Momma won the argument, but then Bart Winslow
described his dream.

"What dream?" Cathy asked.

As I related it to her, it was a dream about
some young girl with long golden hair sneaking
into their room while he was asleep and kissing
him on the lips. I had a suspicion he was talking
about Cathy, and as I told her about it, I could see
in her face that I was talking about her.

It threw me into a rage. How could she risk
our lives like that? Was he so handsome, her
need so much greater than mine? I knew she was
frustrated, but so was I, and I didn't go off and
do anything that crazy. She could say nothing to
defend herself.

I mumbled about how lucky I was that Momma
had insisted they leave, which made it possible for
me to sneak back out. Then I turned away from
her and sulked about it on my own bed. I don't
know how much time passed before I calmed down
enough to look back at her, but she was gone. She
had gone to sit by the window in the moonlight.

I stood there looking at her, looking at how
the moonlight outlined her breasts, her thighs,
and the small of her stomach through the thin

nightshirt. She sensed my presence and looked
at me, unmoving, tempting me with her innocent
new beauty. I told her she looked beautiful sitting
there and that because of the moonlight, she
was as good as naked. She didn't move to cover
herself up.

Suddenly, I thought of her not as my young
sister, Cathy, but as some far more sophisticated
young nymph, a temptress who had so much
confidence in herself that she would dare sneak
up to a grown man sleeping and kiss him softly
on his lips, wanting to taste those lips, wanting to
satisfy her own sexual need. Well, didn't I need
and want that? All I could think, which blinded
me from thinking any other thought, was that she
would have willingly given herself to Bart Winslow
if he had awakened and reached for her. He would
take her on that damn swan bed. She would know
another man's love, not mine.

I was overcome with rage about that. I have
no other way to explain it right now. I shot
forward and seized her and accused her again
of risking everything and wanting him. I told her
she could never be anyone else's but mine, and I
was determined to make her see that. I admit to
losing complete control of myself. I shoved her
down on the mattress. She struggled, fought for a
little while, and then suddenly, she gave up. She
returned my kiss and opened herself to me. I knew
that because we were both virgins, it wouldn't be
easy, it wouldn't be the wonderful experience it

was meant to be for all those who were truly in
love, but I could not stop what I had started. She
cried, but she clung to me as if she was afraid I
would retreat. She dug her fingers into me, and I
pushed on and into her.

We're damned, I thought almost immediately
afterward.

Our dreadful grandmother was right.

We're the devil's spawn.

Kane lowered the diary slowly. He didn't look at me
immediately. He stared ahead. We were both so quiet
we could hear the heat in the pipes and the sound of
a car horn way in the distance. It sounded desperate,
like a lost goose calling for its flock.

Both of us had liked and admired the young
Christopher who was telling us their story. Despite
how frustrated we were by the way he tolerated and
believed his mother, we respected his efforts to keep
himself and his siblings safe. He was, after all, thinking only about their future. From the beginning, he
understood how desperate a situation they were in.
He loved his father, but he was angry at him for leaving them lost and vulnerable, so much so that they had
to tolerate their tortured incarceration in that great
house. Cathy's skepticism had so far proven to be
more accurate than Christopher's unyielding love for
his mother.

Even though Kane looked as shocked as I was at
what he had just read, I doubted that he would deny

having anticipated it. I could shout at him now, if that was what would make me feel better. I could scream that I had told him so, that when he came upon that blank page, we should have done what I suggested. We should have stopped and left the rest of it buried, but I didn't, because I knew in my heart of hearts that I wanted to know just as much as he wanted to know.

Neither of us felt like talking about it immediately. He finally turned to me. "I'm thirsty," he said. "We should have brought something to drink up with us."

I looked at my watch. "We could have some lunch now, anyway."

He nodded. Neither of us would admit that we weren't that hungry, but both of us needed the break. He rose to start after me.

"Leave it up here," I said, nodding at the diary in his hands.

He put it on the chair, and we left the attic.

We descended silently. I think neither of us knew quite how to begin this conversation. I talked instead about what to eat, and we both decided I'd make some toasted cheese and tomato sandwiches. He watched me start by neatly cutting the tomato the way my father had taught me years ago, and then Kane went out to the living room and stood there the whole time looking out the window at the street and the trees. He didn't turn when he heard me come to tell him our sandwiches were ready. He continued staring ahead.

"My father looks forward to winter. He's a good

skier. My sister's a good skier. I can ski passably well, but I'm not crazy about it. My mother likes going to ski lodges and sitting by the fireplaces drinking her Cosmopolitans. She has the best ski lodge fashions, all that white fur stuff and those fancy soft leather winter boots that hardly ever see any snow. My father took us on our first family ski trip when I was just six. He had a ski pro teach me on the children's slope. In those days, my sister and I shared a room. Separate beds, of course, but the same room. She would complain about it, but my father saw no reason to spend money on another room for a six-year-old."

"Did you want to be in the same room with your sister?"

He turned quickly. I thought he was going to say something nasty, but he looked like he was giving my question deep thought. "I wasn't afraid of being alone or anything like that. Maybe in those days, I was closer to her than I am now. I mean, when you're six, you'd hate to hug your sister, but at this age, when we hug, I'm well aware of how beautiful she is. Whatever . . . you've got me questioning my own feelings."

"Me?"

"Christopher, then. You ever go skiing?" he asked, eager to change the topic. I wasn't going to oppose it. These thoughts felt too heavy right now.

"No. When my father looks to recreate, he favors swimming in the ocean. We used to take long weekends in Virginia Beach, I remember, but we haven't done that since . . . for a long time. He says he gets enough exercise at work."

"I'm sure he does," Kane said.

"Sandwiches are ready."

He followed me into the kitchen. I poured us both some chocolate milk, and we sat across from each other at the kitchenette table and ate.

"What did you do to make this so good?"

"I put a little avocado in it. My father does that, and he uses real butter."

"Do you think he'd mind if I moved in?" he asked, smiling.

"Probably not, as long as you did KP duty."

"I keep forgetting he was in the navy."

"Yes. He doesn't have any tattoos."

Kane laughed. "Neither does my father. He used to ask my sister and me if we knew any college graduates with tattoos. It was his way of telling us never to get one."

"Suzette brags about the one she has on her rear end, a hummingbird. Ever see it?"

"Good try," he said. "No, and I don't want to, either."

We both finished our sandwiches, but neither of us stood up. The long pause seemed deafening.

"He was always in control when they were alone," I began. "It wouldn't have happened if he didn't lose control of himself."

"I'm not disagreeing, but somehow I don't hate him for it. I'm not even disgusted about it. I'm just a little shocked is all. I mean, I don't want to go into any deep psychological analysis about it. It happened. They were trapped at just the wrong time in their development, their sexuality. But that doesn't excuse it," he quickly added.

"Do you think it destroyed them?"

"They've survived so much. Why not that, too?"

"Their parents were incestuous by definition, and then they were. The old lady thinks it's inherited evil."

"Why wouldn't she? She believed in original sin. She blamed men more, but it wasn't Adam who screwed up in the Garden of Eden. It was Mrs. Adam."

I finally felt a smile on my face. "Right. You guys are the victims from day one," I said, and cleared the table.

"We've got to finish it now, Kristin," Kane said. "Neither of us will sleep tonight if we don't."

"I know," I said. I glanced at the clock. "We should be able to do that."

"I'm going to the bathroom. I'll meet you upstairs," he said.

I rinsed off the plates and glasses and put everything in the dishwasher. Then I went up to my bathroom. I had the strangest urge when I came out. I don't know if I could ever explain it or why I did it, but in my mind, it was my effort to tell both Cathy and Christopher that I was still all right with them. I even thought Kane knew that when I entered the attic, dressed only in one of my sheer nightgowns.

But he also knew it wasn't my only reason.

Is there a point when a girl says to herself, *It's my time*, a time when you might tell yourself what the poets say, "The stars are perfectly aligned"? When you start to date, you know that behind every small, tentative kiss, even behind holding hands, he's thinking about the possibility, supposedly more than you are. In all the novels I've ever read, especially the ones written in the nineteenth and early twentieth centuries, girls supposedly didn't think as much about having sexual intercourse, certainly not before they were married. In some books, especially those set in the Victorian era, they were practically asexual.

And yet the whole idea of young girls being chaperoned all the time suggested to me that there was a fear that if they weren't, they would succumb quickly, maybe even eagerly. The chaperone wasn't there only to watch the man's behavior. It was the unspoken secret everyone knew: girls were just as interested in and excited by the prospect of making love.

I remembered that old joke a comedian told on television when he was recalling his youth and thinking about his parents making love. To a little boy and a little girl, the concept of how it was done seemed like a big "Ugh!" How could you find pleasure in that place on your body that seemed reserved only for peeing? The comedian said that when he thought about it then, he thought, "My father, yes, but my mother . . . never."

If all those adults who pretended or convinced themselves that girls were essentially different from boys when it came to all this could be flies on the wall in our girls' bathrooms or locker rooms and could listen to the conversations there, they would revise and rewrite the whole thing.

At this moment, I pushed aside all denial. Later I would find a dozen different reasons for that, the leading one being that I was as much in love with Kane as I expected I would ever be with anyone, and I trusted that he loved me, too. Dumb romantic excuse? Maybe, but it worked, at least for now. Another reason that loomed high in my rationale was the fear that it might happen some other time with someone I had half as much feeling for. I'd be a little drunk or go just a little too far to stop, and the result of that would be horrible regret to follow me all my life. *Avoid that at all costs, Kristin Masterwood*, I told myself. *This is your chance to prevent that from ever happening.*

And of course, this was very special. Kane and I had shared so much these past days and weeks. We had invaded those places in ourselves that were locked away from everyone else, even those we were so close to in our lives. Christopher's diary had brought us here. We were in our own attic world, and we were ready to step into that place where we would no longer be able to carry our childhood fantasies with us. We would have different eyes. We would recognize those who had entered with us and those who hadn't.

I could almost feel myself lifting the little girl inside me who clung around my neck away and then placing her behind me. I reached out. Kane took my hand and moved so slowly toward me that it was as if he was maneuvering through a very narrow path between jagged rocks. There was that awareness in his eyes. Carefully, like someone concerned that one wrong gesture, one move too quick, would shatter the moment, he undressed. He had what he needed to keep us from suffering serious regret. We were, after all, thoughtful lovers. We knew where unbridled animal passion could lead. We would not step on that path.

Because we wanted this to last a lifetime in our library of memories, we were moving in exaggeratedly slow motion, each kiss sculpted like a work of art, each touch plotted strategically. There was to be nothing sloppy and awkward here, not now. There was no way we would later claim we had stumbled into it, simply gone too far to turn back, and blame it on a rush of passion. That would reduce it all to some blunder and have nothing to do with our deeper feelings for each other.

I remember thinking to myself that girls like Suzette never knew a moment like this, and absent that, their lives would take a different turn. They would never know love the way I would, even if it was to be with someone else later on. I would always fall in love through this moment, through Kane.

With as much gentleness as we could manage in the throes of our building excitement, we both "crossed the Rio Grande," but safely, with him wearing a condom. I wasn't a girl child. I didn't suffer any real pain. Wave after wave of delicious excitement flowed up and over my breasts, up my neck, and into my flushed face. When I was crying with joy, I remembered having the flashing thought that Cathy Dollanganger would never know this beauty. For her, it was almost a savage leap out of childhood.

There were tears streaming down my cheeks when we were done. Kane kissed away some and held me until the trembling in my body stopped. We didn't talk about it. There were some moments in your life that you didn't want to analyze and review. They happened, and that was all there was. *Don't tempt conscience*, I thought. *Don't go measuring yourself against someone else's ruler of good and bad deeds. What you feel is good is good.* That was all there was to think and believe if you had faith in the goodness inside you.

Kane dressed quietly and then sat on the chair. When he looked at me with the diary back in his hand, I had the momentary thought that maybe what we had just done had all been a dream, a hallucination. He smiled and put his hand over his heart. I straightened myself out, brushed down my nightgown, and lay back.

Take me home, I thought. *Read on.*

Afterward, we went onto the roof, and I apologized. No matter how I said it, it sounded weak. I was doing it as much for myself as for her. My own loss of control shocked me. I was far from the perfect young man I wanted to be. How arrogant of me to think I was always going to be in full control of my emotions, my feelings, my body. I knew Cathy believed I was, and in a way, that made me feel even guiltier, but there was nothing to do now to change what had happened. I even hated my apology. I wasn't absolutely sure, of course, but I assured her that she wouldn't get pregnant. I vowed never to let it happen again, but to be honest, I was afraid it would, as long as we were trapped here. It was September, and I was thinking that with winter coming, we had to rush this escape now. We had almost four hundred dollars. I estimated that if we stole some of Momma's jewelry, we could get by. The twins needed a good physical examination as soon as we arrived somewhere. For many reasons, therefore, we had to move soon.

One early October evening, when we knew Momma was going out, we prepared sacks for our foray into her bedroom. Winter was well on its way. We had to get out before snow began to fall. I was prepared to do everything I had to do, but then the worst thing of all happened.

Cory became very, very ill. He was throwing up so much I knew he would be dehydrated. My first suspicion was food poisoning, maybe sour milk, maybe bad meat. He fell asleep beside Carrie and Cathy, and I stayed up all night watching over him. He was far from better in the morning. It was even more serious than I had first thought. When our grandmother came in to leave our basket of food, Cathy told her how sick Cory was. She left without promising anything, and I was about to reveal that we had our key by going out for our

mother myself, but just before I did, she and our
grandmother came in.

Cory was struggling to breathe by now, and
Momma was standing back, whispering to our
grandmother. Cathy lost her temper and began
screaming at her. Momma slapped Cathy, and to
my astonishment, Cathy slapped her back. I thought
our grandmother would pound her or something,
but she smiled at the confrontation as if it was the
proof she needed that we were evil children or that
Momma was getting what she deserved. I seized
Cathy and pleaded with her to stop and let Momma
do what had to be done. Cathy screamed at her
anyway and vowed to take revenge on her.

Grandmother Olivia surprised me again. She
told our mother that Cathy was right. Cory had to
be taken to a hospital. They both left and didn't
return until the servants were retired. Cory was
in a horrible state. I thought he was practically in
a coma. When they returned, Momma bundled
him up to take him out, and Carrie got hysterical.
Cathy calmed her by telling her that she would go
with Momma and stay with Cory in the hospital. I
told Momma that was a good idea, because Cory
had become so dependent on Cathy, but Momma
shook her head, and they left, locking us all in the
room again.

The three of us went to sleep that night,
embracing each other, clinging to each other,
terrified for our little brother and terrified for
ourselves.

How should I write the rest of this? I am sitting here and struggling with the words. My hand is shaking so hard that I don't think I can write. The words will be distorted on the page. I feel like I'm crumbling inside. My body is turning inside out, in fact. Now Cathy looks like she's the one in a coma. She holds Carrie as if Carrie is made of air, weightless, a hollowed-out doll.

The best way to write this, to get it down, is to tell it straight and factually.

Momma and our grandmother returned.

Momma said she had admitted Cory to the hospital. It was under a different name, pretending he was her nephew.

She said he was diagnosed with pneumonia.

She said he died.

It was too late.

My little brother was dead.

When we asked about a funeral for him, she said it was already done.

Cory was dead and gone.

Momma left without any more details, our grandmother following right behind her.

I am writing all of this coldly, because I'm afraid if I don't, I will not be able to write a word.

I knew better than ever now that we were all dying or doomed, all three of us. Carrie was wilting even more quickly now without Cory at her side. I had read a great deal about the immune system people had normally, and I was convinced that ours were so weakened by our

years of incarceration that we would die from the
smallest germ. I explained it to Cathy, but she
looked like she wasn't hearing anything much
anymore.

I would go out one more time, I told her, and
get everything of value I could, and then we would
leave. We just had to wait until I was sure Momma
would not be in her bedroom. I couldn't imagine
her going out to parties and dinners so soon after
Cory's death.

Finally, I felt the timing was right. I told
Cathy to prepare for our escape. I'd be back with
whatever I could, and that would be that. The little
glimmer of hope that appeared in her eyes urged
me forward to be careful and to be fruitful. I had
to get us out now.

I was shocked at what I discovered when I
snuck into Momma's bedroom. Not only was she
gone for the night; it looked like she was gone
forever. Her vanity table was cleared, the drawers
were empty, the closet was empty, and all the
drawers in it were emptied of anything valuable.
It looked like someone was told to vacate the
premises and leave nothing of any value behind
her. I kept searching. There were heavy mink
coats left, but nothing we could carry out in a
suitcase. I made one last desperate search of
a drawer and was shocked to find our father's
picture. Beside it were Momma's wedding and
engagement rings. These were valuable pieces

we could take, but why would she leave them?
Did she want to forget her past that much?
Did she know we were stealing from her and
Bart and she'd left them for us? How ridiculous
that sounded, and how foolish I was to cling to
the hope that she still cared. Was that the last
remnant of my once love for her, a love I thought
would be undying? I chased the thought from my
mind.

We didn't have enough, I kept thinking, and
decided to take a great risk and sneak into our
grandmother's bedroom. But when I got there, I
could hear that she was there. I peered through
the slightly opened door and saw her sitting on
her bed, her head bald. That hair we had come
to hate was nothing more than a wig. She had
never looked uglier to me. She was holding the
Bible. I heard her asking God to forgive her sins,
to consider that all she had done she had done
to please him. Never did I think of her as more
insane than at that moment. I hated and pitied her
at the same time.

Still worried about not having enough with
which to leave, I ventured down to the rotunda
and then into the library. I saw what had to be
our grandfather's desk and thought it was just
possible that he had money in one of the drawers,
but what caught my attention first was the sight
of all the medical equipment neatly wrapped up
and the hospital bed stripped of everything. How

odd, I thought, but before I could investigate any more, I heard voices and quickly went down on my stomach behind a sofa. Two servants had entered, and I overheard their conversation.

As I write this, my throat feels like it's closing up on me, and I'll soon struggle to breathe. I am writing quickly to get it down and over with.

What I heard before they started to make love right there on the sofa.

Our grandfather was dead. He had been dead for almost a year!

He had left everything to our mother, who hadn't come up to free us and start us on a new, wealthy life.

As far as the servants knew, our grandmother had been poisoning an army of mice in the attic. She had been using arsenic, a white substance. She had been giving us sugar-coated doughnuts, which we all devoured, especially Cory.

When I told all this to Cathy, she was stunned into disbelief. I clung to it, but I knew there was one test to make. I fed Cory's pet mouse the sugar-coated doughnut we had, and as I feared would happen, he died just as any rodent would if it ate arsenic.

Did our mother know what we were eating, how it was slowly killing us, and how it had killed Cory? She left us up here suffering for almost a year longer than we had to.

We decided to leave the following morning. While we were planning, our grandmother appeared for the last time. Cathy thought she had snuck in many times and probably knew we could escape. She left, locking the door, but we had no time to worry about that now. We had to get ready to make our escape. We decided to take some samples of the doughnuts and the dead mouse in a plastic bag. If we were picked up by the police, we would hand it all to them and then tell our story.

Despite all this, there was still a part of me that hoped there was some explanation for what Momma did or permitted to be done to us. I hated myself for clinging to that and went to sleep chastising myself for being such a little boy when it was time to be a man and face up to the ugly fact that our own mother cared more about herself than she cared about us.

We didn't have much of a plan for once we escaped this house. I knew that, but we had no choice. We could get to the train that had brought us here and ride it out and away to a future where we could grow healthy, pursue our dreams, and somehow, someway, bury the horror we had lived, bury it so deeply we could pretend it had just been a bad dream. Our mother had died with our father. Could I convince myself of that? Could Cathy?

I barely slept. While Cathy was getting Carrie ready, I wrote my last lines in this diary. I'm going to leave it hidden up here in a small metal box I found that will lock automatically when closed. There is no key to it that I can find.

As I write these last lines, I know that the diary belongs to the attic now.

Along with the four young children who trusted and hoped and the three who survived.

We were both crying when Kane closed the diary.

He embraced me, and we clung to each other for quite a while, rocking on the sofa.

Then, in silence, we rose, we restored the attic, and still without saying a word to each other, we left. I closed the door softly behind me. It would never be the same place for me. I thought in the near future, I would go through my mother's things, take what I thought I could use sometime in the future perhaps, and then get my father to give away the rest to the local thrift store or some charity.

It was time to let go of things that would not bring back my mother. I would explain to him that we didn't need them in order to remember her. She would live forever in our hearts and minds. I knew he would listen and nod in agreement. He simply needed me to be the one to say it.

"Let's spend as much time today as we can with each other," Kane suggested when we got to my room. "I'll take you to a great restaurant, something lively and fun. Please," he begged. "You said your father won't be home for dinner."

"Okay," I said. I didn't want to be alone, either.

While I showered and dressed and fixed my hair, I kept looking at the diary and thinking. I had promised my father I would give it to him when I was finished, but I knew he would either destroy it or throw it away, and more than ever, I didn't want that to happen now.

Where did it belong?

Not buried away in my room, and not with Kane.

I didn't find the answer until weeks later.

Epilogue

Everyone at school was focused on the Christmas holiday. I felt sorry for our teachers. The closer it was, the more difficult it got to keep our attention on the subject matter. Between classes, the chatter and the laughter in the hallways seemed to be at a higher, more excited pitch. Some of my classmates were going to spend the holidays in Florida and other warmer places, but the majority talked about family gatherings at their homes in Charlottesville. The teachers were looking forward to their break, too, and their annual holiday party. Everyone had more charity in his or her heart, and those who violated rules or stepped out of line found the benefit of a wider embrace of forgiveness.

All my girlfriends, especially Suzette, noticed how much closer Kane and I had become. There were small but telling revelations. More than ever, we held hands almost every opportunity we had. We sat closer to each other wherever we could sit together. We whispered and nudged each other gently. When we could, we kissed, quickly but lovingly. We were with each other almost every free moment after school and on weekends.

Of course, Suzette was the first one to suggest I had "crossed the Rio Grande." All my other girl-friends waited to hear me confirm it. I didn't have to do anything or say anything. My silence brought envi-ous smiles. They knew now that I was in a relationship deeper than most. It was so strong that we were sure to coast easily into graduation together, and then into that time that tests all high school romances. Most didn't survive the distance and the worlds between them. But it was still exciting to think about it. At least, we had something to remember, a time to cher-ish.

My more jealous friends wouldn't miss an oppor-tunity to remind me. In various ways, I heard, "Kane will date lots of girls, and you'll date other boys."

"What a threat," I replied, which didn't give them the satisfaction they hoped for.

Despite all this distraction, I aced my exams and quizzes and began to pull ahead of Theresa Flowman in a big way. Unless I stumbled in some serious man-ner, I was now the odds-on favorite to be our class valedictorian. Only one thing was happening that could have a detrimental emotional effect on me. My father was getting more serious with Laura Oster-house. They dated frequently; she ate at our house as often as possible. Aunt Barbara and I chatted about it on the phone, and I gradually came to accept it. The three of us were going places together, and there was even a night when my father joked and said Kane and I could come along to make it a double date.

Every day, I anticipated my father asking me if I had finished with the diary, but for some reason, he didn't. Perhaps he thought I had become bored with it and had decided it was better not to mention it and get me started reading it again. Occasionally, Kane asked me if I had given it to my father. I just shook my head, and he immediately changed the subject.

The construction at Foxworth had taken big leaps forward. The house exterior was complete, and all the work was now going on inside, which was perfect timing for the change in the weather. My father was busier than ever with it, and because of it, he was being offered some other opportunities. He was talking more about expanding his business and was meeting with accountants, lawyers, and even one or two investors. I saw that Laura was a big help to him during all this. Much of their conversation involved these new ideas and opportunities. Both their lives were fuller and more exciting. There was no room for me to feel or express any jealousy. If I had learned anything from Christopher's diary, it was to cherish the joy your loved ones enjoyed, even if you weren't part of it. Loving someone really meant hoping they were happy with or without you.

That weekend before our holiday break was to begin, my father called me from the building site and asked me to sift through some of his mail from the day before that he had left on his desk. He needed a quote from a tile company, and he had forgotten to include it in his bag when he left for the site in the morning. I was on the phone with him, reading off the companies until I found the right one and gave him the information he needed.

When I put the mail back, I noticed something, a handwritten letter. It wasn't much more than a one-page note, but it was from Dr. West. In it, he made a specific reference to the future resident of the property and the importance of those "ramps to all entrances and not just the front." From the fact that there was going to be an elevator for a two-story home, I already had guessed that whoever was going to live there was handicapped. But there was another interesting detail: "CC: Mr. and Mrs. William Anderson" under Dr. West's signature.

I returned to my father's desk. I sifted through his papers until I found a more formal letter from Dr. West, this time with his letterhead. He had an office in Richmond. Later, when Kane came over, I told him about what I had found.

"What does it mean?" he asked, shrugging. "The house is really being built for this doctor and not the Arthur Johnson who was mentioned in that news story a while back? Maybe one of his handicapped relatives or something?"

"I don't know, but you're right about Arthur Johnson. He was never really the owner."

I told him that my father finally had found out that the owner of the new house was involved in a trust managed by a hedge fund Arthur Johnson ran, but I knew nothing more. Because the property was so different from Foxworth Hall and because of the changes in the landscaping, neither my father nor I gave it very much thought. Kane knew how much my father wanted to put Foxworth Hall into the past. I explained that he was then introduced to this Dr. West, and he and I both concluded that Dr. West had treated Corrine Foxworth when she had been put into a mental clinic.

"My father suspected that, because it was Dr. West who seemed to know so much about the interior of Foxworth Hall, something he would have learned from Corrine."

"So . . . okay. You think he's the real owner now?"

"No. That CC at the bottom of his letter makes me think he's acting on behalf of someone else, this William Anderson."

"But . . . why should we care?"

"What if it's a pseudonym?"

"For whom?"

"What if it's Christopher Jr. who's moving back to Charlottesville—something had happened to him and he's handicapped now?"

His eyes widened. "You really think that's possible?"

"I think we need to find out," I said. "My father has always been a little annoyed at the effort to hide the real buyer and builder. Don't you see?" I said. "Look at how much trouble whoever it is has gone through to hide his identity. First, it looks like this Arthur Johnson is doing it. It's even leaked that way to the press. He's wealthy enough, and he's involved, visiting the site. Then my father discovers there's a trust involved, and the manager of the trust is kept secret. All of a sudden, as more detailed decisions about the interior have to be made, he is introduced to this Dr. West. New designs are introduced to facilitate access to the home for someone who's handicapped. It's almost as if it wasn't until much later in the construction that the real owner and resident decided to go through with it. And now we have this name . . . Anderson," I added.

Kane thought, nodding to himself. "What should we do?"

"I don't want to say anything to my father, of course. We're getting out of school Tuesday. It's a half day. Let's go to Richmond to see Dr. West."

"What makes you think he would tell us anything? And he's sure to tell your father that you went to see him."

"I'll take the risk. If I say something to my father now, he'll forbid me to go or something, and then I'd have to tell him everything about the diary, about reading it with you."

He thought a moment and then gave me that famous Kane Hill shrug and smile. "You could go as a patient, and there would be doctor-patient confidentiality," he kidded. Then he changed expression quickly, seeing the way I was reacting. "We just appear? This does sound crazy. Maybe we're the ones who need Dr. West."

"If you don't think we should, I'll—"

"No. We'll do it," he said. "We've come this far with it. We need to see it to the end."

Because I was so nervous about it and already feeling so guilty that I had revealed the diary to someone else, I was afraid my father would see this new deception in my face and ask me the questions I couldn't answer. Of course, I would have to, and it would be a terrible moment between us. I didn't even try to come up with a fictional story for why I wouldn't be home Tuesday after school had let out for the holidays. I would do it all first, and then I would confess everything.

Luckily for me, my father was very occupied, both with the construction project and with Laura. He rattled off some plans for us over the Christmas holiday and mentioned that Aunt Barbara was going to come visit us again. He then mentioned the possibility that Uncle Tommy would drop by on his way to a Caribbean vacation, staying at some film producer's villa on St. Martin. I thought that would mean using the sofa bed in the den, and I thought I would volunteer to give him my room, but he added that Uncle Tommy was bringing his newest Hollywood girlfriend along, and they would be staying at a hotel in Charlottesville. He laughed about it, but I could see he was more excited than he had been in years.

And here I was, about to disappoint him more than I ever had.

It occurred to me that this was going to be the first time I had taken the diary out of my house since we had found it in the rubble of Foxworth Hall. Kane picked me up in the morning, and to be sure I didn't expose it to anyone at school, we hid the diary under the front seat of his car. I worried about it all day, the way someone might worry about leaving his or her wallet under the seat. I tried to be as excited about the holiday as everyone else in my school, but I couldn't keep my heart from pounding every time I looked at the clock and realized how soon Kane and I would be on the highway to Richmond. When my girlfriends asked me why I was acting this way, I referred to my uncle's and aunt's arrivals and how long it had been since we had all been together. I didn't say that the last time was my mother's funeral, but I think some realized it.

It wasn't until I was in Kane's car and we were heading for Richmond, which was just a little more than an hour away, that he asked me, "So what are you going to say to this psychiatrist?"

"The truth," I replied. "What was found and what we read. I'll make it clear how much we want to return it to Christopher Jr."

"What if Dr. West refuses to see us?"

"We'll camp out on his front doorstep," I said, and Kane looked at me, smiled, and nodded.

"I believe you would. So what if we convince him about the diary and he says he'll take care of it?"

"I'll say no. I don't trust anyone to do this but us now. I won't give it to him. If I have to, I'll threaten to give the story about the estate's new owner to the newspapers. I'm confident that he doesn't want that to happen."

"Then he'll really call your father."

"We'll see," I said, but I was a great deal more frightened than I was showing.

We followed the car GPS and easily found Dr. West's office, which was in an office building on Bremo Road. After we parked, Kane looked at me, hesitating.

"I just want you to be sure about this," he began. "Once you go in there and reveal yourself to him, Kristin, your father will surely find out, and I know how special your relationship with your father is."

"Yes," I said in a very weak, tiny voice. I was clutching the diary the way some religious person might clutch the Bible. "I think when my father expressed how much he wished I wouldn't read this, he was telling me that once I had, it would bring on a major responsibility, an obligation. He was right. We owe it to Christopher now, Kane. He has to know that someone else knows their story, and if William Anderson is really him, he should get it back and do with it what he wishes. You don't have to come in with me."

"Like I would ever let you do this alone. Let's go, then," he said, and opened his door. I opened mine and stepped out, overcoming any hesitation. We walked toward the main entrance of the building and checked the directory to be sure Dr. West's office was here. Then we entered the lobby. There was a festive atmosphere, with Christmas decorations and a small Christmas tree in the lobby. People going to and fro were infected with the joviality, laughing and wishing each other a happy holiday. Kane and I went to the elevator, pushed the button for Dr. West's floor, and then held hands in the elevator, neither of us speaking.

Dr. West's outer office also had Christmas decorations. There was a small Christmas tree on a table to the right. It was a light oak paneled outer office with simple but comfortable imitation leather chairs and a sofa and a dark brown tiled floor. The table in front of the sofa was covered with entertainment and fashion magazines. In fact, there was nothing to suggest that this was a psychiatrist's office and that the people who came here had serious mental and emotional problems.

The receptionist was a woman who looked to be in her early sixties at least. She had short, curly, grayish light brown hair and what I would call a grandmother's pleasant smile, with soft hazel eyes. She wore almost no makeup, but her cheeks were as rosy as the cheeks of someone who had just come in from the cold. She wore a light blue cardigan sweater and a white blouse with a pretty cameo above her right breast. In my mind, she was the perfect receptionist for a psychiatrist, because she gave off a relaxed, friendly demeanor that would help the most nervous person take a breath and feel some desperately sought tranquility. That was how she made me feel. There was a box of holiday candy in front of her for anyone to sample.

"Hello there," she said. "How can I help you?"

"We're here to see Dr. West. It's very important,"

I said, widening my eyes to impress her with just how important it was.

"You haven't made an appointment."

"No. We just drove in from Charlottesville."

"Well, what's this about?" she asked. "Are you related to one of the doctor's patients?"

Kane and I looked at each other.

"In a very distant way, I am," I said. "But that's not why we have to see him. It's very important. He'll want to see us when he learns why we're here."

She raised her eyebrows. "The doctor's not here," she said. "He's on his way back from the hospital."

"May we wait?"

She looked at her appointment book. "He has a patient in about an hour," she said.

"We won't take up much of his time," I promised.

"You may wait here," she said, with the tone of a monitor approving a bathroom pass or something. She suddenly looked less friendly to me, perhaps because we were so secretive.

"Thank you," I said, and we sat on the sofa. I saw the way she was looking at me because of how tightly I had the diary clutched against my body. Maybe I looked like someone who needed a psychiatrist.

Kane started to flip through magazines. The receptionist went back to her paperwork, looking up periodically and then looking down again.

Finally, close to twenty minutes later, Dr. West entered his outer office. He was at least six foot three or four and very slim, with a dark brown, well-trimmed mustache, thick, wavy dark brown hair that showed some ripples of gray, and very thoughtful-looking grayish-brown eyes. I thought he looked to be in his mid-sixties or so. He wore a dark blue suit and a gray tie. His somewhat thin lips curled immediately into a curious smile when he set eyes on us. He looked quickly at the receptionist.

"These two insisted on seeing you, Dr. West," she said with a somewhat apologetic tone. "They wouldn't tell me why," she added. "Nor have they told me their names."

His bushy eyebrows rose like two caterpillars nudged.

"Oh? How can I help you?" he asked, not moving toward his inner office.

I glanced at Kane and at the receptionist before turning back to Dr. West.

"My father is Burt Masterwood," I said, hoping that would be enough to capture his interest. It did.

"Did he send you to see me?" he asked.

"No, sir," I said. "This doesn't have to do with the house construction."

He nodded and indicated his inner office door. We both rose and followed him.

He closed the door behind us and gestured at the more comfortable-looking, real leather auburn sofa on our right. He put his briefcase down on his dark cherrywood desk, which had everything neatly arranged on it, and then pulled a matching cherrywood rocking chair closer to us.

I had never met a psychiatrist, and Kane had never

mentioned either him or anyone in his family ever being treated by any. I was sure his father must know many doctors, including psychiatrists. They all needed good deals on cars. Dr. West leaned back in his chair. If he had any concerns or apprehensions, he didn't show them. He looked relaxed and ready to talk about anything. And yet I had the sense that he wasn't surprised I was here.

"So, what's this about?" he asked, intertwining his long fingers and placing his palms against his flat stomach. He struck me as someone who either jogged regularly or played tennis.

I began at the beginning, describing how my father and Todd had come upon the metal box and the diary. I told him who had written it and in general terms described what it had revealed. The expression on his face changed ever so slightly as I highlighted the most important parts, especially the poisoning of Cory and the deception Corrine and her mother had created to keep the children locked in the small bedroom and attic for so many years.

When I finished, he rocked a little, and then, with his eyes suddenly steely, he looked at me and said, "Why bring this to me? Why don't you bring it to the police?"

"We think someone else should do that, if he wants to," I said.

"To repeat, why bring this to me?"

"You treated Corrine Foxworth sometime after 1972," I said without hesitation.

"How do you know that?"

"I know it. What's the difference how?" I said defiantly. I was gambling on being right. I didn't want him to think my father had told me, but then it suddenly occurred to me that maybe my father really had known and just didn't want me to know for sure.

There was a pause as he rocked and looked at Kane and then at me. "There was a great deal of misery and unhappiness in that grand old house. Maybe it's time to bury it all and let it go. Including that diary," he added, nodding at it still clutched in my hands.

"It's not ours to do," I said.

"Corrine Foxworth died some years ago under tragic circumstances," he said. "I know about it only because some follow-ups were ended, but I know nothing else about her or what happened to her children."

I knew it was quite arrogant of me, a high school senior, even a valedictorian candidate, to look at a psychiatrist and accuse him of lying, but my instincts told me I was right.

"I'd like to hand this back to Christopher Jr., her son," I said, as if he had said nothing. "I think you can help me do that."

He shook his head. "I have no idea where he is. I'm afraid you've wasted your time." He glanced at his watch. "I'm sorry, but I have a patient coming in fifteen minutes. I have some work to prepare." He stood up and put his rocking chair back where it had been.

I looked at Kane. It was written in his face. We had failed. We should go home. We stood up. Dr. West went behind his desk, and Kane went to the door. Just as he opened it, I turned back to Dr. West.

"I'd like to give this to William Anderson, then," I said. "You and I know he would want it. Once I give it to him, as you say, all the misery and unhappiness will be buried, if that is what he wants. Otherwise, all that these children went through will be for nothing."

Dr. West stared at me a moment. I held my breath. "Does your father know you're here?"

"No, sir."

"This was something we did together," Kane said quickly. "It means a lot to us now."

He nodded slowly. "Close the door," he said.

Neither of us said a word until we were in Kane's car and on our way. What we said to each other only had to do with directions to the address. Neither of us was prepared to hear the sort of details Dr. West decided to relate. He understood we had something special in our hands, and I thought that weakened any reluctance he had to share what he knew. He saw how important it was to put it all in perspective. We had only Christopher's viewpoint of events. We knew nothing of Corrine after the first fire. I never intended to feel a bit sorry for her, but learning how her mother tormented her, hated her in a sense, truly upset me.

The doctor had described how her mother had gotten a replica of a child's skeleton and put it in a trunk, suggesting that it was her poisoned child. Dr. West said it was one of the things that sent her over the edge of sanity. Now it made more sense to us.

When we pulled up to the curb, Kane turned off the engine, and we sat there looking at the house. There was a ramp in front for wheelchair access. From my father's work and my own study of houses, I knew this was a classic Colonial Revival, with its gabled roof, entry porch with slender columns and double-hung sash windows with multipane glass. It had a stone veneer. This particular home wasn't the largest on the residential street, but it wasn't the smallest, either. It had a lawn that looked too small for the house, however. There was a dark green van in the driveway. All the curtains in all the windows in the house were drawn open, obviously to gather in the remaining afternoon sunshine.

I knew why Kane was full of hesitation. Dr. West had made it clear to us that William Anderson didn't know ninety percent of what we knew.

"Considering the journey he has made, the pain he has gone through, and the difficulties he has had to understand himself and what had happened to him, and especially how his brother and his sisters felt, it would not be right for me to deny him what you have to give," he continued. "So I will tell you where you will find him. The final decision will be yours to make. You've become part of this now. Whatever you decide to do, I hope you will respect his need for anonymity."

We both swore to that.

"Strange," he said, smiling, "but the thing that most drew him to want to return to that property is the image printed on his mind of that view from the attic window. I can't tell you how many times he's described it to me."

"Which was why it was so important for my father to have a bedroom window that offered that view," I said.

"Yes."

I didn't want to disagree with a psychiatrist, but I had a different reason in my mind for him being drawn back to the Foxworth property.

I confessed that my father did not know that Kane and I had read the diary together, nor did he know we had finished reading it. I revealed that I had broken a promise I had made to my father.

"I want to tell him everything in my own way at the proper moment," I explained.

Dr. West thought a moment and then shrugged. "Normally, there's something about this office that prevents me from revealing what I have heard in it," he said. "I made an exception to that rule today for what I think were justifiable reasons. As for what has gone on between us, however, you can depend on me to keep it within these walls."

I was grateful for that.

But there was no question in my mind what Dr. West meant by "justifiable reasons." What Dr. West had learned treating Corrine Foxworth had caused him to go beyond the patient-doctor relationship and in the end do what he was doing for William Anderson.

"You two are quite extraordinary," he told us in his doorway just before we left his office.

"She's the extraordinary one," Kane said. "I'm just along for the ride."

Dr. West laughed. "Any man who knows how

to compliment his woman will do real well in this world," he told him.

Kane's smile was big and bright enough to light the whole state of Virginia.

"It's still not too late to turn around and drive home," Kane said as we sat in his car in front of William Anderson's home.

"Yes, it is," I said. "It became too late as soon as I disobeyed my father and turned the first few pages."

"Your father is going to hate me," he said.

"He'll be angry in the beginning, but after this, after I tell him all of it, he will understand. He and I love each other too much. Don't worry. He won't hate you. My father will always love everything I love."

I opened the door.

Although Dr. West had not called ahead to tell William Anderson what we were bringing, he had called ahead while we were still in his office to tell him it was all right to see us. Kane stepped up beside me, and we started down the stone sidewalk. We were halfway to the front porch when the front door opened, and William Anderson's wife pushed him in the wheelchair to the entrance. He was thin and fragile-looking. Damage had been done to his nerves and his legs, but he had a full head of beautiful graying flaxen hair and startling cerulean-blue eyes. Even in his early sixties, he was as handsome as I had imagined he might be.

We had learned that he had been given to someone basically to drop off at a hospital emergency room away from Charlottesville. The man had been paid well to do it and disappear.

The boy who would become William Anderson had been saved, but the serious damage had been done. However, there was someone else at that emergency room that day, someone who heard about this child left without anyone to claim him. He was a man of great means whose grandson had died in an accident shortly before and who couldn't get this beautiful sick child out of his mind. He would take him into his home and his heart, make him part of his business, and leave a share of a fortune to him.

That was nearly fifty-five years ago. He had gone through a great deal since, including therapy and eventually becoming a good enough businessman to continue to build on his inheritance.

How ironic that of the four, he would become the wealthiest, with a loving wife and later, as we would find out, a son who was married with two sons of his own. The new house would have someone to inherit it.

Now he raised his hand and smiled at us as if he knew what we were bringing, what his brother Christopher surely had wished with all his heart that, somehow, someone would.

We knew that because of what had happened at Foxworth Hall and what had been made of his family name, it was best for him to return as someone else, even though he would always answer in his heart to his lost brother and sisters when they called, "Cory."

This was the reason I believed he was going back. He was hoping that someday he would hear them call him again.